THE
FEAR
SIGN

By the Same Author

THE FEAR SIGN

AN ALBERT CAMPION MYSTERY

Margery Allingham

CARROLL & GRAF PUBLISHERS, INC.

NEW YORK

This book was first published under the title *Sweet Danger* in England and also as *Kingdom of Death* in the United States.

Copyright © 1933 by Doubleday & Company, Inc.
Copyright © 1960 by P & M Youngerman Carter, Ltd.
Published by arrangement with John Stevens Robling, Ltd. for P & M Youngerman Carter, Ltd.

First Carroll & Graf edition 2000

Carroll & Graf Publishers, Inc.
19 West 21st Street
New York, NY 10010-6805

Library of Congress Cataloging-in-Publication Data is available.
ISBN: 0-7867-0755-0

Manufactured in the United States of America

CONTENTS

THE MILL AT PONTISBRIGHT ON SATURDAY EVENING

COACH HOUSE

MILL HOUSE

RIVER

MILL

ROLLS

WHEEL

DYNAMO

POOL

CHAPTER I

In Confidence

A small window in the sunlit, yellow side of the Hôtel Beauregard, Mentone, opened slowly, and through it a hand appeared, which, after depositing a compact brown suit-case upon the sill, speedily vanished.

Guffy Randall, who was allowing his car to roll in a leisurely fashion, down the gentle slope, to the sharp right-angle turn which would bring him to the front of the hotel and lunch, pulled up and observed the now closed window and the bag with that air of polite yet careless interest, which was his chief characteristic.

It seemed such a foolish thing to do, this leaving of a small brown portmanteau upon the sill of a shut, first-floor window. Mr. Randall was stolid, nordic, and logical. He also had the heaven-sent gift of curiosity, and thus it was that he was still gazing idly at the hotel wall when the sequel of the first incident occurred.

A glazed ground-floor window was opened cautiously, and a small man in a brown suit began to climb out. It was a very small window, and the unconventional departer seemed more anxious to watch what he was leaving than to see where he was going, so that he came out feet first, his knees resting upon the sill. He moved with remarkable agility, and as Mr. Randall watched he saw to his astonishment a hand replace an unmistakable revolver in a strained hip pocket.

The next moment the new-comer had closed the window, hoisted himself carefully to his feet, and stepping on a pipe-bracket, pulled himself far enough up to retrieve the

1

bag. Then he dropped silently on to the dusty path and set off down the road at a sprint.

The young man caught a glimpse of a small, pink, rat-like face and scared red-rimmed eyes.

Naturally the obvious explanation occurred to him, but he felt all the mistrust which the Englishman abroad feels towards any judicial system he does not understand, coupled with a vigorous horror of becoming involved in it in any way. Moreover, he was hungry. The day was as hot and as lazy as only a day on the French Riviera out of season can be, and he felt no personal animosity towards any impecunious hotel guest who must resort to undignified methods of departure, so long as he himself were not inconvenienced.

He turned the Lagonda gently into the palm-lined street, which ran round the bay and drove slowly through the ornate iron gates to the hotel entrance.

As he pulled up in the wide gravel parking place, he noted with relief that the hotel was by no means crowded. Rugby, Oxford, and the shires had produced in Guffy Randall at the age of twenty-eight an almost perfect specimen of the younger diehard. He was amiable, well-mannered, snobbish to the point of comedy and, in spite of his faults, a rather delightful person. His cheerful round face was hardly distinguished, but his very blue eyes were frank and kindly and his smile was disarming.

At the moment he was returning from the somewhat trying experience of conducting an aged and valetudinarian dowager aunt to an Italian spa, and having now deposited her safely at her villa was proceeding quietly homeward along the coast.

As he set foot in the cool ornate vestibule of the Beauregard, conscience smote him. He remembered the place well, and the benign face of little M. Étienne Fleurey, the manager, returned to him.

It was one of Guffy's most charming peculiarities that he made friends wherever he went and with all sorts of people. M. Fleurey, he remembered now, had been the most estimable and obliging of hosts, whose small stock of

Napoleon brandy had been nobly produced at a farewell gathering at the end of a hectic season some few years before. In the circumstances, he reflected, the least thing he could have done was to have given the alarm after the mysteriously departing stranger, or, better still, to have chased and apprehended him.

Regretful, and annoyed with himself, the young man decided to do what he could to remedy his omission, and, giving his card to the reception clerk, desired that it might be taken immediately to the manager.

M. Fleurey was a person of great importance in the little world encompassed by the walls of the Beauregard. Minor strangers spent whole fortnights in the hotel without so much as setting eyes upon the august cherub, who preferred to direct his minions from behind the scenes.

Nevertheless, within a few minutes young Mr. Randall found himself in the little mahogany-lined sanctum on the sunny side of the forecourt, with M. Fleurey himself pumping his hand and emitting birdlike chirrups of welcome and regard.

M. Fleurey was definitely ovoid in figure. From the top of his shining head he sloped gently outwards to a diameter on the level of his coat-pockets, whence he receded gracefully to the heels of his immaculate shoes.

Guffy was reminded of a witticism of the earlier season which had related how M. Fleurey had been tapped on the soles of his feet so that, like Columbus's egg, he should be able to stand.

For the rest, he was a discreet, affable soul, a connoisseur of wine and a devout believer in the sanctity of the *noblesse.*

It began to dawn upon Guffy that M. Fleurey was more than ordinarily delighted to see him. There was an element of relief in his welcome, as though the young man had been a deliverer rather than a prospective guest, and his first words put all recollection of the unconventional departure he had just witnessed out of his mind.

"Name of a name of a little good man," said the manager in his own language, "it is of an astonishing

The Village of **Pontisbright** where it all happened

GT. KEPESAKE

Lugg's Tree

Where Lugg found the body

Gorse bushes

H E

Mill

mill pool

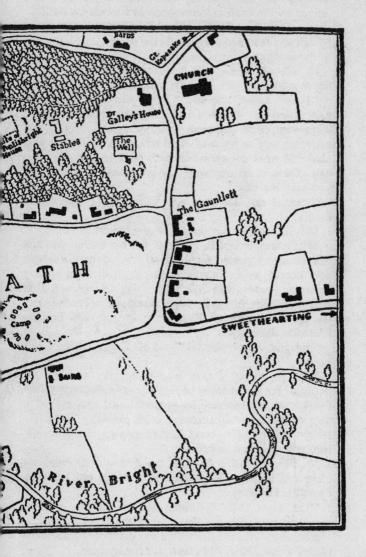

clarity to me that you, my dear Monsieur Randall, have arrived by the express intervention of Providence itself."

"Really?" said Guffy, whose French was by no means perfect and who had only caught the sense of the latter part of the sentence. "Anything up?"

M. Fleurey spread out his hands deprecatingly and a frown ruffled for an instant the tranquillity of his forehead.

"I don't know," he said. "When you came in I was in a quandary—as you would say, in a flummox. And then, when your name appeared, I said to myself, 'Here is my deliverer; here is the man of all others who will most help me.' The *noblesse* are as an open book to you, M. Randall. There is no one with any pretension to title whom you have not met."

"Here, I say, don't pin your faith to that," said Guffy hastily.

"Well, shall we say no one of any importance?"

M. Fleurey turned to his desk and his visitor saw that this glistening pantechnicon, usually so immaculate, was now littered with reference books, most of them ancient volumes, greasy with much thumbing. *Burke* and *Dod* were well to the fore, and a large crested pocket-handkerchief lay upon a square of tissue paper on top of a London telephone directory.

"Imagine my perplexity!" said M. Fleurey. "But I will explain."

With the air of a man who is anxious to relate his troubles, but not without paying due compensation to the feelings of his listener, he produced two glasses and a decanter from a small cupboard in the panelling, and a few seconds later Guffy found himself sipping rare Amontillado while his host talked.

M. Fleurey had a flair for the dramatic. Opening an enormous register, he pointed to three names half-way down the last page.

"Mr. Jones, Mr. Robinson, and Mr. Brown of London," he read. "Is not that sinister? I am no cabbage. I was not born yesterday. As soon as Léon pointed out these entries to me I said, 'Ah, there is mystery here.' "

Guffy, while wishing to congratulate M. Fleurey on his powers of detection, if only in gratitude for the sherry, was not very impressed.

"I've never heard of them," he said.

"Wait . . ." M. Fleurey lifted one finger to heaven. "I have observed these visitors. They are all three young; unmistakably of the *noblesse*. One of them has—how shall I say it?—the manner. The others wait upon him with the care and the deference of courtiers. The manservant is mysterious."

The Frenchman paused.

"Even this," he continued, raising his voice and adopting the throaty murmur of the fashionable *diseur*, "even this would not be in itself of interest. But this morning Léon, my *maître d'hôtel*, received a complaint from a fourth visitor whose room backs the suite occupied by Mr. Brown of London. This visitor—a negligible person—ninety francs a day and *vin du pays*—declared that his room had been ransacked—how do you say?—rendered to bubble and squeak. Nothing had been stolen, you understand."

M. Fleurey lowered his voice on the past participle as though apologizing for using it in the presence of his guest.

Guffy nodded, indicating that, as between one man of the world and another, he was aware that such things did happen.

"I went up to the room myself," confessed the manager like one admitting to a servile act. "It was indeed upsy-daisy. The miserable owner, while he did not actually accuse anyone, indicated that he suspected the manservant, W. Smith, of the affair. Now, my friend—" the manager set down his glass—"you perceive my situation. There is nothing I desire more in my hotel than the presence of royalty incognito, and nothing I desire less than confidence tricksters, clever thieves, or the *hoi polloi* making game. Now this last is impossible; these people are the *noblesse*. I am experienced. I served my apprenticeship. I know. But which of the other alternatives is correct? I have here the handkerchief of Mr. Brown. You see the crest. There is only one like it in all these books of information.''

He picked up a little battered leather-bound volume and, turning over the yellow pages, pointed to a rudely drawn design with the single word underneath it: *"Averna."*

"There is no account in this book of the owners of that crest, and the book is lent to me by the Municipal Librarian. But you see, there it is. The crest, usurped or not, is a genuine crest. What shall I do? If I am unduly inquisitive my visitors will go. If they are confidence tricksters I shall have been fortunate, but if they are not, then my reputation, the reputation of my so beautiful hotel for courtesy, intelligence, and, as you would say, 'wise guyishness,' will be done, gone, exploded—pouf!—like a carnival balloon.''

"I'd like to see these people," said Guffy. "Any chance of my getting a squint at them without them seeing me?"

"My enchanting friend, the thing is no sooner said than done. Come here."

The little plump man tiptoed across the thickly carpeted room as though he feared the floor were unsafe.

Guffy swallowed the last drop of his sherry and followed.

M. Fleurey slid back a little hatch in the panelling, and, to his complete astonishment, Guffy found himself looking through a small round window high up in the north wall of the lounge. The ornate moulding on the other side successfully hid the peep-hole, and the whole of the lounge lay spread out beneath like a new-angle photograph.

"This," said M. Fleurey with pride, "is my quarter-deck. From here I can see my passengers, my crew, the life of my whole establishment. Keep back as much as possible—forgive me, but these subterfuges are necessary.''

Guffy moved obligingly and regarded the scene below with interest, now that his first amazement had subsided. The huge cream-and-amber room below was sparsely dotted with people, but there were enough to make his task difficult had it not been for the excited little manager at his side.

"Look, my friend," he said. "In the corner by the

window. Ah, the palm obliterates the head of Mr. Brown. Nevertheless, wait for a moment. We can already see the others.''

The young man peered down at the elegant little group round the corner table. He saw one sleek brown head, one black one, and the third man was, as M. Fleurey had said, hidden behind the palms.

As Guffy stared, one of the men turned and he caught sight of his face. An exclamation escaped him.

M. Fleurey tugged his sleeve impatiently.

"You recognize them?'' he demanded. "Are my fears at rest? I implore you, my friend, to tell me!''

"Half a minute . . .'' Guffy pressed his face against the glass of the peep-hole in an effort to catch a glimpse of the man in the shadow.

The brown-headed "equerry'' he had recognized immediately as Jonathan Eager-Wright, probably the most daring amateur mountaineer in Europe and a member of one of England's oldest families. He was a shy, retiring person who was seldom in England, and who treated his place in Society with a wholly unwarrantable contempt.

Guffy grew more and more curious. He had no doubt that he would recognize the second man the moment he turned his head. Surely those tremendously square shoulders and those tight brown-black curls, making his head look like the back of a shorn lamb, could belong to only one person in the world: Dicky Farquharson, the brilliant young son of old Sir Joshua Farquharson, chairman of Farquharson & Co., the Anglo-American mining engineers?

Having recognized two old friends, Guffy's first impulse was to reassure M. Fleurey and hurry down to the lounge, but something odd in the behaviour of the pair held his attention and his curiosity. It seemed to him, watching from his place of vantage above them, that Messrs. Farquharson and Eager-Wright were much more subdued than usual. There was a strange formality about their dress and their manner.

The man in the corner appeared to be absorbing, not to say dominating, them.

Although, of course, he could not hear what was being said, Randall received the impression that they were listening deferentially to the other's harangue; that their laughter was polite to the point of affectation; and that, in fact, they were behaving like men in the presence of royalty.

How two such unlikely persons could possibly have come together in such a situation was beyond Guffy's powers of conjecture. As he watched, both young men suddenly drew out pocket lighters and simultaneously offered the third of the trio the flame.

Eager-Wright, it seemed, was the favoured one, and the third man bent forward to light his cigarette.

As Guffy stared, a pale, somewhat vacant face came into view. Sleek yellow hair was brushed back from a high forehead and pale blue eyes were hidden behind enormous horn-rimmed spectacles. The expression upon the face was languid and a little bored. The next instant he had leant back again.

"By George!" said Mr. Randall. "Albert Campion!"

The next moment his shoulders began to heave and he turned a crimson, distorted face to the startled manager.

"You weep!" the little man ejaculated. "You are alarmed—you are amused—yes, no?"

Guffy clutched at the desk for support, while the little manager danced round him like an excited Pekingese.

"My friend," he expostulated, "you keep me in suspense. You bewilder me. Do I laugh or am I abased? Is my hotel honoured or is it degraded? Is it the *noblesse* or is it some racket of malefaction?"

Guffy controlled himself with an effort. "God only knows," he said. And then, as the little man's face fell, he clapped him vigorously on the shoulder. "But it's all right, Fleurey, it's all right. You know—*au fait*—quite the thing. Nothing to get *distrait* about."

And then, before the manager could press for further information, the young man had flung himself out of the door and raced down the stairs, still laughing, to the lounge.

As he went, Guffy reflected upon the beauties of the

situation. Albert Campion, of all people, being seriously mistaken by the good Fleurey for minor royalty was a story too magnificent to be lightly dismissed. After all, it might almost be true; that was the beauty of Campion; one never knew where he was going to turn up next—at the Third Levée or swinging from a chandelier, as someone once said.

As Guffy crossed the vestibule he had time to consider Campion. After all, even he, probably one of that young man's oldest friends, knew really very little about him. Campion was not his name; but then it is not considered decent for the younger son of such a family to pursue such a peculiar calling under his own title.

As to the precise nature of the calling Guffy was a little fogged. Campion himself had once described it as "Universal Uncle and Deputy Adventurer." All things considered, that probably summed him up.

Although what he could possibly be doing at the Beauregard playing prince with two men like Farquharson and Eager-Wright to help him was beyond the scope of Guffy's somewhat inelastic imagination.

He hurried across the lounge, his round face beaming, the pricelessness of the joke still uppermost in his mind. He laid a hand on Farquharson's shoulder and grinned at Campion.

"What ho, your Highness!" he said, and chuckled.

His laughter died suddenly, however. The pale vacuous face into which he stared did not alter for an instant, and Eager-Wright's iron hand closed over his wrist like a vice.

Farquharson rose hastily to his feet. His face betrayed nothing but consternation. Eager-Wright had risen also, but his warning grip did not slacken.

Farquharson bowed slightly to Campion. "Sir," he said, "may I present the Honourable Augustus Randall, of Monewdon in Suffolk, England?"

Mr. Campion, not a muscle of his face betraying a trace of any emotion save polite indifference, nodded.

"Mr. Randall and I have met before, I think," he said. "Perhaps you will sit here, next to Mr. Robinson? Mr.

Jones should have introduced you." He smiled deprecatingly. "I am, at the moment, Mr. Brown of London."

Guffy looked round him in bewilderment, waiting for the explosion of laughter which he felt must be coming at any moment. But on each of the three faces he saw nothing but extreme gravity, and Mr. Campion's pale eyes behind his spectacles were warning and severe.

CHAPTER II

H.R.H. Campion

"Now that the doors of my palatial suite are safely locked," said Mr. Campion some sixty minutes later, "let us adjourn with all due pomp to the state bedroom, and I will tell you in kingly confidence that 'uneasy lies the head that wears a crown.' "

He linked his arm through Guffy's and they walked across the sitting-room into the adjoining bedchamber, whither Eager-Wright and Farquharson had preceded them.

"We're coming in here because the walls are practically sound-proof," Campion explained airily as he swept aside the mosquito net and seated himself upon the great gilt rococo bed.

Guffy Randall, mystified and truculent, stood before him, Dicky Farquharson lounged upon the dressing-table stool, a glass of beer in his hand, the bottle on the floor at his feet, while Eager-Wright stood by the window grinning broadly.

Guffy was frankly unamused. He felt he had been made to look an ill-mannered ass and was prepared to accept only the most abject of apologies.

Farquharson leant forward, his smile wrinkling his forehead until his short, close-cropped curls almost met his eyebrows.

"It's rather a blessing Guffy has turned up at this particular juncture," he said. "He'd never have stood the strain of playing the courtier for long. It's damned hard work, old man," he added, grinning at his friend, "His Majesty being rather a stickler for etiquette. You haven't got the

bearing at all, if I may say so. Bring the heels together
smartly and from the waist—bow!''

Guffy passed his hand over his forehead. "Look here,"
he said, "I'm completely in the dark. I take it you have
some purpose in careering about the place behaving in this
extraordinary fashion. I don't want to intrude, of course,
but if you could give me a clue it'd help considerably.''

Mr. Campion, sitting cross-legged on the bed, his pale
eyes amused behind his enormous spectacles, nodded affably.

"As a matter of fact, you ought to have been in it from
the start," he said. "The army of spies which reports to
me daily scoured London for you about three weeks ago.''

"Really?" Guffy looked up with interest. "I was in
Oslo with the Guv'nor judging some new sort of dog
they're breeding. I'm sorry about that. Frankly, Campion,
I feel this is going to take a bit of explaining. When I
dropped in here this morning I found old Fleurey black in
the face because he thinks he's got a pack of confidence
tricksters in the place. I took a squint at the suspects for
him and I found it was you.''

"Confidence tricksters!" said Eager-Wright, aghast. "I
say, that reflects on us rather badly, Farquharson.''

"Oh, he thought also that you might be minor royalty,''
said Guffy with due fairness. "He suspects you, Campion,
of being the potentate of some little tinpot Balkan state.''

Farquharson and Eager-Wright exchanged glances, and
a faint smile passed over Mr. Campion's pale, foolish
face.

"The good Fleurey is a man of perception," he said.
"You can't fool a hotel proprietor, Guffy. The man's
absolutely right. You are now in the presence of the
Hereditary Paladin of Averna and his entire Court. Not
perhaps very impressive, but genuine. That's the chief
charm about us in this business: we're absolutely *bona
fide*.''

Guffy's blue eyes became dark and incredulous. Mr.
Campion met them gravely. Then he held out his hand.

"Meet Albert, Hereditary Paladin of Averna.''

"Never heard of it," said Guffy stolidly.

"You will," said Mr. Campion. "It's a hell of a place: I'm the king. Farquharson represents the Government of the country. Eager-Wright is the Opposition. I suppose you wouldn't care for an order or two? The Triple Star is natty without being bourgeois."

"It sounds mad," said Guffy. "But I'm with you, of course, if there's anything I can do. I don't want to be offensive, but it sounds as though you're collecting for a hospital."

Mr. Campion's pale eyes became momentarily grave. "Yes, well, there's always that," he said. "And before you decide to join us I feel I ought to point out that there's a distinct possibility that I and all my immediate friends may have to die fighting for my country. I say, Farquharson, have you got that coat?"

Dicky leant over the back of the stool and pulled a suitcase from under the dressing-table. From its depths he drew out a light travelling ulster and displayed a six-inch tear just under the shoulder.

"A bullet?" enquired Guffy with interest.

"As we got on the train at Brindisi," agreed Mr. Campion. "We Avernians live dangerously."

"I'm in it," said Guffy stoutly. "I say, though, where is this place Averna? Ought I to have heard of it?"

"Well, no. Its greatest asset is that very few people ever have heard of it." Mr. Campion's precise tone was still light, but Guffy, who knew him well, realized that he was now approaching the serious. "To be quite honest," he went on, "it's not very hot, as kingdoms go. To begin with, the area's about eight hundred, I should say."

"Square miles?" said Guffy, impressed.

"Acres," said Mr. Campion modestly. "That includes the castle, of course, but not the rockery. I also hold dominion over the left half of a beautiful mountain about four thousand feet high, and the right half of a much loftier affair. Included in this not very desirable property is running water, cold, five hundred yards of sea coast, a truffle plantation, and quite half a dozen subjects, all of whom now have a signed photograph of myself in court dress and five hundred cigarettes. My levée was a stout affair. It was only my personal charm which retained me my throne, although no doubt the uniforms helped. Our red and gold ones are rather good; you must see them.''

Guffy sat down. "I'm awfully sorry," he said, "but it just doesn't sound true. Suppose you tell me about it plainly and simply, as though I were a child."

"It's not a simple story," said Mr. Campion. "However, if you make your mind receptive, put your trust in me and try to grasp one fact at a time, I'll explain. First of all the history of Averna is important, and it goes like this. It all began with a man called Peter the Hermit, who went out to do a bit of crusading in 1090. He took a friend with him called Walter the Moneyless, who seems to have been about as hopeless as his name, and they went off with a rabble and had a frightful time coming through Dalmatia. They expected to be fed miraculously—ravens, and what-not, you know—but the notion wasn't sound, and they finally came to a sticky end on the plains of Asia Minor. You can find all that in any history book, probably not so lucidly put.

"But now we come to more specialized information. With these two birds was a fearfully tough egg called Lambert of Vincennes, who not unnaturally got fed up at half-time and came back. He parted from the other two enthusiasts in the mountains on the Dalmatian coast and had rather a thin time at first. But he had the pioneer spirit all right, furnished himself with a wife—some early Hungarian beauty, no doubt—and with her took refuge in a sort of pocket in the mountains, a pleasant valley with trees and a stream and large protecting walls of rock all round. In fact, my present kingdom."

Guffy nodded understandingly. "All clear, so far," he said.

Mr. Campion continued with dignity. "These two and their followers settled down in the valley for a bit and then the old boy made plans for getting home. The only thing against the valley was, and is, for that matter, that it's a most difficult place to get out of. Once you're in it you're in it, and if the crops fail or the stream runs dry the situation can be most unpleasant. Also, there's no social life.

"Mrs. Lambert and most of the others were left behind while Lambert and a couple of friends set out from home. The extraordinary thing is that they got there. But, home politics being what they were at the time, the Lambert estates had been sequestered and the unfortunate fellow couldn't raise enough money to get back to his valley again. He turned up in England and was received kindly as a sort of holy man. But no one felt like exploring at the time, and finally he died in despair, commending his kingdom, in which no one quite believed, to the English Crown.

"It seems to have been a sort of standard anecdote until 1190, when Richard the First set out to do his own bit of crusading, and then a detachment under a delightful soul called Edward the Faithful left the main expedition in Tuscia, cut across Romandiola to Ancona, and across the Adriatic—whatever it was then called—to a place called Ragusa, where the Dinaric Alps run down to the sea."

He paused and looked at his friend apologetically. "I'm sorry to trot out all this history," he said, "but it's absolutely necessary if you're going to get a clear idea of what we're up to. To carry on with Edward the Faithful: he discovered Lambert's kingdom eventually, and wasn't very impressed by it. There were no members of the original party alive, and Edward seems to have taken a dislike to the place. But he set up the royal standard and claimed it formally from two lizards and a bear, as far as I can make out. Matters weren't improved when someone started a rumour, based on abstruse and erroneous calculations, that the valley was the scene of the incident between Cain and Abel. That settled it as far as Edward was concerned. He christened it Averna and bunked back to England. Later on, when he handed in his report to Richard, the king appears to have been frightfully amused. He rewarded Edward, but presented the kingdom as a kind of royal snub to a perfectly mad family called Huntingforest, the ances-

tors of the Earls of Pontisbright. Two of these lads died on
expeditions to this kingdom, and I imagine that Richard
laughed like fun—or his heirs did—the humour of the
period tending that way.

"Finally, when any of the family became a little uppish
the reigning king used to suggest a trip out to see the old
family possession."

Guffy grinned, and Mr. Campion heartened and went on
with his harangue.

"No one got much out of it," he said, "until about
1400, when Giles, the Fifth Earl, actually went out there,
set up as Hereditary Paladin and built a castle. To him we
are indebted for most of the present palaver. He had a
crown made, drew up articles—the deeds of the place, as
it were, and had 'em signed and ratified by Henry the
Fourth. After this everything settled down normally. Most
of the Pontisbrights preferred to stay at home, and the
family, whose estates in the midlands had dwindled, were
given others in East Anglia and became quite important
people, in with the Governments and that sort of thing. A
few adventurous members of the family looked in at Averna
when they made the grand tour, and 'Hereditary Paladin'
was mentioned in the family titles on state occasions, but
the place was not attractive and of no value, and no one
took much notice of it.

"The last time it came into any sort of prominence was
in 1814, after the rearrangement of Europe. Then the
fifteenth Earl of Pontisbright was quietly financed by the
British Government to enable him to buy his estate secretly
from Metternich, the great real estate pedlar of that time,
so that no row over the little bit of land could lead to any
fighting which might possibly involve us.

"Then in the Crimea the last earl was killed, and the
line came to an end. There you have it in a nutshell, or at
least most of it."

He rose from the bed as he finished speaking and wandered down the room, his long thin figure looking somehow very modern and prosaic after his story.

Guffy was still puzzled. "I've assimilated all that," he

said, "and I may be a complete fool, but I still don't see how you came into it. I thought your family name was—" He hesitated. Mr. Campion's real name was one of the few subjects which were taboo in his presence.

"Ah, well, now we come to the difficult bit." Campion regarded his friend mildly from behind his spectacles. "About eight or nine months ago you either do or you don't remember there was a minor earthquake in that part of the world. Nothing much happened, but it shook up a bit of Italy and broke a few windows in Belgrade. No one thought any exciting damage had been done for a long time until Eager-Wright, holidaying in the Bosnian Alps, discovered there had been a certain amount of recent disturbance among the great ones. Chunks of rock had been hurled about, and that sort of thing. Well, then, this is frightfully important and the whole crux of the matter generally: he discovered on behalf of the British Government that with very little help from a man like Farquharson, Averna could be made a pretty useful spot. You see, roughly it's like this. Until last year Averna was a small oval patch of land entirely surrounded by rock, save for a single narrow tunnel through which a mountain stream ran out to the sea. I believe one of the early Pontisbrights attempted to shoot down this tunnel and never emerged at the other end. But now, since the spot of bother last year, the tunnel is no longer a tunnel, but an open cleft in the rocks, the sea has come up, and Averna now has a minute coast line—quite five or six hundred yards, I should say. Farquharson as the expert has had a look at it, and in his opinion it would now be comparatively simple to carry on the good work done by the earthquake and turn the place into a marvellous natural harbour at a cost of approximately two and sixpence as the politician thinks."

Guffy's round eyes grew rounder. The significance of the harangue was beginning to dawn upon him.

Farquharson leant forward. "That isn't all, Randall," he said. "There's every evidence that on the land behind the castle there's an untapped oilfield. It was discovered, I imagine, years ago, but of course the incredible difficulties of transport made it valueless. Even now I doubt whether it's a commercial proposition to export; but who wants to export it if ships can take it in on the spot? You see the situation now, don't you?''

"Good Lord!" said Guffy. "A natural harbour with natural fuel.''

"That seems to be the general opinion," said Farquharson, and Campion cut in, his quiet, foolish voice sounding odd in conjunction with the importance of his discourse:

"Only no one wants anyone else to have a natural harbour in the Adriatic like that," he said. "There'll probably be a lot of international litigation about it. Litigation is a tetchy business at the best of times, but just now it might be rather awkward if there was much argument or fuss. The European situation being what it is.''

"I see," said Guffy slowly. "I suppose there's no doubt at all that the place actually belonged to the Earls of Pontisbright?''

"Oh, none at all. They had it by right of conquest first, and then, to be on the safe side, they bought it from Metternich. They hold, or at least they once held, the deeds, the charter, the regalia—the receipts, in fact—and if the family hadn't disappeared in the Crimea things would be simple. As it is, however, the family was in low water at the time of its disappearance, and there seems to have been a general mix up at the finish, and, frankly, everything belonging to Averna has been lost. That's where we come in. That's what we're doing. We're on a sort of fantastic treasure hunt with rather a lot at stake. The Powers-That-Be got wind of the affair, first through Eager-Wright and then from their own expert, and, deciding that the matter was one of those complicated slightly under-hand pieces of business which go so well with my person-ality, they did me the honour of calling me in, giving me a free hand, and there you are. Rather pretty, isn't it?''

Guffy Randall sat silent for some minutes reflecting upon what he had heard. His slow methodical mind went over the story inch by inch, and finally he looked up, a suggestion of alarm in his eyes.

"Rather a tall order, isn't it?" he said. "I mean, these proofs may be anywhere."

"That's just it," said Eager-Wright from his corner. "However, we've been more hopeful since someone took the trouble to shoot at us."

Campion nodded. "The good folk in authority have an idea based upon certain enquiries that part of these papers, documents, crowns, and whatnot may be about to fall into the hands of some unscrupulous private agent, who will hold them until the right moment to make a deal. As the feeling in London is that the moment for safety is almost past, they are anxious to make him come out into the open if he really does exist. Our somewhat spectacular descent into Averna and our leisurely return through Europe is a self-advertising stunt. We had intended to wait until we received an offer to purchase and then to freeze on to the vendor with the tenacity of bull-pups. I understand the intention at present is even to revive the Pontisbright title if necessary. But even so, our employers won't cut much ice at the Court of The Hague if they can't produce the documents. So far no one's tried to sell us anything. But someone tried to kill us, and we've been followed most thoroughly ever since we left the kingdom; so it looks as if our good work has not been completely wasted. It's only the delay that is alarming, because, as you can gather, the whole thing is rather serious. As far as I can see, we might have all Europe flaring up if a certain Power thought it worth while to fight for Averna. It is just important enough to make a good excuse."

"I see. Did you catch a glimpse of the man who fired at you?"

"Just a glimpse," said Farquharson. "There were two of them: one, a most extraordinary-looking fellow with a widow's peak that almost touched the bridge of his nose, had been following us for some time, and just as we were getting into the train at Brindisi he took a pot shot at us. Unfortunately we were surrounded by a crowd immediately, and although we made a sprint after the fellows, we missed them. We haven't seen widow's peak since, but his pal, a little rat-faced person with a perpetual sniff, is right here in this hotel on the same floor.''

"Really?" said Guffy with interest. "Is that the man who had his rooms ransacked?"

This innocent enquiry had an instantaneous effect upon his audience. Eager-Wright sprang to his feet and Mr. Campion paused in his stride to regard the speaker sharply.

"Fleurey told me," said Guffy hastily. "That's why he was trying to find out who you were. Apparently some fellow or other on this floor complained that your man, W. Smith, had gone rummaging among his things. Naturally Fleurey was most anxious not to make any complaint until he was certain you were not royalty incognito. Now I come to think of it, I saw a man sneaking out of a window on this floor when I was driving up just before lunch. He was a little rat-faced person in a brown suit."

"That's him," said Eager-Wright. "Lugg must have frightened him."

Mr. Campion, who had become suddenly grave, turned to Eager-Wright.

"I say, would you mind going out and finding Lugg?" he said. "It's the same old Lugg, Guffy; he's only masquerading under the name of Smith, like the rest of us. This wants looking into. I wonder what the cretin's done now."

Five minutes later Eager-Wright returned, his eyes alight with curiosity, and in his wake, lumbering, breathless but indignant, came Mr. Campion's personal servant and general factotum, Magersfontein Lugg.

He was an immense and gloomy individual at the best of times. The lower part of his vast white face was almost hidden by a drooping black moustache, but he had the quick keen eyes of a cockney in spite of the lugubrious expression which he almost always wore. The fact that he had been a burglar before, as he remarked himself, he had lost his figger, tended to make him a very valuable ally to the master to whom he was devoted. Mr. Lugg's knowledge of the underworld was unrivalled.

At the moment the sleek black clothes of the typical

gentleman's gentleman sat oddly upon his ungainly form, more especially as he wore no trace of the subservience which almost invariably accompanies them. He eyed his master truculently.

"Can't even 'ave a little sleep in the afternoon now, can't I?" he said. "It's 'Yes, me lord; no, me lord' the whole time. I get sick of it."

Campion waved his remarks aside impatiently. "Sniffy Edwards has left this hotel by a window. Before he left he complained to the management that his rooms had been ransacked by a person who resembled you very closely."

Mr. Lugg looked completely unabashed. "Oh, 'e saw me, did 'e?" he said. "I wondered if 'e had."

"Look here, Lugg, this is disgraceful. You'd better pack your things and go straight back to Bottle Street." Mr. Campion, it seemed, spoke more in sorrow than in anger.

"Ho, that's it?" said his aide angrily. "It's manners now, is it? I don't like to talk to you like this in front of yer friends, but I didn't know we'd got to put on airs and graces in private. King you may be, but not to me. Very well, I'll go. But you'll be sorry. When I went through Sniffy's rooms I didn't search 'is bags, as you might think. I simply took 'is morning mail. Anybody might 'ave done that. 'E was in 'is bath and I nipped in quick as you please and read the letters the moment after 'e'd done so 'isself. And what's more, I found something. I found the key of the 'ole situation. I was going to show it to you as soon as I got you alone. But am I going to now? Not on yer life! I'm going back to London."

"Cast aside like a worn-out glove, I suppose," said Mr. Campion sarcastically. "The plaything of fate again. Come across with it, Lugg, if it's interesting."

Mr. Lugg appeared mollified but affected not to have heard the interruption.

"So Sniffy went, did 'e?" he said. "I thought 'e would. I left a note on 'is dressing-table sayin' I'd show 'im what it was like to take a good look at the inside of 'is own 'ead if I laid ears to 'is dirty little snuffle again. I left it anonymous, you know, but if 'e saw me that accounts for him leaving sudden.''

"What about this key to the whole situation?" enquired Campion again.

With a gesture of resignation Mr. Lugg removed his coat, unbuttoned his waistcoat, and drew from a small pocket in the lining a crumpled half sheet of paper.

"There you are," he said. "You fight in your gentle-manly way. Say 'Excuse me' and 'I wonder if I could trouble you.' But if you want a thing done, go and do it in the natural dirty way that the Lord meant. And if you don't like to read another bloke's letters, I'll put it back."

"Lugg, there's something positively horrible about you," said Mr. Campion with distaste as he picked up the paper.

CHAPTER III

The Man Higher Up

The fragment of paper which Mr. Campion held and at which the others glanced over his shoulder was thumbed and dirty, but the message was legible enough.

"Gwen's, London. Dear S.,—This is to give you the office. Have heard from P. that the old man is angry. We have both been on wrong track, as I thought. I am off to Fly by Night to-night. The old man's heard of something that may give us the lead in on the doings. There is supposed to be something carved on one of the trees in the garden which will show us the light. Seems like Sweet Fanny Adams to me. Join me careful. You can leave that bunch, they know less than us.—Yours, D."

"There you are," said Mr. Lugg. "That's what I call evidence. It gives it to yer in one."

"I'm hanged if I can see it," said Guffy, who was still frowning over the document. "Can you make head or tail of this, Campion?"

"Well, yes, in a way. It's extremely interesting." The pale young man in the horn-rimmed spectacles continued to regard the missive thoughtfully. "You see, Sniffy's correspondent is inclined to stick to his own vernacular. Translated, I imagine it goes something like this, doesn't it, Lugg? 'Dear Sniffy,—This is to warn you. Have heard from P. that the man who employs us is angry. We have been on the wrong scent, as I thought. I am off to Pontisbright to-night. Our employer has heard of something which may give us a clue to the whereabouts of the proofs. There is alleged to be something carved on one of the trees in the garden'—of the old Pontisbright house, I suppose—'which may give us that clue. I am not very sanguine about this. Join me at Pontisbright, but take care. You can leave Mr. Campion and his friends. They know less than we do.—Yours, Doyle.' ''

"How d'you make out 'Pontisbright?' '' said Farquharson.

"Rhyming slang. It's still used a good deal, especially for proper names. That's only a guess, I know, but I think we're fairly safe in assuming that it's what the man means.''

"Of course you are,'' said Mr. Lugg's sepulchral voice from the background.

"How do you know 'D' stands for Doyle?'' continued Guffy obstinately.

"Well, Peaky Doyle has been with Sniffy Edwards on this job and he's the most likely person to write to his friend on the subject. Also, he spends a lot of his time at Gwen's, a rather shady lodging-house in the Waterloo Road.''

"Peaky Doyle is the man we've called 'widow's peak' all along, the man who fired at us at Brindisi, I suppose?'' said Eager-Wright. "I say, Campion, this is important, isn't it? What do you actually make of it?''

Mr. Campion considered. His pale face was vacant as ever, but his eyes were thoughtful.

"It's an interesting note altogether,'' he said at last. "I see no reason at all to suppose that it isn't genuine, and in that case it puts us on a new scent altogether. In the first place, if Peaky Doyle is going to Pontisbright, I suppose we'd better go too. That's the name of the Suffolk village, by the way, where the Pontisbright mansion originally stood. Well, well, well; perhaps the fun is going to begin at last.''

He was silent again for a moment and stood looking down at the paper.

"I know what you're thinkin','' said Mr. Lugg suddenly. "You're thinkin' just what I've bin thinkin' all along, and it's this: 'Oo exactly is Peaky Doyle's old man?''

Mr. Campion glanced at his aide, and for a moment they regarded each other solemnly.

"Well, why not?" said Mr. Lugg. "It might be. And if so, either you give up the 'ole idea or I 'and in my resignation."

"Nerves troubling you again?" enquired his employer mildly.

"No," said Mr. Lugg stoutly. "I know what's good for me, though. I've never worked a miracle yet and I don't want t'ave to begin now."

Mr. Campion seemed to realize that this cryptic conversation must be very tantalizing to his friends, and he turned to them.

"Peaky Doyle once worked for a very extraordinary person early on in his unbeautiful career," he explained, "and the thought has occurred to both Lugg and me that he might be back at his old job. I suppose you people have heard of Brett Savanake?"

"The financier?" enquired Farquharson, while Eager-Wright and Guffy looked blank.

Campion nodded. "He's an extraordinary man, one of those business geniuses who turn up now and again. He's chairman of a dozen companies of international importance, and how he got there is one of those mysteries that people have given up trying to explain. Early on in his career there were some very queer stories floating about, and just after the Winterton Textile Trust smash he used to go about with a bodyguard of thugs. Peaky Doyle featured rather prominently in that outfit. Since then Savanake's just gone on from strength to strength. He's never photographed, never interviewed, but keeps out of the limelight as much as possible."

"But," said Farquharson, aghast, "would this be big enough for him? Think of the risk!"

Mr. Campion grinned. "I don't think the risk would worry him," he said. "But whether the thing's big enough is another matter altogether. If we're up against him we're up against something pretty exciting. Still, I don't see any way of finding that out immediately. If it arises, it arises.

What is important is this yarn about a clue carved on a tree trunk. We can't afford to ignore a hint like that, can we? Alas, I see the day of my pomp departing. I must get back to work.''

"Look here," said Guffy, "what exactly are we looking for? This may seem rather a trite question to you, but it's been worrying me."

Campion apologized. "I'm sorry," he said with genuine contrition. "I ought to have explained this before. There's three things without which the Powers-That-Be don't consider they could possibly get a favourable decision at the Court of The Hague. The first—it's rather like a fairy story, isn't it?—is the crown which was made for Giles Pontisbright in the reign of Henry the Fourth. He had it made by Italian workmen, and the only description of it we can get is a rather fanciful affair in a manuscript in the British Museum. I'll read it to you."

He sat down on the bed again and took a slip of paper from his note-case. He began to read, the archaic words sounding even more strange in his precise voice.

"*Three drops of blood from a royal wound, three dull stars like the pigeon's egg, held and knit together with a flowery chain. Yet when a Pontisbright do wear it, none shall see it but by the stars.*' "

As he finished reading he eyed Guffy gravely through his enormous spectacles.

"It sounds very difficult, doesn't it?" he said. "That bit about it not being visible when it's on, for instance. Besides, those ancient crowns weren't one of those red-plush bowler-hat affairs with festoons of jewellery. They made 'em almost any shape. Well, then, that's that. Our next little problem is the charter. That's written on parchment, which, according to the stationery bills of the time, must have been either one-half or one-quarter of a whole sheepskin. It's written in Latin, of course, bears Henry the Fourth's seal and his mark. I don't think the fellow could write. And the third treasure, is, as it should be, the most important of all, and simply consists of Metternich's receipt for the money in 1814. Heaven knows what that looks like. So, you see, we're going to have fun."

Guffy's pleasant round face flushed. "It's rather jolly, though, isn't it?" he said. "I mean, I rather like it. Who's got the Pontisbright manor house now? I ought to know that part of the country well, but I can't even remember having heard the name before."

Mr. Campion met Farquharson's eyes and grimaced. "That's where we come up against another snag," he said. "There's no longer any house at all. When the title lapsed the old Countess, who was the only member of the family left, simply sold up everything, lock, stock, and barrel. The entire place was dismantled and sold piece by piece, until nothing but a hole which had contained the foundations was left. It was one of the great acts of vandalism of the Victorian era." He paused. "Not very helpful, is it?"

"But the garden," persisted Guffy. "This fellow Peaky Doyle distinctly mentions the garden."

"Oh, the grounds are still there, we believe," put in Farquharson. "Not kept up at all, you know, but still there."

"But isn't there anyone even remotely connected with the family living in the place? In the dower house, or somewhere?"

"There's a mill," ventured Eager-Wright. "That's inhabited by the family of a man who made an unsuccessful claim to the title just before the war. He was killed in France afterwards, and the family consists of a few kids, I think, but we're not sure about that. You think we ought to go down there, Campion?"

The tall fair young man in horn-rimmed spectacles nodded.

"I think so. After all, as far as we know Peaky Doyle and his friends are the only people who are interested in this affair besides us, and in our present position with nothing definite to lay hands on, let us go and see what the other fellow's got."

"Now that's sensible," said Mr. Lugg with the sublime confidence of a man who cannot conceive a situation when his opinion is not useful. "Only all I say is, find out first 'oo you're up against. And if it's you know who I mean, leave it alone.''

Mr. Campion ignored him. "Look here, Farquharson," he said, "in your position as Equerry-in-Chief, I wonder if you'd mind making all the necessary arrangements? Pay our bills and give notice and see we leave to-night."

"To-night?" expostulated Mr. Lugg. "I've got an appointment to-night. I don't want to leave a bad impression in the place. People get talkin' and it might look funny."

His further expostulations were cut short by a discreet tapping on the outer door. He ambled off to open it, still protesting, and returned a moment or so later to announce that Monsieur Étienne Fleurey was desolate, but could he have a word with Mr. Randall?

Guffy went out in some surprise and was still more astonished to find the little man himself standing on the threshold. He was pink and apologetic, and Guffy, who realized the blow to his dignity which he must have suffered by being forced to attend to anything personally, regarded him enquiringly. The manager could hardly speak.

"Monsieur Randall, I am prostrate with regret. You will accompany me?"

He led the young man into an unoccupied suite farther down the corridor and closed the door with every show of caution. Having satisfied himself that he could not be overheard, he presented a shining face to his visitor which was adorned with such an expression of woe that all Guffy's sympathies as well as his curiosity were aroused.

"Monsieur, the situation in which I find myself is, as you would say, putrid. I am annihilated. My world has come to an end. It would be infinitely better if I were dead."

"That's all right," said Guffy, not knowing quite what else to say. "What's up?"

"The unspeakable imbecile who complained," Monsieur Fleurey continued, tears in his eyes, "he has gone. He has departed, crept out of the hotel like a veritable odour, but that is not all. Circumstances which I dare not divulge, circumstances which you, my dear Monsieur Randall, will as a man of honour understand and respect, machinations of fate over which I have no control, compel me to insist that the man Smith return anything which he may have taken—no doubt in some perfectly pardonable error—from the room of this *canaille* whom we all so justifiably detest.''

"I say," said Guffy, trembling between a sense of guilt and a desire to help, "this is going to be rather awkward, isn't it?''

"Awkward? Never in my career have I experienced such a sense of embarrassment such as now overwhelms me! But what can I do? I tell you my entire life, the fortunes of my hotel which are my very existence, depend upon the recovery of a certain"—Monsieur Fleurey gulped—"a certain letter which the man Smith doubtless suspected was one of his own."

Guffy made up his mind. Apart from the fact that the little manager appeared to be on the verge of hurling himself weeping at his feet, Mr. Randall had very strong ideas concerning the ethics of Mr. Lugg's escapade.

"Look here," he said, "I imagine there's been some mistake. Suppose in about fifteen minutes or so you search the room occupied by Sniff—I mean your late client. You never know with letters. They slip behind beds, or get tucked under carpets, don't they?''

Monsieur Fleurey's little bright brown eyes met the Englishman's for a second. Then he seized Guffy's hand and wrung it.

"Monsieur Randall," he said with a gulp which he could not quite repress, "you are a veritable hero. The— how shall I say?—the pineapple of your race."

Guffy went back to the royal suite and delivered his ultimatum. Mr. Lugg was inclined to be truculent, but Campion was instantly obliging.

"That's rather a good idea on the whole," he said. "You slip out and throw the letter behind the bed, Lugg. After all, we've read it. Don't be a fool."

When the big man had gone off grumbling on his errand he turned again to Guffy.

"I shouldn't think many things would arouse our friend Étienne so thoroughly, would you?" he said slowly.

"Rather not. The poor fellow seemed on the verge of suicide." Guffy was still amazed.

Mr. Campion moved over to the telephone. "Little Albert has had one of his rare and illuminating thoughts," he said, and put through a call to Paris.

After some moments' rapid conversation in French with some oracle in the capital, he hung up the receiver and faced the trio. There was a curious expression in the pale eyes behind the spectacles, and for the first time that day a faint tinge of colour on the high cheek-bones.

"That was my good friend Daudet of the Sûreté," he said. "He knows everything, although this question was simple enough in all conscience. It occurred to me that the only thing that could produce such a state of hysteria in the good Fleurey was the fear of losing his job, of relinquishing the eminent position he has worked so hard to attain. I enquired of Daudet the name of the proprietors of this hotel, and he tells me that this, the Mirifique at Nice, and the Mirabeau at Marseilles are owned by the Société Anonyme de Winterhouse Incorporated. And that interesting little combine, my pretties, is chairmaned and practically owned by that beautiful soul Brett Savanake. D'you know, I really think things are going to begin."

CHAPTER IV

"Here's Mystery"

"Across the face of the *East Suffolk Courier and Hadleigh Argus,* Fate's moving finger writes, and not very grammatically either," said Mr. Campion cheerfully to Guffy, who sat beside him in the back of his venerable Bentley thirty-six hours later.

Lugg was driving, and by his side Eager-Wright dozed peacefully.

Campion glanced at the paragraph in the local newspaper they had bought on the way down which had occasioned his remark. Its headline, "Mysterious Attack in Suffolk Village," had caught his attention, and he re-read the few words below for the fourth or fifth time during the journey.

"Miss Harriet Huntingforest, a resident of Pontisbright, near Hadleigh, Suffolk, has been the victim of a remarkable attack by an intruder yesterday, who entered her house and ransacked it without removing anything of value. Miss Huntingforest, who surprised the intruder, courageously ordered him out of the house, but was brutally felled to the ground, which rendered her unconscious. The only description of her assailant with which Miss Huntingforest can furnish the local police officer is that he was of unusual height and the possessor of an extraordinarily pronounced widow's peak."

"Pretty, isn't it?" he said, handing the paper to Guffy. "That's a sort of sign and portent, a direct message from Providence to say, 'Albert, you're on the right track.' "

33

"It's extraordinary," said Guffy. "I'm glad I came with you. Since Farquharson has had to stay behind to hand in his report, I feel the Court of Averna would be a bit depleted without me. I see myself as a sort of Watson with a club."

Mr. Campion shrugged his shoulders. "I don't know whether it's going to be that kind of a party, unfortunately," he said. "Although I don't know what on earth Peaky Doyle's up to, beating up old ladies. Still, we must wait to find that out until we get there—if ever." He glanced round him at the desolate country through which they were passing as he spoke.

The scenery was growing more beautiful and more rural at every mile. Once they had left Framlingham the loneliness was extraordinary. They seemed to have travelled for miles without seeing a soul. Plump little white houses were hidden among great overblown trees; even the fields seemed to have become smaller, and the flint roads were dusty and in places extraordinarily bad.

Just as he had finished speaking, at a particularly confusing five-way cross, Lugg pulled up the car and turned an exasperated face to his employer.

"Now where are we?" he demanded.

"How far have you been driving blind?" countered his employer mildly.

Mr. Lugg had the grace to look startled. "I was relying on you," he said bitterly. "I thought you'd sing out if I was going wrong. I didn't expect you to sit there like a dummy while we see England first. When I've bin in doubt I've bin taking the road to the left; and I've bin in doubt since we left Ipswich."

"At that rate," said Mr. Campion affably, "we ought to be just approaching it again. There's a map in that pocket by the side of you, Guffy. As for you, Lugg, you hop out and have a look at the signpost."

Still grumbling, Mr. Lugg obeyed, and came back a moment or so later with the information that the two roads on their right both seemed to lead to a place called Sweethearting, they were headed for Little Dunning, and had apparently come from Little Sweffling.

"There's nothing but a boy scout mark to show where that road leads to," he added, pointing to the remaining way. "Probably the poor bloke 'oo wrote the signpost didn't know and 'adn't got the energy to go and see. Shall we go and 'ave a look?"

"Boy scout mark?" enquired Campion, and as Lugg's great flail of a hand indicated a gate which led into a ploughed field on their right, the young man rose slowly and, climbing out of the car, went over to examine the sign chalked upon its surface.

He was so long away that Guffy, his curiosity aroused, went to join him and found him looking down at a round patch on the wood where the old and dirty surface had been scraped away. In the centre of the white wood thus displayed was a mark in red chalk. It was carefully made and consisted of a cross surmounted by a cedilla.

Mr. Campion was frowning. "How extraordinary!" he said. "It must be a coincidence, of course. Ever seen that mark before, Guffy? It's probably the most ancient symbol in the world."

Eager-Wright, who had now joined the group, looked puzzled.

"I have seen it somewhere before," he said. "What is it? A tramp sign?"

Campion shook his head. "No. It's most odd." There was a new inflexion in his voice and they regarded him with interest. He stretched out his hand and rubbed the chalk gently. "It's a perfect example of the ancient God-help-us mark," he said slowly. "Frankly, my dear old birds, you've no idea how ancient it is. It's probably the sign that the Children of Israel chalked up on their doors in times of persecution. The Ancient Britons used it when the Norse pirates swept down upon them. At the time of the Black Death you could find it on practically every door and house wall. The last time I saw it, it was scribbled upon a piece of corrugated iron in a devasted area in France after the war. You can never tell where it's going to turn up. It isn't an appeal to a Christian god, even. The symbol of the cross is much older than Christianity, of course. Usually this thing is found in terrorized districts, rather than in places where the danger has already struck. It's a sort of—well, it's a fear sign. It's very remarkable to find it here.''

"If we could find a 'public,' " said Mr. Lugg, on whom the phenomenon had made little or no impression, "we could ask our way. Then we should feel we were getting somewhere, and we wouldn't be wasting our time any'ow.''

There was no gainsaying the wisdom of this remark, and they trooped back to the car thoughtfully. The green countryside looked very peaceful and lovely in the late afternoon sun, but there was no telling what cloud might hang over this gentle unspoiled area, what secret might be hidden in its lush meadows or behind the branches of its leafy overhanging trees.

It was eight o'clock in the evening when Lugg, who seemed to have developed a beer-divining gift, steered the ancient Bentley slowly down the hill into the wide valley in which the village of Pontisbright lay. The main bulk of the place was built round two sides of a square heath comprising some twenty acres of gorse and heather, interspersed with short wiry grass. The principal road, down which they came, skirted one side of the heath and dipped suddenly, to swerve at right angles at the base of the valley and struggle off northward, leaving upon its left a small winding river by the side of which was an old white mill with a largish house attached.

The occupants of the car made a note of the mill. This, then, was the home of the Fittons, the children of a pretender to the Pontisbright title.

On the opposite side of the road from the mill was a considerable strip of woodland, and they guessed that the site of the original Pontisbright Hall must have been somewhere here.

They caught a glimpse of another house set squarely in the far corner of the wood, a structure whose white walls and slate roof looked curiously out of place in comparison with the antiquity around.

Lugg turned at right angles to the main road and brought the Bentley up with great pride before the entrance of one of the most delightful inns in a county famous for its hostelries.

The "Gauntlett" was shaped like an E without the centre stroke, and in the recess screened by its yellow walls was a cobbled yard, very fresh and clean. A row of benches bordered the yard and a large sign hung from a post planted in the cobbles. The rudely painted board was much faded, but the outline of a great mailed fist was just discernible on a blue ground.

The building was thatched, and its latticed windows were set crazily in the walls among the clematis which covered them.

The bar door was open, and two old men sat drinking beer in the last rays of the sun. They looked up with interest in their little watery eyes as the big car appeared. It was evident that the arrival of visitors was doomed to cause a certain amount of commotion. Startled faces appeared at the lower windows and the chatter from within died down.

Mr. Lugg sniffed as he clambered out and held the door open for his passengers to alight.

"Pretty as a picture, isn't it?" he said. "Look lovely covered with snow. Let us 'ope," he added solemnly, "that the quality of the beer don't make it all a mockery."

Mr. Campion ignored this pious wish and led the way into the bar, where they interviewed the landlord. This worthy turned out to be a stocky, rather startled little man in shirt-sleeves and a cloth cap. He seemed very dubious about providing them with accommodation, and they got the impression that he was genuinely put out by their unexpected arrival. Finally, however, he fell a victim to Guffy's powers of persuasion, and his wife, a large, red-faced woman, who shared her husband's faintly scared expression, conducted them upstairs to big unspoiled Tudor bedrooms.

As it was too late to go visiting, the personnel of the Court of Averna contented themselves with an evening devoted to deliberately casual enquiry. Eager-Wright and Guffy joined the dart players in the bar, while Mr. Campion engaged Mr. Bull, the landlord, at shove-ha'penny on the taproom table, polished to glass by long years of eager play.

The landlord was a past master with the five coins, and at sixpence a game was quite content to beat the harmless-looking young man from London until closing time and after.

Shove-ha'penny is a great leveller, and as the evening wore on, Mr. Bull and Mr. Campion reached a state of amity which might have been achieved only by years of different fostering. Mellowed, Mr. Bull revealed a streak of conscious virtue which his acquaintances somewhat naturally discredited instantly from his very insistence upon it.

"I wouldn't cheat you," he said to Mr. Campion, fixing the young man with a softening eye. "I wouldn't cheat you because that wouldn't be right. When I pick up my glass I might flip a coin into the bed with my sleeve." He illustrated the point with remarkable dexterity. "But I wouldn't do it. I wouldn't do it because that'd be cheating and that wouldn't be right."

"I wouldn't do it, either," said Mr. Campion, feeling that he was called upon to make some sort of echo to this important statement.

The landlord depressed his chin until it disappeared into the folds of his neck.

"Very likely not," he said. "Very likely you wouldn't. And very likely you couldn't, either. Takes a bit of prac-tising, that does. There's some people in this house now"—he nodded to an innocent-looking old man swig-ging beer in a corner—"who've been trying to do it for fifty years and never have, not without being caught. But I tell you what," he went on, breathing hops and confidence into Mr. Campion's ear, "there's one man you want to be

careful of at shove-ha'penny, and that's Scatty Williams.
Scatty Williams is a clever one.''

Mr. Campion appeared to be momentarily off his game.
''Sounds an attractive bird,'' he ventured.

''Bird?'' said the landlord, and spat. ''He's just an
ordinary old man. Looks a bit like a bird, now you come
to say so. Bit like a duck. Bald head and a long yeller
nose. Not bright yeller, mind you; about the colour of
these walls.''

Mr. Campion glanced at the mellowed plaster and his
mental picture of Scatty Williams grew from the merely
interesting to the fantastic.

''He works up at the mill,'' continued the landlord.
''Him and Miss Amanda practically run the business.''

Mr. Campion's expression became vacant almost to the
point of imbecility and he watched the landlord carefully
as he stepped back and screwed up his eyes preparatory to
taking a shot into the top bed.

''She's a one with the wireless,'' Mr. Bull remarked
without further explanation. ''That's what the mill's mostly
used for nowadays. They've got electric light down there.''

It had not occurred to Mr. Campion before that the mill
might be a running concern, and his interest in the Fitton
family grew.

''I shouldn't have thought there was enough grain around
here to support a mill,'' he said stupidly.

''Oh no,'' said Mr. Bull. ''No, there's very little corn. I
don't suppose Miss Amanda mills twenty sacks in a year.
She runs a dynamo. Charges up wireless batteries. She
told me she could put me up a light outside the house here.
Said she'd write my name in lights if I liked. Seems
funny, and that's a fact. So it is now.''

His opponent refrained from pointing out that as apparently the entire population of Pontisbright gathered at the
''Gauntlett'' already, not much purpose would be served
by any such ambitious scheme, but his interest in Miss
Amanda Fitton increased.

''She's clever for her age,'' was Mr. Bull's next remark, ''and I'm not trying to deceive you. Even if there

was any reason for it I wouldn't do that. But I reckon she must bring in quite thirty pounds a year, and her only seventeen. Of course they work hard for it, her and Scatty, but they get it."

"Seventeen?" said Mr. Campion, who was getting a remarkable mental picture of the two millers of Pontisbright. "Does this astonishing young woman live alone at the mill?"

"No, no. There's three on 'em. Three Fittons. There's Miss Mary, the eldest; she's twenty-three. Then comes Miss Amanda. Then there's young Mr. Hal. He's only sixteen. He'd be a lord of the land if the law was what it ought to be. He's a Pontisbright all right. You wait till you see him. Looks like the burning bush coming along; yes, yes, so he does now."

Mr. Campion had no time to enquire into this startling simile, for the landlord was still talking.

"They've got a foreigner staying with them, a fine upstanding old lady. Miss Huntingforest, her name is. Got knocked down by a burglar yesterday." He became thoughtful for a moment and then turned to Campion with the expression of one who has had a vision. "Now I *hev* thought of something," he said. "If you gentlemen want to stay here you'd better get took on at the mill as paying guests. I reckon they'd be glad to have you. Scatty was talking to me about borrowing the paper to see if there was anybody advertising for a place."

"That wouldn't be a bad idea at all," said Mr. Campion. "In fact, that'd be a very good idea. But I thought we'd fixed up here?"

"That'll be all right," said Mr. Bull vehemently. "Don't you worry about that. Some people'd complain and make a fuss about being put out, but I wouldn't. I ain't and I shan't. I don't feel it and I shan't say it. I'm honest, though I do say it myself."

"Quite," said Mr. Campion foolishly. "Quite. You're not very keen on visitors here at all, are you? I thought it was rather strange when we came in."

"Ah," said Mr. Bull, "strange it is, and I shouldn't be an honest man if I didn't admit that."

They went on playing until long after closing time, legal and actual. Eager-Wright and Guffy retired, and Campion remained with the landlord alone in the big empty taproom. An oil lamp had been lighted, and the uncertain shadows it cast over the table gave the landlord such an advantage over his opponent that it evidently seemed to him a waste of good money to suggest finishing the play.

Mr. Campion remained vague and foolish-looking, but the scared expression which had lingered in his host's eyes earlier in the evening returned as the shadows deepened, and towards eleven o'clock, while they were still playing, Mrs. Bull appeared in the doorway, a coat thrown over her nightgown. Her face was very pale, and when her husband stepped over to speak to her the indolent figure by the table caught a stifled sentence. The words were ordinary, but there was a thrill in the whisper in which they were uttered.

"It's out there again!"

Campion stepped over to the window, not wishing to eavesdrop, and, pulling back the short red curtain, looked out into one of the most perfect moonlit nights he had ever seen. The moon was nearly full and it streamed into the room like a flood-lamp. Outside it was so bright that colours were almost distinguishable.

Campion was standing there surveying the prospect when a quick step sounded behind him, and the next moment the curtain was jerked from his hand and thrust back into position across the window. He turned in polite surprise and caught sight of the landlord.

The man was very pale, his small eyes were starting and his lips quivering.

"Don't let that in here," he said huskily. "Don't let that in here, whatever you do."

He went into the bar and was pouring himself out a drink when Campion came in. The young man paused in the doorway, looking slight and ineffectual as ever.

"Something funny going on?" he enquired affably.

Mr. Bull swallowed his drink before replying. Then he lowered his voice and said unsteadily: "The powers of darkness, sir, God help us!"

As he spoke he traced something with his forefinger in the dregs on the bar, hastily wiping it off with a cloth immediately afterwards. Campion had just time to catch sight of a cross surmounted by a little hooked sign before it vanished beneath the duster.

The young man went slowly upstairs to bed. He did not undress, but stood for a long time at the window of his bedroom, looking over the moonlit garden of the inn. Since his room was at the back of the house he could not see the heath. The garden ran some way up the hill down which they had come into the village. Everything looked very peaceful in the brilliant light, and the air was warm and flower-scented. It seemed incredible that anything should be seriously amiss in such a lovely valley, or that any terror could walk abroad to alarm such guileless souls as the good people of the inn.

Mr. Campion was still standing motionless, his pale eyes thoughtful behind his spectacles, when the latch of his door clicked softly and he turned round just in time to see Lugg's enormous bulk and great white face looming into the room.

Mr. Campion surveyed him coldly. "Come for a night-light?" he enquired at length.

" 'Ush," said Mr. Lugg, holding up a warning hand. " 'Ush. Something's up. I 'aven't 'alf seen something. My legs is shaking so I can 'ardly speak."

Mr. Campion went over to his side, treading softly on the creaking oak boards.

"You're getting a bit eccentric, Lugg," he murmured. "Heard any voices?"

Mr. Lugg plumped himself down squarely on the bed.

"I've been out for a walk," he said. "I 'ad a touch of indigestion and I thought I'd walk it off. It seemed a nice night." He wiped his forehead and looked up at his master knowingly. "Thought I might get 'old of a bit of information about the place, and I 'ave. There's something very queer going on around 'ere. I found a corpse to start with.''

"A what?" said Mr. Campion momentarily taken aback.

"Corpse," said Lugg complacently. "I thought that'd make yer sit up. There it was lying out in the moonlight all wrapped up in a sheet. It give me a turn when I saw it. I emptied me flask at one go."

"Yes, well, what you want is a good rest," said Campion soothingly.

"It's lying out on the 'eath," Mr. Lugg persisted. "Come and 'ave a look at it. Just the thing to make yer sleep. I was walking along, just as you might be, 'ands in me pockets, and whistling soft to meself, when I come to a great patch of gorse. I was going round it when I see a gleam of white in a clearing in the middle of it. The moon was very strong and it picked out everything nearly as clear as day. I worked round the gorse till I come to a little path, and then I saw the corpse. It was all wrapped up in a shroud, just the face showing. There was pennies on the eyes and the jaw was dropped. It was a man—old man by the look of 'im—and stiff as you like. I just 'ad one look at 'im and came back 'ere like bingo."

Mr. Campion removed his spectacles. "It sounds worth seeing," he said mildly. "Come on."

They went quietly out of the inn, tiptoed across the cobbles and sighed with relief as their feet sank into the silencing turf of the heath.

"It's over there," said Lugg, pointing to a dark patch of gorse on the uninhabited side of the stretch. "Seems funny, don't it? A corpse is one thing, but a laid-out corpse on a blasted 'eath is another. Something shockin' about it."

Campion was silent, but he quickened his pace and gradually the patch of furze came nearer. When they were within a few yards of the outside edge, a stray cloud passed over the moon and left them temporarily in shadow.

" 'Ere we are." Lugg's voice was unusually husky. "This is the path."

He plunged down a narrow track, sweeping aside the overhanging branches of prickly yellow flowers as he went.

The moon came out from behind the cloud just as they entered the clearing, and the whole scene was once more lit brilliantly.

The clearing was empty, save for themselves.

Mr. Campion turned to the speechless Lugg.

"If we had a snare we might get a rabbit," he said conversationally.

"I saw it," said Mr. Lugg hysterically. "Look 'ere, you can see for yourself. This is where it was lying."

He pointed to a roughly made bed of dry bracken and hay in the centre of the clearing, where the moonlight fell uninterrupted.

Campion stepped forward and picked up something lying half hidden by the shadow under a gorse bush. It was a piece of linen about as big as a man's pocket handkerchief. He shook it out gingerly and Lugg grunted.

Scrawled upon the cloth was the sign again, a cross with a cedilla at the top.

"Well," said Mr. Lugg, whose vocabulary had deserted him. "Well, I ask you!"

Mr. Campion dropped the rag and wiped his long, pale fingers fastidiously with his handkerchief.

"Don't, my dear old bird," he said. "Don't. I don't know."

CHAPTER V

The Miller

"But yesterday a king," remarked Mr. Campion as he walked across the heath to the mill with Guffy and Eager-Wright the following morning. "To-day, a poor gentleman come about the trouble. There's a natty line in cheap philosophy somewhere there."

"We drop the Hereditary Paladin business, then?" said Eager-Wright, not without relief.

Campion nodded. "From now on," he said primly, "I get no more respect than my naturally superior intellect deserves."

Guffy, who had not been listening to the conversation, but who had been surveying the scene with approval, turned. On the soil of his own county he was no longer the diffident, affable soul he had been on the Continent. Here he was a man of information.

"What a pity they took down the old house," he said. "It must have been rather fine." He indicated a mound of parkland which rose out of a wooded stretch on their right. "Quite a nice little bit of shooting, still, I should say," he went on. "Not hunting country. That must be the rectory over there by the church, I suppose."

The three young men glanced towards the slate roof of the modern house they had noticed from the car, and Eager-Wright uttered the general thought.

"It may not be very easy to go prowling about in those woods," he said. "Still, I imagine we've got the place to ourselves. Widow's Peak would hardly hang about after his colossal blunder in attacking Miss Huntingforest, or whatever her name is."

45

Guffy, who was becoming more of the fine old country gentleman at every step, beamed.

"Now we're actually here," he said, "I feel that no beastly London magnate with his dirty little crooks can put up much of a show against us," he said.

Eager-Wright grinned, but Mr. Campion remained impassive.

"I don't know whether it's occurred to you," he said diffidently, "that our big business friend, Savanake, is employing Widow's Peak and Sniffy Edwards at the moment because he's at the disadvantage of having led a more or less upright life for the past year or two. Any moment now it may occur to him to get hold of something rather better class in the crook line. That's why we've got to hurry. You know: haste is essential. The early birds get the worm. First reasonable offer will conclude deal. You all know how I got the V.C. at Rorke's Drift, but in spite of my well-known intrepidity, which you all admire so much, I should be glad to get the Mother's Union prizes safely under lock and key before Savanake undertakes the job himself. Hullo, here we are."

They had left the heath now and turned down the narrow lane to the mill. Here, spread out before them, was the real rustic loveliness of Suffolk at its best. In spite of the industry of Miss Amanda and her assistant it was evident that the mill did little business, for the track was grass-grown and culminated in a rough patch of green which sloped gently down to a white-flecked race. The mill itself, a great white wood and brick building, sprawled across the stream into the meadow on the opposite bank, and beside it stood the house.

If there had been any doubt that the millers of Pontis-bright had once been prosperous folk, it must have been instantly dispelled. The house was a nearly perfect example of late fifteenth-century architecture. Its wattle-and-daub walls were plastered over and ornamented with fine mouldings. Big diamond-pattern casement windows bulged beneath rust-red tiles, and the whole rambling place suggested somehow the trim blowsiness of a Spanish galleon.

The charm of the place was increased by faded chintz curtains billowing through the open windows, and the gleam of polished wood from within. Even a remarkably complex wireless aerial festooned across the roof had a rustic and archaic look.

There was one startling anachronism, however. Drawn up before the door was an extremely ancient but unmistakable electric brougham. This remarkable vehicle had been painted crimson by an inexpert hand, and now sat, squat and self-conscious, blushing violently for its own age.

As they came nearer they saw that the original upholstery, long since defunct, had been replaced by the same variety of faded chintz that adorned the house.

Guffy stared at the apparition in respectful astonishment.

"That looks like the thing the guv'nor paid a man in Ipswich ten quid to take away, the year of the war," he said. "What an extraordinary thing!" He paused and looked about him dubiously. "I say, there's rather a lot of us," he ventured. "Suppose you two go and make the arrangements? I'll wait for you."

"Grand old man seized with social funk," said Eager-Wright. "Come on, Campion."

From the moment they approached the front door, an air of faintly hilarious unreality descended upon the whole proceedings. As soon as Eager-Wright knocked the door was swung open with suspicious celerity by a person who was easily recognizable from the landlord's description as Scatty Williams.

The man really was amazingly like a duck. His head was very bald and very white, but his face was a yellowish tan. There was a ring just above his ears which showed quite clearly where his hatband finished, and his face and neck were exposed to the elements. Two little bright blue eyes almost hidden by shaggy grey eyebrows were set close together beside the narrow bridge of an enormous nose, which splayed out at the tip so very like a duck's bill that one almost expected him to quack. To add to the incongruousness of his appearance he was wearing a white dress waistcoat of ancient cut which had been fitted with white sleeves, so that it faintly resembled a cocktail jacket. For the rest, however, he was arrayed in corduroy trousers, enormous boots and a very bright blue shirt without a collar.

He beamed at the visitors, and it dawned upon them that he was one of those people whose natural qualities unconsciously exaggerate every emotion they may happen to feel. His smile of welcome was transformed, therefore, into a horrific grin of pure joy.

"Come in, come in," he said before they could speak, and then, pulling himself together, he added with a gravity which was as portentous as his delight had been vivid: "You'll be the gentlemen who were thinkin' o' staying here? What name shall I tell the lady?"

Eager-Wright shot an enquiring glance at his companion.

"Mr. Wright and Mr. Campion," said the pale young man firmly.

Their guide, mumbling the names over to himself so that he should not forget them, led the visitors over a sweet-smelling, stone-flagged hall into a low, very dimly-lit room in which dark masses of furniture loomed indistinctly.

The room really was absurdly dark. Eager-Wright stumbled over a chair as soon as he entered and regained his feet with a muttered apology, to find himself looking down at someone who had come forward to meet him with outstretched hand.

"Hullo," said a clear, unexpectedly vibrant female voice. "I mean, how do you do? I'm Amanda Fitton. The house is extremely old and very picturesque. There are remarkable fac—fac—well, advantages for bathing, boating, fishing, walking, and—er—motoring."

There was a pause for breath and a clatter as Campion kicked a side table in his attempt to step up beside his companion.

"Perhaps you saw the car outside?" continued the voice with a barely concealed note of pride in its tone.

"The food is good," she hurried on. "Home-cooked and—er—liberal. If you are delicate the water is very good here. You can have as much milk and butter and eggs as you can eat."

As the visitors made no sound, if the laboured breathing of Eager-Wright could be discounted, the voice continued, this time with a hint of desperation in its depths:

"There is rough-shooting in the autumn and, no doubt, golf on the heath. The food is good," she repeated rather lamely, "and would five guineas be too much? There are three of you, aren't there? Three and a man?"

"Five guineas each?" enquired Eager-Wright.

"Oh, no! Five guineas altogether. Or we could make it pounds. We can take you for as long as you like, and the beds are good."

There was a pause and the voice became unexpectedly wheedling.

"You will come, won't you? We've got electric light in some of the rooms, and the mill doesn't make much noise, really, and Scatty and I—I mean Williams—can work it when you're out."

"That sounds very fine," said Mr. Campion's vague, idiotic voice out of the dusk. "Let me give you our recommendations. We're all house-trained, to start with. Good-tempered, and, except for Lugg, remarkably well-mannered. We dislike hot and cold water, modern improvements, inside sanitation, central heating, and expensive wall-paper. My friend here—Mr. Wright—who appears to have fallen over something else, is engaged on a book about rural Suffolk, while I am partly assisting him and partly on holiday. Lugg is very useful about the house, and we had intended to pay three guineas a week each. Do you think we shall suit you?"

Once again there was silence in the gloom and then the voice remarked unexpectedly: "Do you mind shabby furniture? Tears in things, I mean."

"Nothing, in my opinion," said Mr. Campion firmly, "gives a house more old-world charm than tears in furniture."

"Oh, well," said the voice, "in that case let's have a little light on things. Stand by while I pull up the blinds."

They heard her moving cautiously across the room and then, with a great rattle of rings, the curtains were thrown back, and what had once been a pleasantly furnished room came into sight.

It was certainly true that there were tears in the furniture. Even the best brocade wears out in time, and the delicate rose and blue coverings of the formal settees and wing armchairs had been mended and remended until they would stand repair no longer. The Brussels carpet was so threadbare that only faint indications of pattern remained, and everything in the room which age could mar, in spite of care, had been spoiled long before.

Miss Amanda's visitors, however, were oblivious of these details. Their interest was not unnaturally centred upon the girl herself.

Amanda Fitton, eighteen next month, was at a stage of physical perfection seldom attained at any age. She was not very tall, slender almost to skinniness, with big honey-brown eyes, and an extraordinary mop of hair so red that it was remarkable in itself. This was not auburn hair nor yet carroty, but a blazing, flaming, and yet subtle colour which is as rare as it is beautiful. Her costume consisted of a white print dress with little green flowers on it, a species of curtaining sold at many village shops. It was cut severely, and was rather long in the skirt.

There was something artificially formal in her whole appearance. Her hair had been dressed rather high on her head and certainly in no modern fashion.

She eyed them calmly with the inquisitive, but polite, regard of a child.

Eager-Wright was staring at her with frank admiration. Mr. Campion, as usual, looked merely foolish.

She shrugged her shoulders eloquently. "Well, now you've seen the room," she said, "and you know the worst. Or very nearly the worst," she corrected herself quickly. "All the rooms want doing up a bit, but the beds really are good. And the food really could be absolutely marvellous if you did pay three guineas a week each," she added with a sudden burst of naïveté.

"Oh, well, then, that's fixed up," said Eager-Wright with tremendous satisfaction.

She smiled at him, a wholly disarming gesture which opened her mouth into a triangle, and revealed very small white even teeth.

"Wait!" she said. "You'll have to find out sooner or later. You may as well hear it all. Of course this is very awkward, but then you can always have one of those flat round ones, and I don't mind fetching water. We could have the copper alight all day. And if you wanted one when you came in—in the evening or anything—we could just get it out of the copper in a pail. Four pails makes a really good one. Besides, if you've never had one in those round things it's rather fun. After all, you are on a holiday and there'll be bathing."

"I know," said Mr. Campion happily. "You haven't got a bathroom."

She looked at them wistfully, and wrinkled her nose engagingly.

"Does it really matter—awfully?"

"Not in the least!" said Eager-Wright, who was quite prepared to forswear baths for ever and a day should she desire it. "I could always get the water," he continued helpfully. "I mean, if you showed me where the copper was and all that sort of thing."

"I tell you what," said Amanda with sudden enthusiasm, "we could have a pump from the copper all worked by electricity. Scatty and I have got some marvellous gadgets. You'll have to see them. How long can you stay?"

"A week," said Campion quickly, before Eager-Wright could engage the room for life.

"Oh, well, that's splendid," she said. "Are the others like you? Oh, and will you have your food by yourselves or will you eat it with us? It's rather fun eating with us and it doesn't make so much work. Oh—and do you think your man would mind sharing a room with Scatty? He needn't, of course, because I can always sleep in the mill. We could put up an army in the mill if we cleared away some of the things." She stopped abruptly. "I'm not putting you off, am I?"

"Good Lord, no," said Eager-Wright, who could not take his eyes off her face. "I'm only worrying if you'll be able to put up with us. There's such a lot of us and—"

"There's Lugg, of course," said Mr. Campion. "He lowers our stock considerably."

She waved his words away airily. "Oh, well, that's marvellous," she said. "Now you're here and it's all fixed up, what shall we do first? Come and see the rest of the house. It really is rather jolly amd the beds are good. And the food ought to be all right. We've got one P.G. already; Aunt Hatt. She's been with us three years now. She came over from America on a visit and stayed with us for a bit, and then she sort of took over everything. We're really the nonpaying guests, as a matter of fact. Scatty and I don't make a lot at the mill, and our hundred a year doesn't go very far. And"—she paused and looked at them delightfully—"it isn't really queer my telling you all this, because if you're going to live with us for a week you may as well know all about us and then you won't be surprised by anything. First of all, about Scatty. He opened the door to you just now. Well, he isn't really a butler. Only when old Honesty Bull sent down this morning and told us that there were some people who wanted to stay down here for a bit he said you had an enormous car. And so I thought we'd better smarten up a bit. That's why I've got this frock on, and I made the drawing-room a bit dark. We had two women hikers once, but I'm afraid the drawing-room put them off. So I determined it shouldn't happen again. Scatty and I work the mill."

She stopped breathlessly.

Mr. Campion smiled. "Just the place for Wright and his book," he said. "As soon as I heard it was a mill I said 'Just the thing. Nothing like running water for inspiration.' And wheels within wheels, and that sort of thing."

Amanda shot a dubious glance in Mr. Campion's direction before she hurried on again.

"Oh, well, come and see Aunt Hatt," she said. "I

expect she's in the kitchen. She cooks so much better than Mary that she took over after she'd been here a week. Do you like American food? Scatty and I fixed her up an electric waffle iron. It works all right, but it's a bit big—the blacksmith made the actual grill—and you get waffles about a foot across. But I think that's all the better. Come on."

She led them across the hall again, whose carved king beam was at least as old as the Wars of the Roses, and through an archway into a great kitchen.

This was a vast apartment with whitewashed walls and a red stone floor. Standing by a table, which looked as though it had been built to hold machinery, was a tall grey-haired woman with a big apron tied over her brown walking skirt and blouse, and a pair of golden pince-nez on her nose.

Her whole appearance suggested a brisk practicalness in direct opposition to Amanda's more inconsequential personality. At the moment she was engaged in lifting little round currant buns out of an oven-tray, and the golden heap on the wire stand looked very inviting.

"Well, did you have any luck?" she said, and shut her mouth quickly, as she realized that Amanda was not alone. But the next moment, as she caught sight of the young men, a smile spread over her face and she laughed like a girl.

"There's four of them," said Amanda. "And they're paying three guineas a week each, and they don't mind there not being a bath. Oh, wait a minute: Mr. Campion, this is Aunt Hatt—Miss Huntingforest. And this is Mr. Wright, Aunt. Where's Mary? Over at the mill?"

Miss Huntingforest ignored the question. She was surveying the young men with critical, but friendly eyes.

"You're on holiday, I suppose?" she enquired.

Mr. Campion repeated his little speech about Eager-Wright's history of Suffolk, and Miss Huntingforest seemed reassured.

"Really? An author?" she said, looking at the young man with quickening interest. "Well, isn't that nice."

Eager-Wright looked uncomfortable and muttered a few words of modest depreciation.

Aunt Hatt relieved his embarrassment by offering them all a bun. As they stood round in the kitchen nibbling her gift, the slight formality which had momentarily fallen on the party was dispelled.

Miss Huntingforest went on with her cooking, talking the whole time with that complete lack of self-consciousness which seemed to be the keynote of the whole household.

"You'll forgive my enquiring what you are doing down here," she said, stooping down to peer into the enormous oven. "I'm not a nervous woman as a rule, but since that attack on me the other day I have certainly been a little alarmed."

"Oh yes," said Amanda quickly. "I ought to have asked you; do you mind burglars?"

"Not at all," said Mr. Campion easily. "Do you have many?"

"Only one so far," said Miss Huntingforest grimly. "But that was not enough. If he hadn't struck me down before I realized what he was up to I could have managed him. But you don't expect such things in a civilized country. I was alone in the house," she hurried on. "The children were in the village and I'd just come out here to see if the bread was rising, when I saw him come creeping out of the dairy. He must have got in by the back window. I said: 'Young man, will you please inform me what you're doing?' He spun round and looked at me and I had just time to see that he was a stranger, and had the most remarkable peak of hair coming down right over his forehead, and then, as I went for him, he put up his hand and caught me on the chin. I went down and hit my head on the table, rendering me completely unconscious. It's a miracle I didn't swallow my dentures and choke to death. I wrote to every paper in London about it."

She paused.

"A horrible experience," said Eager-Wright, while Mr. Campion looked foolish and sympathetic at the same time.

"And, of course, he didn't take a thing," said the good lady.

"Adding insult to injury," put in Amanda, and she and her aunt laughed immoderately.

Miss Huntingforest turned to the young men. "I don't know whether Amanda's put you wise to the family," she said. "It's a rather curious arrangement, but it works very well."

"I told them practically everything," said Amanda consideringly. "You see," she went on, turning to the guests, "when mother died four years ago we decided we'd have to make the mill a going concern and take paying guests and carry on generally. Well, so far the paying guest department is the only really paying line. We've only had one guest of course—Aunt Hatt—but from our point of view that's been a howling success."

Miss Huntingforest seemed to think it was her turn to explain a little, although why either of them should have been so courteous was beyond Mr. Campion's powers of divination.

"Well, it was like this," she said. "My father was an Englishman, and, although he never talked about it, I knew he came from this part of the world. And some years ago I thought that as I was planning a little globe-trotting I might come down here and see what the home town of the Huntingforests looked like. Well, when I got here I took rooms in the village at first. And then I met these children and I realized, of course, that they must be distant connexions of ours. And so I came to stay here. I hadn't been in the house a week before I decided that I must take things in hand. There was Amanda, if you please, running about like a Milwaukee Indian, without a mended stocking to her name. It wasn't nice to have two pretty young girls without a chaperon in the heart of the country like this. It wasn't nice and it wasn't safe. I'm emancipated, I hope, but I'm no fool. So I put my foot down and here I am."

She drew another great tin of cookies out of the oven as she finished speaking, and Amanda helped herself, motioning them to imitate her.

Miss Huntingforest beamed at them. "If you can eat cakes at eleven o'clock in the morning you're all right," she said. "It's an acid test, in my opinion. If a man can eat two cookies before noon and enjoy them there's not much wrong with him."

"Well, look here," said Amanda, "I'll take you round the house and Scatty'll get your things. I'll go up with him and cadge a ride back in your car. I've never been in a really decent car. Mine goes by electricity, you know."

"Goes!" said Miss Huntingforest with good-humoured contempt.

Amanda blushed. "Aunt Hatt's very rude about my car," she said. "But it's really very useful, and not at all bad, considering that I bought it off a higgler for a pound, and Scatty and I made it go. There's only one thing against it; you can't go more than five miles in it. Two and a half miles out and two and a half miles back: then the batteries have to be recharged. That doesn't cost very much because of the mill, you see. There's as much power as you want there. It means a lot of work in the winter, seeing to the sluices and that sort of thing, but it's worth it. I left it outside the door this morning because I thought it might impress you. It did, didn't it?"

"It certainly did," said Mr. Campion truthfully.

"There you are! I had a row with Hal about it. He said it'd put anyone off. I must go and help Scatty push it back to the shed in a minute, because the battery's being charged and we've only got one."

"Let's all go and push it," said Eager-Wright, who seemed anxious to serve in some way or other.

She turned to the door, but was restrained by Miss Huntingforest.

"Amanda, that's your one respectable dress."

"Oh, yes, of course. I forgot. I'll go and change. They've said they'll stay, anyhow, and I don't suppose my working clothes will really put them off."

Miss Huntingforest seemed to have doubts on this point, but she said nothing and the girl hurried out.

"If you're interested in antiquities—" began Aunt Hatt, but got no further on this subject, for at that moment there was a certain amount of confusion in the hall outside, and Guffy's voice was heard distinctly.

"Really, it's quite all right," he was saying. "A bit of a scratch—nothing else."

At the same time the kitchen door was opened and a girl who could quite clearly be no one else but Mary, Amanda's elder sister, appeared with Guffy in tow, while a boy about sixteen followed them.

Mary Fitton had Amanda's hair, Amanda's eyes, but not Amanda's pep. In exchange, Nature had endowed her with a grace all her own and an attractive, but serious, expression.

The boy resembled his sisters as far as the hair was concerned, but already he had developed a certain pugnacity of expression.

Both strangers were tremendously excited, and Guffy, looking pale and slightly flustered, strode between them. He was in his shirtsleeves, and his right hand was closed tightly over his left forearm, which was covered with blood.

"Come on, put it under the pump," said Mary.

She spoke as though she had known her companion a long time, and it occurred to Campion that she, too, must have the family gift for making friends.

They all crowded round Guffy as he stood by the sink, while young Hal pumped streams of water over the injured arm.

"Well, for crying out loud!" said Miss Huntingforest. "That's a nasty scrape. Where did this happen?"

While introductions were hastily effected, Guffy explained.

"I—er—I was prowling round the mill," he said, "when Miss Fitton here took pity on me and introduced herself. I was investigating a loom there is up there—most interesting—when I lost my footing and crashed through one of the floorboards."

"Dry-rot," said Miss Huntingforest. "I've said it over and over again. You might have killed yourself."

"I was all right," said Guffy hastily. "Only struggling back, like a fool, I caught my arm on a six-inch nail. I'd taken off my coat to give a hand with the loom and, of course, this is what happened. It pierced the skin."

"Pierced the skin!" said Aunt Hatt. "You'll have to

have stitches in that. Wait a minute: I'll make a tourniquet and then you can wash it as much as you like.''

Mary glanced at her aunt. "I think he'd better go up to Doctor Galley," she said. "You be quiet," she added, as Guffy opened his mouth to speak. "You can't wander about with a tear like that. It'll get awfully sore if you don't have it sewn immediately.''

Hal smiled at Guffy, as from one superior being to another.

"She's a bit bossy," he said. "But I think she's right, you know. Look here, we'll walk up with you. Galley's a very good man; he hardly hurts at all. He takes out teeth as well—if you need it.''

Eventually, after a certain amount of protestation, Hal and Mary set out with their captive for the doctor's, and prevailed upon Eager-Wright to accompany them.

Mr. Campion appeared to have been forgotten, and he sat in a little recess in a corner of the hall and looked through the open doorway at the quivering leaves and dancing water without. The old house seemed very quiet after the hullabaloo. It was really amazingly attractive. Like all very old houses it had a certain drowsy elegance that was very soothing and comforting in a madly gyrating world.

He allowed his thoughts to wander idly. He noticed the delicate Gothic carving of the stone fireplace, sniffed appreciatively at the mingled odours of wallflower and baking cookie, and wondered how the rabid busybodies who leap upon ancient monuments and tear them stone from stone that they may grace the dank loneliness of museums could have overlooked such a perfect unspoiled gem.

He was disturbed in his reflections by the reappearance of Amanda dancing down the staircase in her "working clothes." At first sight she appeared to have put back her age ten years or so. Her slender figure was covered by an old brown jersey and skirt which had shrunk with much washing until they clung to her like a skin. The only concession to vanity was a yellow-and-red bandanna handkerchief knotted loosely round her neck.

"Hullo," she said. "Where are the others?"

Mr. Campion explained. Amanda looked crestfallen.

"Has that floor gone at last? Scatty and I wondered if we couldn't re-board it with faggot poles. They wouldn't be comfortable to tread on, but they'd be safe. I'm very sorry. Is he badly hurt?"

"I don't think so. He seemed to be enjoying it," said Campion truthfully. "Your sister was looking after him. She's taken him to the doctor now."

Amanda was silent. A shadow had passed over her face.

"I didn't think I'd go myself," Mr. Campion continued. "It was rather like joining the crowd round an accident, I felt. By the way, I hope your doctor is not too rustic. Not the cobbler in his spare time, or anything like that?"

She shook her head. "Oh no. Old Galley's all right, really."

She stood fidgeting in the middle of the hall, looking absurdly young.

Something prompted Mr. Campion to take a shot in the dark.

"I must get back to Lugg," he said. "That's my man. He's getting very temperamental. He went for a walk on the heath last night and came back with a ridiculous story about finding a corpse on the heath."

He stopped abruptly. The girl was looking at him with a mixture of alarm and defiance in her eyes.

"Don't you think it would be nice?" she said in a tone which warned him not to continue as clearly as if she had said the words. "Don't you think it would be nice if we went to see the mill?"

"Splendid idea," said Mr. Campion affably.

His tone and expression were friendly, but his pale eyes behind his spectacles were keen and searching, and it had not escaped him that Amanda's cheeks were very white and her lips were trembling.

CHAPTER VI

Tongues in Trees

"Ease her a bit! Ease her! Now hang on or she'll go in the river."

Amanda, breathless and crimson with exertion, clung to the archaic steering arm of the old brougham.

Mr. Campion, who was pushing the cumbersome vehicle up the dangerous slope to the coach-house of the mill, did as he was told.

"If only Scatty was a proper chauffeur," Amanda observed, as they tucked this great-great-grandmother of electric transport into an old striped-canvas shroud. "If only Scatty was a proper chauffeur he could do all this shoving."

"That's right," said Mr. Campion brightly. "Or if he was a horse."

Amanda regarded him coldly. "You admitted the car looked very well outside the house," she said with dignity. "You're probably one of those people like Hal who don't believe in appearances. But I do. Appearances matter an awful lot."

"Oh, rather," said Mr. Campion. "I knew a man once who carried it to excess, though. His name was Gosling, you see, so he always dressed in grey and yellow, and occasionally wore a great false beak. People remembered his name, of course. But his wife didn't like it. Of course, he had perfectly ordinary children—not eggs—and that was a blow to him. And finally he moved into a wooden house with just slats in front instead of windows, and you opened the front door with a pulley on the roof. It had a natty little letterbox on the front gate with "The Coop" painted on it. Soon after, his wife left him and the Borough Council stepped in. But I see you don't believe me."

"Oh, but I do," said Amanda. "I was his wife. Come and see the mill."

The shadows of the leaves made dancing grey patterns on the white walls, the water was very clear, and the air was warm and sunny, as they came across the yard and turned into the cool, slightly musty-smelling building.

"There isn't much to see up here," said Amanda, "except my dynamo, which is rather fun. That's our principal possession. Then there's Mary's loom. She makes homespun scarves and things. They go to a shop in London. She doesn't get much for them, but they're very pretty. That's all there is except the oak, and that's Hal's."

"The oak?" enquired Mr. Campion.

She nodded. "It's right up in the mill tower. It isn't much to see, but it's the only Pontisbright heirloom we've got. It isn't really an heirloom at all, because I suppose we stole it. But nobody wanted it except us."

She paused, and stood leaning against one of the pillars which supported the crazy floor of the apartment above. An old sack-shoot trap stood open, and through it was a vivid picture of green meadows, overblown trees, and a little winding stream which flowed gently on to the crimson and yellow of a distant osier bed.

She made such a fantastic figure in her tight brown jersey and red-and-yellow kerchief that Campion, regarding her owlishly behind his spectacles, wondered if the whole adventure were quite real.

He sat down on a pile of sacks, and the girl's next remark was in keeping with his mood.

"Of course," she said, "Hal's the proper Earl of Pontisbright. That makes it all the more fun, don't you think?"

Mr. Campion blinked. "It all depends what you mean by fun," he said cautiously.

"Oh, well—the missing earl and all that sort of thing. You know; the wicked great-grandmother, the babe in the snow, and justice gone astray. It's so nice when it's true. Shall I tell you about it?"

It was evident to him that the query was superfluous. Amanda, always informative, was in chatty mood.

"Well," she said before he could assent, "the last proper Earl of Pontisbright—that is, the last man who lived at the Hall—had two sons; a young one called Giles and an older one called Hal. Well, Giles went off to America and was never heard of again until Aunt Hatt turned up. She's his granddaughter. But the elder son stayed on with his father and mother, who was an absolute terror called Josephine, until he was about twenty-five, when he fell in love with an absolutely beautiful girl called Mary Fitton, and they got engaged.

"Mary Fitton lived over at Sweethearting with her father, who was just a knight."

She paused. "You don't look very intelligent," she said. "Are you taking it all in?"

"Every word," said Mr. Campion truthfully. "Aunt Hatt's grandfather's eldest brother was engaged to Mary Fitton, whose father was just a knight. I suppose he had trouble with his parents? A battle of snobs in high life, as it were."

"Oh, no. Only with great-great-grandmother Josephine," said Amanda quickly. "His father was rather keen on the marriage, and, anyway, they did get properly engaged. And then, of course, the Crimea happened, and one day Hal rode over to tell Mary that he'd got to go off to the war next morning. And so he said could they get married at once? And she said Yes. And so they went to the clergyman and persuaded him to do them. And it wasn't very legal, but he did. Then Hal and his father both went to the war and got killed, and the Countess Josephine had the nerve to say that Hal and Mary hadn't been married at all, and so the little Hal wouldn't be the heir when he arrived. And she bribed or frightened the parson, who must have been an awful fool, anyhow, into saying there hadn't been any marriage, and so the title lapsed, and the Countess Josephine sold up everything and had the house pulled down. Still clear?" she demanded, somewhat breathlessly.

"Yes," said the valiant Mr. Campion. "Can I tell you the story of my life after this?"

Amanda ignored him and went on: "Mary Fitton got into trouble from her relations, but the little Hal, although he was poor, was an awfully fierce sort of person, and clearly a Pontisbright. He went off to London and made some money and got married, and his son was called Hal, too, and that was my father. He came down here and bought the mill and fought the claim, really because he had promised his father he would for the first Mary Fitton's sake. But it was very awkward, and he had no documents, and so he lost. Then he got killed in the war, and his money was lost in the war, too, all except a hundred a year, which we've got. But you see how it all happened, don't you? I mean, the Countess Josephine business, and why Hal is the proper rightful earl. You believe it, don't you?" she went on anxiously.

Mr. Campion's pale eyes smiled from behind his enormous spectacles as he looked from the girl in the shadow to the green and lovely scene without. After all, he reflected, if the electric brougham were true, why not the story of the rightful earl?

"Of course it's true," said Amanda, breaking into his thoughts. "That's why we stole the oak. Would you like to see it? These steps aren't very safe, so you'll have to take care."

She led him across the uneven floor to a very tottery open staircase, which led up to the apartment above.

"There isn't time to show you all this now," she said, pointing vaguely to the big dusty barn in which they stood. "The oak's in the tower. It took six men to get it there, besides me."

The tower of the mill proved to be a small wooden room, built on above the main structure, and as they climbed into it the air smelt hot and stuffy, and there was an ominous scampering in one corner.

"Rats," the girl remarked cheerfully. "There's dozens of them about. Ratting's rather fun. Well, here you are. Here's the oak."

She displayed a huge cross-section of an oak bole, about four inches thick, which leant up against the wall under the window.

"We stole it; or at any rate we took it," she said proudly.

"Very determined of you," murmured Mr. Campion affably. "Where was it?"

"On the tree, of course," she said. "If you're interested I'll tell you about it, but if you're not I'll save it for some other time." As usual she hurried on without waiting for a reply. "First of all, the oak tree that this belonged to was supposed to have been planted by the first Pontisbright that ever was, hundreds of years ago, and it stood up in the park by the Hall. It was famous all over the county. And then a long while ago, probably about seventeen hundred, a part of it blew off. So they cut the rest down quite short, until it was about as high as a table from the ground, and they fixed a brass sundial over it. When the Countess Josephine sold the house she sold the sundial, too, and it was unscrewed and taken away. Well, we found the tree—or rather, Father and Mary did, when Mary was quite young—and we stole this slice off it. It was a tremendous business to cut, I believe. I wasn't old enough to know much about it then, but anyway here it is."

Mr. Campion's pale face was perfectly blank. "Very nice, too," he said. "But what for?"

"The inscription, of course," said the girl. "It was on the wood under the sundial, rather badly carved and a bit mossy when we found it. But that's gone now. I scrubbed it. If you could help me push it back a bit—it's frightfully heavy, so be careful—I could show you what I meant."

Mr. Campion was fast learning that association with Amanda always entailed strenuous physical exertion. He took off his coat, and between them they lowered the great disc gently to the floor. The underside of the wood, which now lay revealed, had roughly gouged signs upon its blackened surface. Cracks had defaced the letters in some places, but the tremendous depth of the carving and the size of the ciphers had helped to preserve their character.

There appeared to be eight lines of lettering, each character being a good three inches high.

Mr. Campion said nothing, and the girl dropped upon her knees and with a somewhat grubby forefinger traced the words as she read, while the young man, bending over her, followed her finger, an expression of complete stupidity on his pleasant, vacuous face.

"If Pontisbright would crownèd be,
Three strange happenings must he see.
The diamond must be rent in twain
Before he wear his crown again.
Thrice must the mighty bell be toll'd
Before he shall the sceptre hold,
And ere he to his birthright come
Stricken must be Malplaquet drum."

"Rather jolly, isn't it?"

Mr. Campion looked more vague than ever. "I say," he began diffidently, "this would probably be of great use to old Wright in his book. I'd like to take a copy of it for my album, too. There's one thing I don't follow: if the tree was blown down about seventeen hundred, and the sundial was put on the stump then, how did this carving come to be on the wood itself?"

"Oh, we worked that out," said Amanda. "It's quite simple, really. You see, we imagine this inscription was meant to be a secret affair, and we think the man who wrote it was the father-in-law of the Countess Josephine. He was always writing bits of verse. Mother had some of his letters, and he often broke out into doggerel in those. You see," she went on earnestly, striving to make herself clear, "we think this writing was not done before the sundial was put on, but after. Someone unscrewed it, did the carving and then put the sundial back. We worked this out from the condition the letters were in when we found it."

"That would make the date of the inscription about eighteen-twenty, I suppose?" ventured the young man, glancing up from the envelope on which he had been scribbling. "I say, this'll help Wright tremendously in his book. There's nothing like a secret inscription or two to give an author's work the authentic touch. Then the publishers can say: 'Mr. Wright, who is, of course . . .' Well, well, he will be pleased."

"Isn't it about time," said Amanda, regarding him steadily, "that you dropped all this holiday business? We know who you are. That's why we were so keen on your coming to stay with us. That's why I've shown you this. Does it interest you, or doesn't it?"

For some moments Mr. Campion was silent. Amanda looked slightly uncomfortable.

"Look here," she said with one of her sudden bursts of confidence, "perhaps I'd better tell you all about it now. You see, about a week ago a most unpleasant person, pretending to be a professor of some sort, presented himself at the front door and put Mary and me through a thorough cross-questioning about inscriptions; had we got any? had we heard of any in the wood? and all that sort of thing. Naturally we shut up like oysters and I had the oak moved up here for safety."

"I see," said Mr. Campion soberly. "This professing person, was there anything odd about him?"

"He hadn't a widow's peak, if that's what you mean," said Amanda. "He was just an ordinary, scrubby little soul. Not bad enough to throw in the race, you know; but we didn't like him."

"Quite," agreed Mr. Campion. "Tell me, was it the honest manliness of my appearance which made you confide in me with such touching spontaneity?"

"No," said Amanda. "I told you, we knew about you. Aunt Hatt used to be a great friend of Mrs. Lobbett and her husband, down in the South somewhere, and she heard all about you from them. D'you remember them? She used to be Biddy Pagett."

Mr. Campion gazed thoughtfully out of the window. "Oh yes," he said. "I remember Biddy. I remember Biddy very well."

Amanda shot a shrewd, quick glance in his direction and changed the subject.

"When old Honesty Bull sent down to us this morning to tell us some people wanted to stay, he also told us your names. We had a council of war and decided that you were just the man to get into the house. It doesn't really matter, does it?"

Mr. Campion turned to her and there was unexpected gravity in the eyes behind the spectacles.

"Amanda," he said, "this has got to be kept quiet."

She nodded. "I know." She put back her head and passed a finger across her throat. "Not a word," she said. "Only, if there's anything we can do, let us in on it, won't you?"

He seated himself upon the window-ledge. "How much of my illustrious life have you been able to mug up?"

"Not a lot," said Amanda, crestfallen. "Aunt Hatt didn't know much. She only knew your name and that you were in the adventure over at Mystery Mile. And we know you live in Bottle Street, and have a man-servant who's an ex-convict."

"An ex-burglar," said Mr. Campion. "Forget the convict. Lugg doesn't like his college education mentioned. It's a tradition with old Borstalians, I believe. Anything else?"

"That's all," said Amanda. "It isn't really an acquaintance-ship, is it? Only when you arrived I did hope something was going to happen. And now we're on the subject I should like to point out that I would make a very good aide-de-camp."

"Or lieut," said Campion. "I often think that's what the poet meant when he said Orpheus and his lieut."

"Very likely," said Amanda. "They made trees, didn't they? That reminds me, let's put this thing back."

When the oak was once more hoisted into position and Mr. Campion had resumed his coat, they went down into the mill again. Just before they came out into the yard he laid a hand upon her arm.

"What happened on the heath last night?" he enquired.

The girl started and glanced behind her involuntarily, as though she feared some intangible audience. When she turned to him again her small face was very grave.

"That doesn't come into it," she said. "I can't explain it, but that's got to be forgotten."

Mr. Campion followed her out into the sunshine.

CHAPTER VII

Cain's Valley

"It's the friendliness of the village I like," said Eager-Wright as the three paying guests of the mill walked across the heath that evening after dinner.

"That's right," said Guffy expansively. "You don't get this curious clubbable atmosphere in many country places. What do you say, Campion?"

The pale young man in the horn-rimmed spectacles who was wandering along beside the others, his habitual expression of affable idiocy very much in evidence, glanced up.

"Oh, it's all very nice," he said cheerfully. "All very nice indeed. Let's hope it doesn't lead to membership of the oldest club in the world."

"What's that?" said Guffy.

"Club on the head," said Campion promptly.

"In my present mood I should enjoy it," said Eager-Wright. "She's rather an amazing girl, don't you think?"

"Charming," agreed Guffy with unexpected warmth. "Charming. None of this modern nonsense about her. Sweet, and, you know, well—" he coughed—"womanly. Gentle, discreet, and all that sort of thing."

"Eh?" said Eager-Wright. "If you think working a mill, with dynamos, sluices, and general sack-heaving is a womanly occupation, I don't know what you expect of your hoydens."

"Oh, Lord, I wasn't talking about the brat!" said Guffy with dignity. "I meant the elder sister. You aren't baby snatching, I hope, Wright?"

"You only saw her in her 'working clothes,' as she calls

them,'' said Eager-Wright. "She looks a bit young in that
get-up, I admit."

"She looks about ten," said Guffy coldly. "How old is
she? Fourteen? But they're nice people. It seemed a pity
that the bar-sinister crept in in the fifties."

The three young men were paying a call. Earlier in the
day a note had arrived from the white house opposite the
church, in which Dr. Edmund Galley, after describing
himself as a "lonely old scholar remote from modern
enlightened conversation," had begged the three "visitors
to our little sanctuary" to drink a glass of port with him
after dinner.

Campion had the note in his pocket, and he took it out
to re-read it. It was an odd document, written in such
appalling script that Amanda alone had been able to deci-
pher it at first. The paper was yellowed with age but of an
expensive variety, and the address, oddly enough was
"The Rectory."

This peculiarity had been explained away by Amanda.
The village of Pontisbright no longer possessed a parson.
A visiting curate bicycled over from Sweethearting every
other Sunday to take a service in the little Norman church.

Guffy glanced at the paper in Campion's hand.

"He's a rum old boy, isn't he?" he said. "He stitched
up my arm quite satisfactorily this morning, though. Looks
like a gnome, by the way."

"Did it occur to you," remarked Eager-Wright, "that
the people up at the mill seemed rather dubious about our
coming along here to-night?"

Guffy turned to him. "I thought that," he said. "Why
were you so keen on going, Campion?"

"Educational reasons mostly," said the young man in
the spectacles. "There is no pastime more calculated to
instil into the young gentleman a Thorough Knowledge of
Life and a Dignity of Manner than the exercise of polite
conversation with his elders. That's on the first page of my
etiquette book."

"By the way," said Guffy, ignoring this outburst, "I'd
forgotten. There's rather a sweet story about this old doc-

tor. Apparently he inherited the house, furniture, library, everything, from his great-uncle, the last incumbent of the living. The uncle's rectory had been inadequate, so he built himself that white house. He lived to ninety-five or so, and died leaving the whole thing and a small income to this man Edmund Galley, who was a penniless medical student at the time, on condition that he lived there. Galley accepted the legacy and simply set up as a doctor. It must have been about forty years ago. There was no other medical man in the place, or for a radius of ten miles for that matter, and so he's done very well for himself.''

Mr. Campion remained thoughtful. "If the uncle was ninety-odd and our present friend, the hospitable doctor, whose port I trust is inherited with the house, has been here forty years, the probable date of his uncle's appointment as Rector of Pontisbright would seem to be about 1820. In which case he may very well have been the foolish cleric who was under the thumb of the wicked Countess Josephine.''

"I don't know what you're talking about,'' said Guffy with dignity. "Do you?''

"In the main, yes," said Mr. Campion judicially. "Well, since we've arrived, let us walk up the garden path looking as though we might be able to dispense modern enlightened conversation, and let the bravest of us pull the bell.''

The white house, which had looked so modern compared with the thatched cottages of Pontisbright proper, proved, upon nearer inspection, to be much more old-fashioned than they had at first supposed. The garden was well kept without being trim, and the flower borders were filled with herbs whose pungent scents hung heavy on the evening air.

The steps up to the porch were green with age, and as they climbed them they found that the hall door stood open. From the darkness within an odd figure materialized, and with a chirrup of appreciation Dr. Edmund Galley came out to meet his guests.

At first sight he appeared somewhat eccentric, in costume at least, for above a pair of ordinary grey flannel

trousers he had arrayed himself in a smoking jacket which
must have first seen the light in those days when men hid
themselves away in little morocco dens, dressed themselves up, and settled down to a pipe as to some secret and
ceremonial rite, requiring fortitude and patience in its
accomplishment.

Above this display of magnificence the doctor's face
was round and smiling, albeit a little wizened, like an old
baby.

He greeted Guffy as a friend. "My boy, this is very
good of you to take pity on an old man. How's the arm?
Mending, I hope. You want to be careful in this district!"

Guffy introduced the others, and, after the ceremony
was over, they followed their host through the dark hall to
a room on their left, whose long windows looked out over
an expanse of flowers.

The whole house seemed to be permeated by the scent
of the herb garden. The effect was extraordinary, but not
at all unpleasant, though their first impression of the room
they entered was that it had been undisturbed, even by the
housemaid's brush, for many years.

It was a ridiculous room to house such a queer little
person. In spite of its windows it contrived to be dark, and
the furniture had one disconcerting peculiarity: it was almost all serpentine. Guffy judged that the original Rector
of Pontisbright must have had a pretty taste and considerable means for a man of his calling.

Practically all one wall was taken up by a huge serpentine bureau which curled and curved its undulating length,
a baroque monstrosity if ever there was one. Even the
chairs had this engaging habit of sprawling and curling
until they looked as if one saw them in a trick mirror.

The little doctor noticed Eager-Wright's startled expression and chuckled with unexpected humour.

"What a room to get drunk in, eh, my boy?" he said.
"When I first came down here I was about your age, and
when I came into this room I thought I *was* drunk. Nowadays I'm used to it. When I feel I'm a bit under the
weather I go and have a look at my surgery-table and if

that appears to have legs like this cabinet, then, damme, I know I'm drunk.''

He seemed to concentrate upon Eager-Wright, and the reason for his interest was soon apparent.

"I hear in the village you're writing a book?" he remarked, after waving them to chairs round the window. He had a curious birdlike voice and the likeness was enhanced by his habit of speaking in little staccato sentences and holding his head slightly on one side as he put a question.

"You mustn't be surprised," he went on as the young man looked at him blankly. "Strangers are an event here. Everybody talks about 'em. When I went on my rounds this morning everyone was full of your arrival. A man who writes a book is still something of a rarity here. I'm proud to meet you, sir."

Eager-Wright cast a savage glance at Campion and smiled at his host with suitable gratitude.

Guffy, his huge frame balanced on one of the ridiculous chairs, gazed mournfully in front of him. The evening, he was convinced, was going to be wasted.

"A glass of port?" said the doctor. "I think I can recommend it. It's from my uncle's cellar. I'm not a great port drinker myself, but I've come to like this. The cellar was full of it when I came."

He opened a totally unexpected cupboard in the panelling and produced a decanter and glasses of such exquisite cut and colour that they were easily recognized as museum pieces. The deep rich red of the wine promised well, but it was not until they tasted it that the truth came home to them. Guffy and Campion exchanged glances, and Eager-Wright held his glass even more reverently than before.

"Did you—did you say you had much of this, sir?" he ventured.

"A cellar full," said the doctor cheerfully. "It's good, isn't it? It must be very old."

A gloom settled over the party. That a man could live for forty years with a cellarful of priceless wine, and drink it, perhaps even—sacrilegious thought!—get drunk upon

it, without realizing its value, was, to Eager-Wright and
Guffy at least, a tragic and terrible discovery.

As they drank, the little doctor's affable pomposity
became less noticeable. Seated in a huge arm-chair with
the priceless glass in his hand and the shadows of the room
enhancing the depth of colour of his jacket, he became less
of a person and more of a personage; a queer little personage in his big aromatic mausoleum of a house.

The conversation was very general. The doctor was
surprisingly uninformed upon most present-day subjects.
Politics had passed him by and the only names which
interested him were those of a bygone era.

Once they touched upon the architecture of the church
opposite, however, and he blossomed out immediately,
displaying a wealth of archaic knowledge backed up by
sound original thought which astounded them.

Gradually, as the evening wore on, the light failed and
the shadows at the back of the room deepened until the
baroque bureau had melted into the background. The three
young men became aware that the indefinable something
about the little doctor they had noticed all the evening was
growing stronger and had become recognizable. The man
was waiting for something. He was quite evidently marking time, waiting for some psychological moment which
must now surely be close at hand.

The talk became uneasy and fitful and Guffy had glanced
at his wrist-watch once or twice with pointed interest.

Their host stirred finally, hopping up from his seat with
a birdlike agility which was vaguely disconcerting. He
moved to the window and looked up at the sky.

"Come," he said. "Come. You must see my garden."

Why he should have waited until it was almost dark to
display this part of his establishment he did not explain,
but he seemed to take it for granted that there was nothing
odd in his behaviour and led them out of the room, down a
passage to a side door and out into the tangled wilderness
of flowers and herbs whose scent in the late evening air
was almost overpowering.

"These are all plants under the government of the Moon,

Venus, and Mercury," he remarked casually. "It's rather a quaint conceit, don't you think? The flowers of the Sun, Mars, and Jupiter are in the front garden. I think my garden is my only hobby. I find it very interesting. But that isn't what I brought you out here for. I want you to come along to the end of the garden, right up here on the mound. It's a barrow, you know. It's never been opened and I don't see why it ever should. I don't believe in prying about in graves, even in the service of science."

He went on ahead of them, scrambling up the round artificial hillock, the burial mound of some prehistoric chieftain, hopping through the trees and looking more gnome-like than ever.

"What the hell are we up to now?" muttered Guffy under his breath to Eager-Wright as they brought up the rear of the little procession. "Going to see a poppy under the influence of Neptune?"

"Going to be seen by a poppy under the influence of drink," said the other softly. "Or there may be fairies at the bottom of the garden, of course."

Guffy snorted and they ploughed on until, upon reaching their host's side on the top of the mound, they found themselves looking down upon a wide-sweeping valley. Pontisbright lay like a cluster of dolls' houses in the southern extremity, and, among the uncultivated fields which followed the winding valley, little dwellings nestled snugly. Even Guffy was partially mollified.

"A wonderful view, sir," he said. "By jove! You can see the whole of the Bright Valley, nearly."

The little doctor looked at him sharply, and when he spoke his voice had an unexpected gravity which startled them.

"The Bright Valley," he said. "No, my dear young sir, I see you don't know the local name. In these parts we call it Cain's Valley."

The phrase brought them back to the business in hand with a jerk. It seemed strange to hear the ancient title from this little man in his queer clothes, standing on the top of a barrow at the end of his garden.

But this was only the beginning of the oddness of Dr. Edmund Galley.

"The Valley of the Accursed," he repeated. "And that, alas! my friends, is what it is."

He stretched out his hand and his voice sank to a whisper.

"See?" he said. "See the little lights coming out?"

They did, and it was a very pretty sight. In one cottage after another the lights sprang out, making little sick yellow patches against the fading sky.

"Look," he said, "there are very few of them. Every year they get fewer and fewer. There's a blight on this land that we can never shake off, a curse from which we can never escape."

Guffy opened his mouth to remonstrate, but there was something in his host's expression which silenced him. The little man had changed. Eager-Wright could not be sure if the shadows were responsible for the transformation, but the puckered face seemed to be altered completely by some giant emotion. The eyes looked strangely fixed and the lips were drawn back over the gums like the lips of a maniac.

But in an instant the expression had faded, and when he spoke again it was in his normal conversational tone, save that it now carried a little more of solemnity than usual.

"This is a great responsibility I take upon myself," he said slowly. "A serious responsibility. But if I don't tell you I don't know who will. And if I tell you, it may be too late. Still, a doctor has a public duty as well as a private one, and I think perhaps in these circumstances the course I am taking is the only one open to me."

He turned to them and addressed them collectively, his little bright eyes watching their faces anxiously.

"I am a good deal older than any of you," he said, "and when I heard you'd come here this morning I made up my mind that, whatever the risk of appearing a mere busybody, I would do my best to have a chat with you and put the facts before you; and when you answered my invitation—rather an odd one from a complete stranger—I realized that my task would not be as difficult as it had seemed at first. I saw that you were sensible, courteous men, and after talking to you this evening I am more than convinced that I should have been a positive villain had I neglected this self-imposed duty.''

The young men had stood looking at him while he made this extraordinary announcement with a mixture of curiosity and polite astonishment in their eyes. Guffy, who had privately decided that a man who could drink '78 port without recognizing it was a lunatic and not fit for human society anyway, was inclined to feel uncomfortable, but Eager-Wright was plainly interested. The doctor continued:

''My dear young people,'' he said, ''you must get away from here as soon as you possibly can.''

''Really, sir!'' expostulated Eager-Wright, who had been completely taken aback by the culmination of the harangue. ''I believe in keeping the country for country folk, but after all . . .''

''Oh, my boy, my boy,'' protested the little doctor sadly, ''I'm not thinking of anything of that sort. I'm thinking of you, of your safety, your health, your future. As a medical man I *advise* your instant departure; as a friend, if you will allow me to call myself one, I *insist* upon it. Look here, suppose you come back to the house. I can tell you about it better there. But I brought you up here because I wanted you to see the valley. Now, come along, and I will try to justify myself for what must have seemed to you a very inhospitable outburst.''

Back in the baroque sitting-room, with a paraffin lamp at his elbow, Dr. Galley surveyed the three young men in front of him thoughtfully. He had lost much of the dignity and impressiveness which he had displayed in the garden, but, nevertheless, he spoke as a man in authority and his quick, bright eyes took in each face in turn.

The three young men responded according to their temperaments. Guffy was inclined to be irritated, Eager-Wright was puzzled, and Mr. Campion apparently concentrated with great difficulty.

The little doctor spread out his stubby hands. ''You see

how difficult it is for me to say all this," he said. "The place is my home, the people are my friends and patients, and yet I find myself reluctantly compelled to tell you a secret. But first I must beg that none of you will ever think of giving these facts to any newspaper. We don't want any Royal Commissions, any gigantic hospital, to rob us of our freedom."

He wiped his forehead, which had been glistening. There was no doubt that he was suffering under some great emotion, and their curiosity was roused.

"Has it occurred to you," said the doctor with sudden deliberation, "has it occurred to you that there's something queer about this village—about the whole valley, in fact? Haven't you noticed anything?"

Eager-Wright spoke without glancing at Campion. "There was the mark on the gate," he ventured.

The little doctor seized upon his words. "The mark on the gate," he said. "Exactly. The ancient God-help-us mark, no doubt. You recognized it? Good. Well, let me explain that. When I told you that this village was under a curse I said no more than the literal truth. I suppose the thought that ran through your minds when you first heard me use the word was of something supernatural, something fantastic. Well, of course, that is not so. The curse that lies over Cain's Valley and the village of Pontisbright is a very real scourge; something that no exorcism can destroy; something from which there is only one escape, and that—flight. That curse, gentlemen, is a peculiarly horrible form of skin disease akin to lupus. I will not worry you with its medical name. Let it be sufficient to say that it is mercifully rare but absolutely incurable."

They stared at him.

"Oh, don't think me a crank," he said. "I'm not the man to advise you to leave a delightful holiday spot because two or three people have contracted a contagious disease in this district. When I said a curse I meant a curse. The place is poisoned. The air you breathe, the soil you walk upon, the water you drink is impregnated, soaked, drenched with the poison. There is no escape from it. If the facts were broadcast what would happen? Our county council would be forced to take action, people who have lived here all their lives would be driven from their homes, and the place would become a hunting ground for bacteriologists and no good purpose would be served. I ask you to leave here immediately, for your own sakes."

Guffy rose to his feet. "But this is incredible, sir," he said with more brusqueness in his tone than ever. "I beg your pardon, of course, but what about the Miss Fittons? What about Miss Huntingforest?"

The little doctor sighed. He seemed to find Guffy extraordinarily dense.

"I should have explained myself more fully," he said patiently. "I thought you understood. As is usual in cases of this sort, the natives of the poisoned area are rarely, if ever, affected. Nature provides their blood with a natural antitoxin. The Miss Fittons are Pontisbrights also, and one of the peculiarities of that family has always been immunity from this disease. As a matter of fact, I believe Behr mentions it in his treatise on the subject. Miss Huntingforest is also a member of the family, and so far she, too, has escaped."

He sat there regarding them solemnly, the beads of sweat still standing out on his forehead, his hands folded in his lap.

"The legend hereabouts is that one of the early Pontisbrights brought the disease with him from the Crusades, and that it is his poor skeleton mouldering in the churchyard over here which still infects the whole valley. But, of course, that is a fairy story."

Guffy wandered up and down the room in perplexed silence. Mr. Campion leaned back in his chair in the darkest corner and peered at the proceedings through his spectacles, while Eager-Wright kept his eyes fixed upon Dr. Galley.

"May I ask, sir," he said quietly, "how you have managed to escape all these years?"

"I wondered if you'd ask me that," said the little man triumphantly. "I made an experiment on myself when I first came here. I've often considered it was quite the most remarkable thing I've ever done. I inoculated myself before the serum had been located and officially recognized by the B.M.S." He grimaced. "I nearly killed myself, but I was successful in the end. It was not a pleasant business, and I will not bore you with a description of my procedure. But in the end it was successful, and here I am probably the best authority on the disease in the world. By the way, I must ask you not to mention our conversation this evening to the good people at the mill. Poor young people! I'm afraid the shoe pinches sometimes. My behaviour this evening has been a tremendous breach of etiquette, as I'm sure you have noticed, but in the circumstances I do not see what other course there was to take. I hope I have persuaded you to go back to London."

"I'm afraid you haven't," said Guffy stoutly. "After all, I'm determined to do my bit of holiday-making, and here I stay."

It was evident that Dr. Galley did not approve of this decision, and he spread out his hands.

"I'm sorry," he said. "I'm sure if you could see some of my patients in my more westerly districts you'd change your mind. They are not a very pleasant sight. Still, the affair is your own. I'm sure you will understand I was only doing what I considered my duty in warning you."

"Oh, quite right, quite," said Mr. Campion's foolish voice out of the dusk. "But my friend Mr. Wright has made up his mind to write his book here. You know how difficult authors are—temperament and that sort of thing. It puts us in rather an awkward hole, don't you see? What do we do to protect ourselves from this—er—frightfully unpleasant complaint you've got about? I'm sure Wright and I would do anything within reason. Cold baths are very beneficial, aren't they?"

The little doctor peered through the gloom at his third visitor and appeared to consider Mr. Campion's odd enquiries for some moments.

"Well," he said at last, "there's really very little you can do. If you took my advice, of course, you would leave in your car this evening; but as far as protection is concerned, I don't know what to suggest. Unless, of course, you'd care for some of the stuff I made up for my own use. This isn't an injection—merely an ointment. You smear it on the palms of your hands, behind the ears and in the elbow crease, in the evening before going to bed."

He was speaking reluctantly, as though the offer was being forced from him. He looked from Eager-Wright to Guffy and smiled nervously.

"I'm afraid you'll think that this is rather extraordinary coming from a medical man," he continued, "but there's nothing like familiarity with a disease to produce a preventive. The recipe for this stuff was given me by an old man who used to live on the other side of the heath about thirty years ago. He was a strange old fellow—something of a herbalist—and this stuff, whatever it is, does sometimes work. I'll get you some, anyway."

He picked his way across the room with the quick daintiness of a bird and hurried out into the passage.

The Hereditary Paladin and his aides-de-camp had barely time to exchange glances before he had returned, however, bearing a little stone jar tied down with a piece of paper.

"Here it is," he said. "I always keep a supply handy. I often use it, but I may warn you it's seldom efficacious. You try it this evening. Rub it well in. But if I were you I think I'd simply go back to London. After all, perhaps, I wouldn't take this," he went on, stretching out his hand to take the jar from Guffy.

Mr. Campion intervened by shaking the outstretched hand.

"I say, this is really awfully kind of you, awfully kind," he murmured idiotically. "I don't mind telling you you've given us the scare of our lives. After all, it's a drawback to a place, a thing like that. I realize that. If it weren't for old Wright's book we'd clear out. As it is, Art must be served and all that. Which reminds me; I nearly forgot what we meant to ask you. Where is the Pontisbright Malplaquet drum?"

If he expected the little doctor to show any surprise he was disappointed. Dr. Galley merely appeared puzzled.

"I've never heard of it, my boy," he said genially. "Malplaquet? Let me see, that was Marlborough, wasn't it? No, I'm afraid I can't help you. Ask Amanda. She's an extraordinarily intelligent child. She'll probably tell you anything like that that you want to know. But," he went on with returning seriousness, "you mustn't think that these are the ramblings of an old man. This is a serious matter we've been discussing and I know what I'm talking about."

He stood on the step and waved to them as they went down the drive. The moon had risen and they saw him quite plainly, an odd little figure in his ridiculous smoking jacket.

They walked along in silence until they were well out of earshot, and it was Eager-Wright who spoke first.

"I say," he said, "if this is true, it's rather filthy, isn't it?"

Mr. Campion said nothing, but Guffy spoke.

"I suppose it must be true," he said. "But I think we'll stay. We must stay. It's ridiculous. I expect that stuff he gave us is no great use, but we can try."

He took the jar out of his pocket and they gathered round him. There was sufficient light still for them to see the thick black marking on the cover. This consisted of a rough diagrammatic drawing of the sun, but no words surrounded it.

Guffy removed the paper carefully and they stood looking down into the jar, which appeared to be half full of some dark greasy-looking substance which gave off a peculiarly pungent odour.

Mr. Campion thrust a forefinger into the stuff and rubbed a modicum into the palm of his left hand. Then he stood for some moments, his head slightly on one side, a thoughtful expression in his eyes. Suddenly he began to laugh.

"Old Doctor Displays Unexpected Humour," he remarked, and scrubbed his palm with his handkerchief.

"What is it?" Guffy took the jar and sniffed at it

gingerly. "Stop laughing like an idiot, Campion. What's this infernal stuff made of?"

"Sea onion," said Campion mildly. "Or, as we botanical eggs like to think, *Scilla maritima*, or Ye Common Squill. One of the most powerful irritants known to ancient herbal medicine. In fact, rub this well into your palms, behind your ears and into the creases of your elbows, and to-morrow you'll have a fine crop of blisters. Quite terrifying symptoms, in fact; serious enough to make any unenlightened bird hare back to London for expert medical advice. Too bad that poor old boy didn't allow for a modern education. He evidently hasn't heard of the 'How to Cure Uncle at Home' school of literature which has made us all so bright. His tale of plague was pretty, but not circumstantial enough to pass our modern boy."

Guffy stared at him in frank astonishment. "D'you mean to say the fellow was lying?" he demanded.

"But, good heavens," Eager-Wright expostulated, "the man was positively sweating with sincerity."

The Hereditary Paladin cocked a thoughtful eye at his followers.

"He was, wasn't he? I noticed that," he said. "But not with sincerity. Hang it all, people don't perspire with truth."

"Of course," said Guffy slowly. "A man sweats with fear."

"That's what I thought," said Mr. Campion. "Odd, isn't it?"

CHAPTER VIII

Unwelcome Stranger

"Talking of poetry," said Mr. Campion unexpectedly, as the three young men continued thoughtfully across the heath towards the mill, "many a useful thought has burned in verse that Shelley would have spurned. Likewise, the stuff to put your pennies on is not concealed in Tennyson."

"Interesting, no doubt," commented Eager-Wright good-humouredly, "but in the circumstances not very helpful. This is no time for blathering, Campion."

The Hereditary Paladin looked hurt but not offended.

"I'm not blathering," he said. "I think like that. I spend so long at the movies that I've picked up their culture. But if you want more dignity, in the words of the Prime Minister, I have just had a bewtiful thoat which I am about to brodecast—not to the wurrld, but to you two, my trusty co-lleagues.' Consider this: *If Pontisbright would crownèd be, Three strange happenings must he see. The diamond must be rent in twain Before he wear his crown again*—you can't have anything clearer than that. *Thrice must the mighty bell be toll'd Before he shall the sceptre hold, And ere he to his birthright come Stricken must be Malplaquet drum*. There you are; there's the whole thing in a nutshell. A fine old-fashioned treasure-hunt with clues complete. Now it's all simple and straightforward. We just have to think round, split the diamond, toll the bell and beat a rousing tattoo on Malplaquet drum.

"To avoid," he continued, his quiet precise voice sounding somehow absurd in the moonlight, "a great many tedious and irritating questions, I will tell you how I came

84

by this information, poem, valentine, or what-have-you. Pay attention, because I do not wish to have to repeat myself.''

He launched into a brief but truthful account of his adventure with Amanda in the mill that morning and dutifully repeated the doggerel when they asked for it. Guffy was inclined to be excited.

"I say—well—that is, rather—er—conclusive, isn't it?" he said, his face glowing with enthusiasm. "That accounts for everything we've got to find. The crown, the sceptre—which corresponds with the charter and the birthright, which is the title deed. Why did you keep quiet about it so long, Campion? I mean, the whole thing's practically settled. Now we just have to hunt round and get the things. Rather a clever little bit of poetry too. Hang it, what are we waiting for?"

"Three things," said Mr. Campion gently. "The diamond, the bell, and the drum. And, of course, there's always the possibility that the whole thing's a sort of joke in bad taste. After all, it doesn't follow that because a thing's been written a hundred years it's true. Consider Joanna Southcott.''

"All the same," said Guffy, who was a little hurt by the production of these awkward details, "it is a help, isn't it? I mean, the hoax theory is absolutely absurd. I once carved a girl's name on a tree. Only three letters, but it nearly broke my wrist. No one would carve all that out if he hadn't got some very good reason. Things are livening up, anyhow. That old doctor was an interesting bird, and then this coming on top of it—well, really!"

He smiled with tremendous satisfaction. Eager-Wright, who had been silent throughout the discussion, now glanced up.

"I say, Campion," he said. "It comes back to me now. When we were in the pub last night playing darts, one old fellow was being teased about his lack of skill and someone bet him he wouldn't get five bulls in ten shots, and he said he would when the Great Bell rang again. I gathered it was a sort of local saying, meaning, you know, the next blue moon, or, as one would say, 'Come domesday.' ''

"That's right," said Guffy. "I heard him say that. What an extraordinary thing!"

"The catch being," said Mr. Campion, "that the Great Bell is the local Mrs. Harris. There ain't no sich thing. If you want to know, it used to hang in the tower of Pontisbright house and was the sort of Big Ben of the county. Unfortunately, it was sold with the rest of the house and melted down to make guns for the Zulu War. There's only one like it in the world—the convent bell of St. Breed in the Pyrenees. I asked Amanda this afternoon. She's a mine of information. Apparently, our only chance of hearing the 'owd Bell of Pontisbright' is an earthquake, hurricane, air-raid, or other calamity, when its ghostly and muffled voice is heard in the village. Still, we can hardly rely upon that. The other minor difficulties include the fact that no one's ever heard of a diamond in the family, and the only drums in the vicinity are the battered pieces of work on the trophies in the gallery of the church. There are nearly a dozen of them, so we can go up and have a musical evening if we feel like it. None of them are of the Malplaquet period, I hear, and anyway they're dropping to bits. Not very comforting, what?"

They turned into the lane leading to the mill as he spoke. Eager-Wright grunted sympathetically, but Guffy was inclined to be obstinately cheerful.

"We'll get to the bottom of it, you'll see. I'm only afraid the thing may be too easy."

"I shouldn't let that cloud trouble you," said Eager-Wright bitterly. "That's not disturbing you, I suppose, Campion?"

Mr. Campion did not reply. A shadow had disentangled itself from the hedge and now clutched his arm. It was Amanda.

She was breathless with suppressed excitement, and, as she stood before them in the moonlight, she presented a slightly fey appearance in her tight brown clothes, her burnished hair dishevelled and her eyes sparkling distinctly in the faint light. It was evident that she was bursting with some great news, but there was also an indefinable flavour of alarm in her whole attitude.

"I say," she began, with her now familiar rush of inconsequential confidences, "it's going to be frightfully awkward, I'm afraid, but it is rather good. He fought like a fiend and Scatty hadn't the least idea who he was until Lugg sat on his chest. Lugg is a delightful person. He and Scatty are going into partnership if ever you get tired of him. But, of course, we can't talk about that now. There's him to think of. I suppose we could hush it all up, but it would be so awkward if it all came out. We couldn't plead self-defence then. Oh, I say, be careful. Nobody knows except me and Scatty and Lugg. I thought I'd wait here and catch you before you went into the house. Still, they did deserve it, creeping about the mill like that. I knew it wasn't rats. And, of course, the noise was tremendous when Scatty and Lugg got there. They were playing cards in the kitchen at first. It was awfully dull, because Scatty hadn't got any money, and they were so glad that something had happened that they got overexcited and—well—"

Eager-Wright clutched his forehead. "For heaven's sake, what's happened?" he demanded.

"I'm telling you," said Amanda's voice plaintively out of the dark. "Don't make such a noise."

Mr. Campion sat down on the bank by the side of the lane.

"Suppose you start from when you decided it wasn't rats," he said gently.

"Well," said Amanda, planting herself before him, "I'll go through it all again if you like, but we're wasting time. I remembered that I hadn't put the dust cover over my dynamo. I look after it rather specially because it's the most important thing I've got. Scatty says it's silly to wrap it up at night, but it doesn't do it any harm, anyway.

"Well, I sneaked out into the mill without taking a lantern, because I know the way, and while I was there I heard someone moving upstairs in the loft where the oak is. So I shouted 'Oi!' quite loudly, because I thought it might be one of the Quinney children ratting. And then there was an awful crash and someone swore. Of course, I guessed what had happened. Someone had knocked over the oak, which was enough to bring the whole mill down. When I heard the swearing I knew it couldn't be the Quinney children because Mrs. Quinney does try to bring them up well, in spite of what they say in the village. And, anyway, it was a strange man's voice.''

She paused for breath whilst they waited, trying to sort out her story from the mass of irrelevant details which she showered upon them.

''Well, the next thing that happened was nothing at all,'' she said. ''Absolute silence. And, although I wasn't afraid—I wasn't, really—I thought, well, suppose I'm not able to get them down alone. So I crept out so softly that they couldn't possibly have heard me and rushed into the kitchen. As you were paying so much every week I bought a lot of beer, and, of course, I forgot Scatty.

''Anyway, he and Lugg were playing cards, and there was a lot of beer about, and when I told them what had happened they just sprang up and charged out into the mill.''

She sighed. ''They made so much noise that I thought the others would be sure to hear them and come out, but I expect they just thought it was you coming back from the doctor's and they were polite enough to keep quiet.''

''But what about the *man?*'' cut in Guffy, whose impatience was verging on exasperation.

''Listen,'' admonished Amanda severely. ''There were two men, but one got away. Scatty and Lugg caught the other one just as he was coming down the staircase. I didn't see the fight because it was in the dark, but apparently Scatty got the idea that there were lots of people there. Anyway, he kept shouting to them to come on, all of them. Lugg only made a sort of grunting sound, but I found afterwards that he'd got his head in the poor man's stomach and was trying to push him through a door that wasn't there.

''I went back to get a lantern when I couldn't hear any

noise at all except them breathing, and when I came back Lugg was sitting on the man's chest showing Scatty how to use a life-preserver. They were both awfully happy, but I stopped it. I'm afraid it may be awkward, aren't you?''

She stood fidgeting from one foot to the other, waiting for their verdict.

"It sounds like a drunken brawl," said Mr. Campion. "Scatty and Lugg seem to be a pair of daisies, as we say on the Bench. There's only one interesting point which arises. Did you notice who their unfortunate playmate was?"

"Oh, I thought you'd guess that," said Amanda. "That was all right. It's Widow's Peak. Serve him right. There's only one thing that makes it so very difficult. I'm afraid they've killed him."

A muttered exclamation escaped Eager-Wright, Guffy whistled, and Campion rose to his feet.

"Oh, dear!" he muttered deprecatingly. "Oh, dear!"

"Perhaps he's not quite dead," said Amanda hopefully. "But you see, Lugg and Scatty were getting so excited that I shut them up in the garage and bolted the door. They can make as much noise as they like in there and no one will hear them. I sent them in to find me a spanner and then I pushed the door to and bolted it. Then I went back and had a look at the man. I put a couple of sacks under his head and I couldn't be sure whether it was his heart beating or if it was mine. You know how when you're— well—just a bit frightened, your own heart seems to be louder than anything else in the world. I gave it up after a bit and came out here to wait for you. I began to dislike the mill without a light.''

"I say, you poor little kid," said Eager-Wright, moved to comment by this frank avowal of humanity.

"Not at all," said Amanda stiffly. "I wasn't afraid. I was only put out, as anybody would be, and very cross with Scatty. I think he was showing off to Lugg. Still, it's the man we've got to think about, even if he did attack poor Aunt Hatt. He still looked very queer when I had a peep at him about ten minutes ago.''

Campion cut off down the lane. "I'm sorry Lugg's breeding has let him down again," he said, but his tone was grave, and as he strode on his face was anxious in the moonlight.

Amanda pattered along beside him, and Guffy and Eager-Wright hurried after them.

It was a grim and silent party which entered the mill some three minutes later. Curious sounds which had been emerging from the garage ceased abruptly as they passed. Amanda produced a hurricane lamp from behind a corn measure and turned up the wick.

Then she led the way up the dangerous staircase to the first floor. The yellow light glinted on her wonderful hair and the brown skin of her unstockinged legs. They followed her into the great dusty apartment above and she stopped and pointed to an alarming bundle stretched upon the boards near the open sack shoot.

"There he is," she whispered, and held the lantern high.

Campion and Guffy dropped on their knees beside the prostrate man and it became evident that in spite of her alarm Amanda had retained sufficient presence of mind to loosen the man's collar and prop up his head.

After a rapid examination Mr. Campion heaved a sigh of relief.

"Thank God he's all right," he said. "His little friend was lucky to get away. We'll leave these two thugs to cool their heels till the morning if you don't mind, Amanda. Meanwhile, there's this person to be attended to. He looks as if the depression had found him out. Still, I think he'll live to be beaten up another day. Really, this is most unfortunate. I don't know what he'll think of us."

He produced a flask from his hip pocket and poured enough spirit between the livid lips to lay out an ordinary undergraduate. The man groaned and stirred.

As he lay there in the light of the oil lamp they had ample time to examine him. At the best of times he could not have presented an attractive appearance, and of course at the moment the odds against him doing so were heavy.

He was a great lank individual, loosely but powerfully made, with a face heavily creased and lined beneath a single day's growth of beard. But by far his most interesting feature was the tremendously deep peak of hair which slanted down across his high forehead to meet the bridge of his nose.

"Extraordinary-looking egg," said Eager-Wright judicially. "He's the chap who fired at us at Brindisi all right."

"Still, a rather bad effort coming here alone and being set on by two murderous heavyweights. Rather a sitting bird, what?" said Guffy, in whom the sporting instinct was strong.

"Not a very good effort, beating up poor Aunt Hatt," observed Amanda dryly. "And Scatty's no heavyweight. It was the beer."

Eager-Wright switched the conversation into more pertinent channels.

"An unpleasant-looking man," he remarked. "Got a gun in his pocket, I see. I suppose they hit him before he had time to draw. Any idea at all who he is, Campion?"

"Alas! poor Yorick," said that worthy. "I knew him, Horatio, a fellow of infinite pest. But I don't think we'll go into that now. Dear, dear! This is unfortunate. He never liked me. We shall never be all boys together now. Look here, Amanda, could you get me an old blanket—one that you don't really care if you never see it again? We'll meet you outside in five minutes. I wonder if you, Mr. Randall, and you, Mr. Wright, would help me carry him downstairs? Treat him very tenderly. He's quite one of our nicest enemies."

When Amanda returned with the blanket they met her in the yard, the limp body of Widow's Peak between them.

The journey down the lane to the heath was tedious, since he was unexpectedly heavy, but they accomplished it eventually, treading cautiously to avoid making any unnecessary noise and taking care to jolt their burden as little as possible.

When at last they reached a convenient patch of heather,

sheltered alike from the road and the wind by a gorse bush, they set him down gently, and Campion covered him with the blanket, using extreme solicitude.

Eager-Wright bent over the man for an instant and emitted a little grunt of satisfaction as he took a scrap of paper from the waistcoat pocket.

"I thought so," he said. "See? He's copied down the rhyme. Amanda didn't disturb him soon enough. He'd finished his work when she heard him. Let's hope he's forgotten it when he comes to himself."

Mr. Campion sighed and, taking the paper from the other man's hand, returned it carefully to the pocket.

"There," he said. "I think that's the least I can do in the circumstances. That may compensate him a little for the inhospitality of the *crétin* Lugg."

They stared at him. "What on earth are you doing?" Guffy demanded. "It's mad enough to leave this fellow here when we've got a perfectly good excuse to drop him into gaol while we hunt round at leisure. Just because a fellow gets beaten up by accident you don't have to give him the game."

Eager-Wright did not join in this outcry. He was regarding Campion speculatively, trying to discover the logical reason which he felt must be beneath this apparently imbecile behaviour. Guffy, who was more single-minded, persisted in his objections.

"Let's put him in the car and cart him off to the county police headquarters." He moved over to his friend and looked earnestly into the pale vacant face. "Look here, Campion," he began, "I appreciate your sporting spirit, old fellow, and I think it's a very fine thing. But I can't help feeling that we're up against something rather serious just now, you know. It's too important a thing to take chances with. We've got to fight, and even to fight dirtily if it comes to it. There's a lot at stake."

"Stout fella," said Mr. Campion affably, shaking the embarrassed Guffy's hand with awful fervour. "But consider, my dear old flag-wagger, how on earth do you imagine this beautiful soul down here ever heard about the oak? He heard about it because little Albert sent him a note with 'Look what I've found in the mill loft, Ducky,' or words to that effect, neatly written above my usual signature.''

As Guffy fell back in shocked amazement and the others regarded the pale young man dubiously, Mr. Campion stirred the figure in the blanket with the tip of his shoe.

"This fellow isn't very bright. In fact, his cleverness is barely more than low cunning, but since he's working for the old firm, as it were, we have one of the most astute brains in the world against us. That's why I thought he was just the man to be supplied with this information as soon as we got hold of it. If it wasn't a riddle it'd be different, of course, but in this case it was senseless to try and hold it back, especially when time is so precious.''

"Well, I'm hanged if I see it,'' said Guffy stoutly. "I think you've gone completely nutty. Why? That's what I want to know; why?''

Mr. Campion linked his arm through the other's.

"Because, little inquisitive,'' he said, "two heads are better than one. That's all.''

CHAPTER IX

Question Time

"If I were in residence, so to speak," said the Hereditary Paladin from his seat of honour on the work-bench which ran along a wall in the dynamo room of the mill, "I should have you two beheaded. As it is, you'll be lucky if you get off with the sack."

He made anything but an impressive figure seated cross-legged on the bench, his knees drawn up to his chin and his trouser-legs flapping; but his eyes were severe behind his spectacles and his curious personality dominated the scene.

Amanda, very solemn and subdued, had perched herself on a heap of sacks in a corner, while Eager-Wright and Guffy kept guard over the delinquents, who, after their night in the garage, looked considerably the worse for wear in the morning sun.

Scatty had apparently decided to take his tone from Mr. Lugg, for whom it was evident he had formed a tremendous respect.

That worthy was more truculent than apologetic, and was still inclined to treat the whole incident in the light of a night out rather than an affair of serious import.

"The sack," said Mr. Lugg grandly, "doesn't come into it. Me and my pal 'ere 'ad a scrap with a party discovered on enclosed premises, probably with felonious intent. Lumme, we didn't ought to get the sack for that. We ought to get the price of our time."

"Don't say 'didn't ought,' " said the Hereditary Paladin absently. "And," he went on with more judicial solemnity, "the price of your time is good! What would have happened if that man had died, as he probably would have done if it hadn't been for Miss Fitton, who had the presence of mind to lock you two homicidal maniacs up for the night?"

"Self-defence," said Mr. Lugg promptly. "Peaky Doyle always carries a gun. It was Peaky, wasn't it?"

"It was Peaky, as it happened," conceded Mr. Campion. "But, as far as I can gather, in your condition last night it would have been all the same to you if it had been the local bobby."

"No, it wouldn't," said Mr. Lugg earnestly. "Not with my instinct. My instinct never tells me wrong. As soon as the young lady 'ere come in I said to myself, 'That's Peaky in the mill. Let's go and bash 'im up and that'll be a real help to his lordship.' I did say that, didn't I, Scatty?"

"Yes," said Scatty with the awful fervour of a man lying to save his skin. Of the two he made perhaps the more lamentable spectacle. He had a scar across the dome of his head, drowned eyes and a round pink tip to his nose. He studiously ignored Amanda's reproachful gaze throughout the proceedings. It was evident that since he had put his faith in his new friend, although not sanguine, he was hoping for the best, or, at least, that the worst might not be unbearable.

"Now look here," said Mr. Lugg, eyeing the assembly warily, and at the same time favouring them with a horrific, but conciliatory smile, "let bygones be bygones. Me and my friend 'ere got a bit lit and p'raps we done a silly thing. But seeing as 'ow it's all right and no 'arm done, let's put that from our minds. What 'ave we learnt from the events of the last evening? Consider that; what 'ave we learnt?"

Eager-Wright's lips began to twitch ominously, and although Mr. Campion remained cool and unfriendly the tension in the room had lessened considerably and Mr. Lugg sensed that he was making headway.

"We've learnt one 'orrible thing," Lugg continued, his voice sinking with fine dramatic effect. "Peaky Doyle is prepared to risk 'is skin, and for a funk like Peaky Doyle that means only one thing—that 'e's workin' for his old boss. And if 'e's workin' for 'is old boss, then the sooner we get 'ome and put the 'ole thing out of our minds the better.''

There was silence after this remark, which was broken unexpectedly by Mr. Lugg's partner in adversity. Scatty Williams emitted the wheezy rasp of an alarm clock about to strike.

"Seems like—er—seems like, Maggers, that 'owever dangerous that be us ought not to run away."

Mr. Campion's factotum was completely taken off his guard by this sudden avowal of courage on the part of his ally. He dived after the countryman's retreating respect.

"If you was to know 'ow dangerous that lot are you wouldn't stand there swankin'," he said. "If you'd been through what I 'ave you'd know that there are times when it's the article to retire graceful.''

"Rather a sordid argument, don't you think, Lugg?" Mr. Campion's tone was enquiring.

Mr. Lugg was not abashed. "You can talk," he said. "You always could. And what does it amount to? A lot of poppycock. 'Igh-sounding, I grant you that. 'Igh-sounding poppycock. I've looked after you like a perishing nurse-maid for never mind 'ow long, and I know you. 'Ave we bin up against Peaky Doyle's boss before? No. That's why we're 'ere to-day; stop me if I'm wrong. I'm all for loyalty and doin' the job, but I don't ask for trouble. Let me go and get out the car and we'll all go back to town."

"An indecent revelation of a nauseating mind," observed the Hereditary Paladin judicially. "You will now go and clean the car, taking Mr. Williams with you. Meanwhile, we shall consider whether we shall keep you here under observation or whether we shall ring up the governor of your old college to see if he has got a vacancy. You can go."

Mr. Lugg's small eyes flickered. "Bloomin' fatigues!" he said to Scatty, and they heard his husky confidential remark to the other man as the two offenders shuffled off down the stairs. "If you 'adn't 'ave bin with me you'd 'ave bin for it. 'E trusts me."

Eager-Wright began to laugh.

Mr. Campion affected not to have heard. "Peaky Doyle was carrying a gun," he remarked. "Old Lugg might have been killed. You may think it odd of me, but I should have been sorry."

"Look here," said Guffy, whose bewilderment of the night before had not abated with the morning light. "I don't understand what's happening at all. I didn't know you knew this fellow Doyle personally, Campion."

"We don't know one another well," murmured the young man deprecatingly. "We met in the house of a mutual friend in Kensington. There was a fight going on at the time. Mr. Doyle hit me over the head with a life-preserver. It wasn't exactly a formal introduction, but I've always felt we were at least on bowing terms since then."

"I'm talking about the letter you said you wrote him," persisted Guffy. "Were you serious last night? You see, I didn't even know he was in the village. Where did you send the note?"

"That," said Mr. Campion modestly, "was rather clever. A pure guess, but it happened to come off. You'd be surprised how it cheered me up. Yesterday afternoon something occurred which gave me the idea."

"The only thing that happened yesterday afternoon," said Amanda practically, "was the invitation from Dr. Galley."

"Exactly," he agreed. "As soon as I received the one I wrote the other, addressed it to Peaky by name, and when we went up to the doctor's house I stuck it on one of the railing spikes where it could easily be seen from the windows. I performed this feat with my natural skill and unobtrusive dexterity and neither of you spotted me. I deduced that Peaky would see that we were all visiting and that therefore the fort would be undefended, and would take advantage of our absence to reconnoitre. As it happened I was perfectly right."

"But why on Dr. Galley's railings?" Guffy demanded.

"Because our friend Peaky is a guest at the house," said Mr. Campion. "See how the plot thickens."

They stared at him, and Amanda was the first to speak.

"But this is absurd," she said. "I've known old Galley all my life, but he wouldn't protect a man who'd attacked Aunt Hatt—really he wouldn't. He's queer, I know; awfully queer in some things." Her voice sank a little on the last words, but she controlled it and her final announcement was firm. "He just wouldn't do it."

Mr. Campion said nothing but remained where he was, perched on the bench, a more foolish expression than ever upon his pale face.

"It's the clue that's worrying me," said Guffy. "That verse on the oak bole. I had a thought," he continued modestly. "That diamond, you know, might be just a diamond-shaped piece of glass, a window panel or something."

Eager-Wright nodded gloomily. "I know," he said. "That's the trouble. The house is no longer here. When the message was carved on the oak I imagine no one ever dreamed that it would be destroyed."

"Another thing's rather odd," ventured Mr. Campion from the bench. "The last two hints in the book of instructions refer quite definitely to sound. You see, 'Thrice must the mighty bell be toll'd Before he shall the sceptre hold'; and likewise, 'And ere he to his birthright come, Stricken must be Malplaquet drum.' It's the musical element which confuses me. I mean, this snappy lyric may simply be the instructions for the ceremony at the accession party; directions to the local choirmaster and whatnot. It's all very mysterious."

"It strikes me as being very mysterious that Peaky Doyle had vanished from the heath this morning and has not yet been heard of in the village," said Eager-Wright. "It looks as though either his friend came back for him or else there are more people about the place than we know of. Someone must have looked after him."

Before anyone could offer any suggestions on this subject Aunt Hatt's clear vibrant voice sounded from the floor below.

"Mr. Campion! You have a visitor. Can I send him up?"

Before Campion could reply Mr. Lugg's sepulchral tones floated up to them.

"That's right, ma'am," they heard him say affably, and add in the more familiar tones he kept for Mr. Campion's intimate friends: "Step up this way, sir, if you please. Look where you're goin'. Every other step's a mockery. 'Is 'Ighness is givin' audience in the boiler room this mornin'."

Footsteps sounded on the stairs and presently a head appeared through the trap.

"Farquharson!" said Guffy, starting forward. "Well, this is delightful. Mind that hole in the floor, old boy. Let me introduce you. Miss Amanda Fitton: Amanda, this is Farquharson, an old friend of ours, a charming fellow."

"Quite the little society matron, isn't he?" remarked Campion, grinning. "What news?"

The new-comer took a copy of *The Times* from under his arm and handed it to the speaker.

"This morning's paper," he said. "Personal column. Fourth paragraph down. I know one doesn't get the papers till the evening in these country places, so I brought it along. I thought I ought to be on the scene of action, anyway."

Campion took the paper and glanced at the paragraph. Then he began to read the message aloud:

" 'If A.A., late of Bottle Street, Piccadilly, will call at Xenophon House, W.C.2, on Wednesday at 4:30, the documents we have prepared for him will be ready for him to sign. X.R. & Co.' "

"Extraordinary way of doing business," said Guffy. "You'll put it off, I suppose? Unless—by jove! it's a sort of code. Good Lord, how amazing!"

"Hardly a code," ventured Mr. Campion gently. "That 'documents ready to sign' bit had a certain forthrightness, I thought."

"Well, it can't be a trap," said Farquharson cheerfully. "The great insurance offices may be viewed with suspicion in some quarters, but I never heard of them taking in unwary visitors and knocking them on the head."

Eager-Wright was looking at Campion with interest.

"Whom will you see?" he demanded.

Mr. Campion's pale eyes were thoughtful behind his spectacles.

"Well, really, I don't know," he said. "But as a matter of fact, I've rather got the feeling that I'm in for a half hour with the boss."

"Who is the boss of Xenophon?" said Farquharson, and then as an incredulous expression crept into his eyes he turned to the other man. "That's Savanake himself, isn't it?" he said.

Mr. Campion nodded. "If I've got to see him at half-past four I'd better hurry, hadn't I?" he said.

CHAPTER X

Big Business

"Mr. Campion," said the pale young man with the tooth-ache, "Mr. Campion. About the papers."

"I beg your pardon?" said the beautiful but efficient young woman at the enquiry desk, eyeing him coldly.

"Campion," said the young man again. "A hot, fiery plant under the jurisdiction of Mars. And I've come about the papers. Large flat, white things. You must have heard of them. I'm sorry I can't speak more clearly, but I've got a toothache. I'll sit down here, shall I, while you ring up about me?"

He smiled at her as well as he could round the enormous pad of handkerchief which he held against his cheek and wandered away from the desk to seat himself on what appeared to be a coronation chair at one side of the tessellated marble hall. Apart from the toothache, Mr. Campion's appearance was in keeping with his surroundings. His dark suit proclaimed business, his neatly-rolled silk umbrella good business, and the latest thing in bowlers business in the superlative.

He sat there for a long time, the one sober spot in the welter of magnificence which greeted the visitor to Xenophon House. He was gazing idly at the baroque Italian candelabra in the painted dome above his head and reflecting how much more jolly it would have been if the posturing Loves and gilded *amoretti* had been replaced by lifelike models of the Board of Directors, when a subdued feminine voice in his ear startled him to attention. It was the young woman from the enquiry desk.

"Did you say 'Campion,' if you please?"

"That's right. About the papers."

"Will you come this way, sir?"

The change in her manner was very noticeable, and Mr. Campion followed her through the hall, a person of importance.

A giant lift which Mr. Campion innocently supposed to be of solid gold deposited them on a mezzanine floor, where the scheme of decoration had leapt on a century or so and hundreds of impressive persons scurried among furniture of chromium steel and glass.

Mr. Campion forgot his tooth long enough to admire this picture of ruthless efficiency and found himself handed over to a soft-voiced, grey-haired man who moved very close when he spoke, as though his business were of some very personal and slightly undignified nature.

"Mr. Campion?" he murmured. "Quite." And then with a gasp, as though he felt his lungs would not contain enough breath for him to finish the sentence: "About the papers? Yes? Will you come this way?"

They entered the lift once more and Campion, ever anxious to be affable, smiled wryly round his handkerchief.

"Two little birds in a gilded cage," he murmured foolishly.

The man started and glanced at him with such cold shrewd eyes that the fatuous smile faded from the half of Mr. Campion's face that was visible, and it relapsed into its usual state of placid inanity.

The other became more deferential than ever.

"Thank you, thank you," he murmured. "Very kind of you, sir." And taking a pencil and paper from his pocket, he jotted down a few hieroglyphics.

Somewhat startled, Campion looked over his shoulder.

"Goldbaum and Cazeners advance two points," he read.

He was still pondering over this incident when he was ushered out of the lift into a corridor inspired by the neo-Byzantine or latter-day Picture Palace school of thought.

"Perhaps you would be so good as to wait in here, sir."

Mr. Campion's feet sank into a depthless carpet. His

eyes became accustomed gradually to sacred gloom. The door shut noiselessly behind him and he sat down in yet another variety of state chair and found himself looking round a room which had all the marble and mahogany solidity of a reading room at one of the better clubs. Immense oil paintings of the company's liners surrounded the walls. A fireplace as big as a church organ and very like it in design filled the far end of the room, and he gazed over a mahogany table which reminded him of a skating rink and nursed his face.

He had just accustomed himself to living in Gargantua when a sudden draught assailed the back of his neck and the next moment a little sandy man who had quite obviously only brains to recommend him paused at his elbow.

"Er—Mr. Campion," he said, holding out his hand. "Pleased to meet you. You've come about the papers, I presume. What's the matter with your face? There's nothing so nasty as a nasty tooth. That's right, keep it warm. Does it hurt you much?"

Mr. Campion shook his head.

"Oh, well, that's all right," said the other. "Glad to have you up."

Mr. Campion smiled shyly and sought for some really suitable return for this greeting. "Nice little place you've got here," he said at last, conscious that he had found the *mot juste*.

The other shrugged his shoulders deprecatingly but with a certain pride. He shot Mr. Campion a sudden penetrating glance.

"You saw the ad?" he enquired.

"In *The Times*," said Mr. Campion.

The new-comer still hesitated, and Mr. Campion felt in his breast pocket.

"I brought this along," he said, "in case you wanted to see it."

He placed an ordinary British passport on the table. The little sandy man's face lighted up.

"Now that's what I call intelligent," he said. "I see

you and me'll get along. My name's Parrott—er—two t's, of course.''

"Of course," murmured Mr. Campion gravely.

Mr. Parrott turned over the pages of the passport, glanced at the photograph and then at Campion. He seemed satisfied, for he returned the document.

"Well, you'd better come along," he said. "The private lift's in here."

Once again Mr. Campion set out on his travels. They skirted the table, Mr. Campion trotting obediently behind his guide, and, after traversing quite a considerable distance, came at last to a small door in the panelling which gave this time on to a Tudor lift; the sort of lift, as indeed Mr. Parrott pointed out, in which Queen Elizabeth might have ascended had the idea of such a thing occurred to her.

"You are now going," said Mr. Parrott impressively, "into The Suite itself. This is the ante-room."

Mr. Campion, still clutching his handkerchief to his swollen cheek, but contriving at the same time to look dutifully impressed, stepped into a cool cedar-scented atmosphere and found himself almost ankle-deep in velvet pile. This great walnut-panelled apartment hung with green was peopled with immaculate young persons of either sex who moved silently, rustled papers softly, coughed discreetly.

A willowy young man detached himself from his fellows and came towards them. The well-known lineaments of a famous family were easily discernible in his face, and his voice had the soft, attractive quality of old-time diplomacy.

Mr. Parrott, who appeared to know that he was out of place in these surroundings, murmured a confidential "This is Mr. Clinton-Setter, one of The Secretaries." And then in a still lower tone to the younger man: "Mr. Campion. About the papers."

Mr. Clinton-Setter smiled, coughed, waited until Mr. Parrott had departed, and spoke again in a lowered voice to Campion.

"Mr. Savanake will see you immediately. Would you like toe—er—leave your hat and umbrella?"

Denuded of his hat and umbrella, Mr. Campion felt he

might now be permitted to see the exhibit without further fuss. But it was not to be.

Mr. Clinton-Setter conducted him through immense double doorways into yet another apartment where an incredibly important-looking person champed and fidgeted with the broad ribbon of his eyeglass.

Mr. Campion followed his escort, his head bent devoutly, his handkerchief still clasped to his jaw. They entered a small corridor and Mr. Clinton-Setter put up his hand warningly.

"This is The Room," he whispered, and tapped discreetly. Then, throwing open the door, he stood aside and announced firmly: "Mr. Campion. About the papers."

The young man with the toothache stepped into the room with the conviction that what you see on the pictures is sometimes true.

He had been prepared for a palatial office, but not for this. Here was a shot from one of the more fanciful German films. The clean lines of glass walls were interrupted by mysterious machines. A gigantic desk which sprouted bulbs, switches, telephones with televisor attachments, and which must have contained, Mr. Campion imagined, enough equipment to befuddle any ordinary office, was set facing the door with a steel arm-chair behind it.

The young man looked about him, searching for the owner of all this efficiency. He had just decided that the room was empty when someone stirred behind him and he turned to see another desk set in an alcove behind the door, and at it, looking very businesslike, a completely unexpected small, plump elderly lady. This person had a lumpy forehead, shrewd eyes, and the faint air of indefatigability of a Labour cabinet minister. She smiled at Campion reassuringly.

"You're two minutes early," she said, revealing a comfortable, homely voice with an unexpected North Country accent. "But it doesn't matter. Mr. Savanake will see you in the private room. That's a great privilege for you. He doesn't often see people there. Try to keep that handkerchief down from your face," she went on. "If he sees people looking ill he's sorry for them and that disturbs him. It makes him waste his mind on unimportant things. That's right. Now go straight in when I open the door. Sit down at the chair in front of the desk and remember there's nothing to be afraid of."

She pressed a button on her desk and, after receiving an answering light, presumably worked from the inner shrine, she smiled at Campion again.

"There you are," she said, and released a lever in the floor with her stout black shoe.

A section of the plate-glass wall slid aside, like the door of a tube train, and Mr. Campion passed within.

CHAPTER XI

The Grand Manner

The ingenuous mind of the pale young man in horn-rimmed spectacles expected solid gold and nothing else, with a small plutocrat, possibly, enthroned within. But the room into which he stepped was even more surprising.

It was small and stuffy, with green distempered walls, and worn brown linoleum on the floor. It appeared never to have been dusted. Old-fashioned spike files lay in piles in the corners. There was a small gas ring with a kettle on it in the fender and a Charles Dana Gibson girl pinned up over the mantelpiece.

The visitor's chair, worn and inkstained, stood before a varnished desk so littered with papers, cigarette ends and odd bottles that there was no clear space upon it at all.

But Mr. Campion noticed these things only slowly. At first his entire attention was taken up by the man who sat hunched behind the welter of papers, the demi-god who controlled the destinies of the fantastic palace beneath him and its slaves.

Brett Savanake was a man of startling appearance. To begin with, he was what in more romantic times would have been called a giant. He was still comparatively young, being nearer fifty than sixty, and his grey-black hair was cut close to his enormous head. He had a round pale face and intense grey eyes. He looked at Mr. Campion without speaking or smiling, and waited until the young man had seated himself before his heavy white lids so much as flickered. Then he grunted.

This minor explosion shook his entire frame, and might

well have startled a more impressionable visitor. But Mr.
Campion remained blank, unassuming, and apparently engrossed in his toothache.

"D'you read *The Times* yourself, or did someone show
you that advertisement?" said the personage fiercely.

"A friend showed it to me," said Mr. Campion truthfully.

"Did you tell him you were going to answer it?"

"Yes," said Mr. Campion.

"That was indiscreet. I don't know if you're the man I
want."

With a sigh, Mr. Campion rose from his chair and
moved towards the door.

"In that case I will repeat my journey through the
wonder house," he said over his shoulder.

"Sit down. Don't be a fool. I've got no time for fools."

Savanake rose to his feet and held out, rather surprisingly, a packet of Players. Mr. Campion appeared mollified, but he shook his head.

"I—I can't with this tooth," he said. "Thanks awfully
all the same."

As he sat down again he noticed that the other had
undergone a complete change of mood. His bullying vanished and he seemed to have decided to become hearty.

"Well, my boy," he said, "so you've come about the
papers. Rather good that, eh? It sounded interesting. Didn't
give anything away. Now, I've been hearing a good deal
about you, one way and another, and I've sent for you
because I think I can put something in your way that may
interest you."

Mr. Campion peered round the corner of his handkerchief.

"Very nice of you, as long as it isn't a spoke in my
wheel," he murmured idiotically.

The personage favoured him with a long and penetrating
stare. Then he leant back in his chair and sighed.

"Well, Campion, let's get down to business," he said.

He was now neither hearty nor aggressive, but himself,
an intelligent personality, a tremendous personal force.

Mr. Campion remained quiet and rather foolish-looking.

With another prodigious sigh the huge man lunged forward, and planted one immense arm among the papers.

"You don't speak Spanish, do you?" he enquired.

"Not often," said Mr. Campion cautiously. "And then only to people who don't understand English."

"Oh, you do? Well, that makes things much easier. The fact is, Campion, I've got a job for you."

If Mr. Campion was surprised at this announcement he did not show it, but remained sitting up looking pleasantly interested.

"It's a difficult job, a ticklish job, but from what I've heard of you you're the man for it. Ever been to South America?"

Mr. Campion nodded. "Once."

"You have? Well, this is splendid!" A gleam of enthusiasm shone for a moment in the grey eyes. "That settles it. You *are* the man we want. It's difficult, dangerous, but the reward is enormous. The latest revolution in Peru has proved very unfortunate for our interests. What we want is someone with brains and resource, someone without ties, to engineer a counter-revolution. Wait a minute—wait a minute. Don't say anything yet." He stretched out a large hand warningly. "It's not so impossible as it sounds. The machinery is all there. It simply needs the right man to take it over. Think of it, my dear boy. You could make yourself president, if you liked."

The Hereditary Paladin of Averna was still hesitating when the other man went on:

"We'll keep you there as long as you do your best to protect our interests. This firm is a world power; do you realize that? This is no ordinary chance, as you can see for yourself. You'll never forgive yourself if you miss it. You're the man I want. I don't know if you're interested in money, but there might be as much as twenty-five thousand pounds and all expenses in it if you succeed. You can make what you like on the side, too. It's not an unattractive offer, is it?"

Campion stirred. His face had lost its inanity and had become thoughtful.

"It's a great deal of money," he said. "But frankly that doesn't interest me so much. The job sounds interesting. I should enjoy it."

Savanake nodded. "You would. That's why I chose you rather than some brilliant young soldier. Frankly, it's a job for an adventurer."

"Just what I was thinking," said Mr. Campion, and his eyes behind his spectacles became almost wistful. "What a pity," he added. "It really is a pity. I suppose you couldn't hold the offer open for a week or so?"

The big man glanced at him shrewdly. "No, I'm sorry, but that's absolutely impossible. The thing must be done now if it's done at all. It'll take you a month to get to the place. There's been some delay already. We've had difficulty in locating you. What's the matter? Thinking about this little business you're engaged on at the moment? Let me see, my enquiries tell me you were down in Suffolk somewhere. My dear boy, leave it. This is the chance of a lifetime."

He ruffled the papers on his desk and finally discovered the memorandum he sought.

"Here we are. It's a little government job, isn't it? Government business is notoriously thankless. You take my advice and put it straight out of your mind. Just walk out and leave it. With a bureaucracy of the type which governs this benighted country the chances are that no one will ever notice that you've resigned. And, anyhow, if they do, what does it mean? A long enquiry, a period of unpopularity perhaps which will be safely over by the time you return. By then another government will probably be in power and the whole thing might never have happened."

Mr. Campion remained dubious, and the personage, having pressed home his point, became more practical.

"I have all the paraphernalia here," he said. He unlocked a leather file and displayed its contents. "There's your reservations on the boat—one of our own liners, of course—here's a letter to the captain, here are your instructions upon arriving on South American soil, here's a letter which we will go into afterwards, and here's five hundred pounds in notes. You'll find it all arranged most thoroughly. I congratulate you, my boy, on seizing this chance of a lifetime."

Mr. Campion looked pleasantly vacant. "When you say the matter is immediate," he said, "just how immediate do you mean?"

Brett Savanake glanced up from the papers in his hand and for an instant his cold, grey eyes held Campion's own.

"When you leave this office," he said, "one of my secretaries will take you down to the ground floor, where a car will be waiting. He will drive with you to Croydon, whence you will both fly to Southampton to catch the *Marquisita*. My secretary will accompany you on board and will conduct you to the captain's cabin. You will remain there until the boat is under way. For obvious reasons you will travel under a pseudonym, and I have prepared passports under the name 'Christian Bennett.' "

He paused, and Mr. Campion peered at him round the corner of his handkerchief, which still covered half his face.

"Fine," he said. "I hope you've remembered to pack my woollens?"

"Your usual tailor has supplied a complete tropical outfit, which is waiting for you on board the *Marquisita*."

"Splendid! Now all I've got to think about is a bottle of Mothersill, and a bag of nuts for the natives, I suppose."

"That facetiousness," said the personage. "I've heard about that. I find it very irritating myself."

The young man looked sympathetic. "I'm sorry," he said. "Still, we are but what we are, and I'm going definitely out of earshot. May I congratulate you on your intelligence system? You've found out quite a lot about me."

Savanake shrugged his shoulders. "It's all here," he said.

"Your real name. I see your brother is still unmarried. You'll come into the title some day, I suppose. Rather unpleasant, a thing like that hanging over you. I should imagine that the life of a country squire with a seat in the Peers' Gallery would not appeal to you."

"Oh, there are compensations," ventured his visitor gently. "You get a lot of free theatre tickets and people send you samples. Not just a packet of razor blades, but big things: mangles, and patent mackintoshes, and thousands of British cigars.''

Savanake went on impassively. ''I know your successes, your association with Scotland Yard. Let me see, you are unmarried, unattached.''

''Fancy-free,'' remarked Mr. Campion mildly, ''is the term I've always liked.''

''You are thirty-two years old,'' the voice went on inexorably. ''You are reputed to be comfortably, but not lavishly provided for. You are reckless, astute, and quite extraordinarily courageous.''

''I take number nines in shoes,'' said the young man with the toothache with sudden irritation. ''I always wash behind my ears, and in my mother's opinion I have a very beautiful tenor voice. Suppose I decide not to play revolutions with you?''

''I don't think you would be so stupid.'' Once again the cold grey eyes peered into Mr. Campion's face. ''Besides, a refusal does not come into the question. I only put this matter up to you as a proposition because it seemed more polite to do so. As it happens there is no alternative. After careful research into your record, habits, and personality I have chosen you.''

Mr. Campion rose to his feet. ''What about my friends?'' he enquired. ''If I desert them now how can I ever look again into those clean but honest faces?''

''I hate that manner of yours,'' said the personage irritably. ''Sit down. All that has been arranged. *Must* you hold that handkerchief up to your face?''

''Yes,'' said Mr. Campion ungraciously. ''I suppose you're going to tell me now that you've written a letter to Mr. Randall, whom I've known for many years, and that a I have to do is to copy it out?''

''Sign it,'' said Savanake. ''It's typewritten on a machine borrowed from your flat. I shall now read it to you.''

He cleared his throat.

'' *'Dear old thing,'* '' he read solemnly, '' *'I am afraid this is going to come as a bit of a shock to you. But don't think too hardly of me. The fact is something has come along which has a spice of real danger in it, the one thing, you know, that I could never resist. I am leaving the childish affair upon which we have been engaged in your hands. Regards to the others. Yours ever . . .' "*

"Bert," suggested Mr. Campion helpfully. "I say, I hate to hurt your feelings, but you can't send that. Guffy would smell a rat immediately. The idea's all right, but I'd better touch it up for you. You needn't be afraid of codes and whatnot. Don't post it until after I'm gone."

He took a fountain pen from his pocket, and began to scribble on a piece of typing paper lying on the desk. The note was very short, and as soon as he had finished it he threw it over. Savanake read the message aloud, no expression in his voice or face.

"Dear old bird: I know when I'm beaten. Something more entertaining has turned up which will take me out of the country, and I'm jumping at it. Please accept my sympathy. I know of nothing more beastly than to find that a man one rather liked was a toot after all. Still, these things have an educational value, and anyhow I should hate you to forgive me. Yours, A.C."

Savanake nodded. "It is better," he said. "You will not, of course, be allowed to send wireless messages from the ship. Now I think that completes your interview. I will send for my secretary and you shall go."

"Just one moment," Mr. Campion raised a pale, detaining hand. "I have a condition which seems very reasonable from my point of view. This firm runs a sideline in insurance, doesn't it? I rather fancy I should like to insure my life for the sum of fifty thousand pounds with you for a short period. Can you arrange it?"

The grey eyes regarded him sharply. "You may find it difficult to get yourself covered if you're going on an errand like this," he said. "As soon as you get to your destination there will be a certain amount of danger. I thought that was what you wanted."

"Ah," said Mr. Campion brightly. "You misunderstand me. The period to which I referred was the time between the moment I leave this office and that at which the *Marquisita* sails.''

For a moment the great face looked at him blankly, and then Brett Savanake put back his head and laughed until the tears rolled down his face.

"I believe you have a sense of humour after all," he said. "I see it now. Very well, I'll fix it up."

"I want it done properly," persisted Mr. Campion. "In fact, I should like it put through by my own brokers. If you'll lend me your telephone I'll ring up my man and tell him to come round and see you immediately."

Savanake shook his head. "Crude stuff, my boy."

Mr. Campion looked hurt. "If you have a telephone directory there," he said, "you can look up the firm yourself and get the number for me. I have a particular reason for wishing that someone whom I shall name will receive a substantial sum of money in event of my death. It's also a hint to your secretary to be careful with me."

Savanake picked up the telephone directory. "What's the firm?"

"Poulter, Braid, and Simpson of Pall Mall. You've probably heard of them."

The personage seemed reassured. The firm was one of the largest of its kind in the world.

"I do my business through a man named McCaffy. If you'd ask for him I should like to speak."

The speed with which the call went through moved Campion to comment, but the personage cut him short.

"We've got no time to waste. Tell him to come round here within half an hour, and I'll have the thing put through for you."

Mr. Campion took the instrument. "Hallo, McCaffy," he said. "This is Campion speaking. I'm insuring my life. Yes, I've got Xenophon to take me for a short period. I'm afraid it's urgent. Could you come round and fix it all up? I've got to get away, but I'll sign everything and leave it for you. I'm sorry, old boy, but you must come immediately. Haste is essential. No, I didn't say that you were inconsequential: I said that haste was essential. Come at once. They won't trouble to go into that; I'm obviously perfectly healthy. Nothing faintly wrong with me except toothache at the moment. You know where it is; Xenophon House. Good-bye. Come along right away, there's a good fellow."

He hung up the receiver. "Are you satisfied?"

Savanake nodded. "That's all right, so far."

A certain amount of delay might have been expected in the transaction of a piece of business of this magnitude, but a murmured word on the telephone to the efficient old lady in the next room and the necessary papers were instantly forthcoming and duly filled in.

"The premium will be paid out of my twenty-five thousand," announced Mr. Campion, striving to look business-like. "And in event of my death I want the whole of this money to be paid to a private individual. That can be arranged, can't it?"

"Certainly. Can I have the name?"

"Miss Amanda Fitton, The Mill, Pontisbright, Suffolk."

Savanake appeared surprised. "But you've only known this girl a week, haven't you?" he enquired. "What on earth do you want to give her fifty thousand pounds for?"

"Need we go into it?" objected Mr. Campion wearily. "You seem to know such a lot about me. Find that out for yourself. Besides, it isn't, I hope, a question of giving her fifty thousand pounds. I trust it won't be necessary: don't we all?"

When at last the formalities were over, Savanake touched a bell upon his desk.

"The time has come to wish you good-bye and good luck, Campion," he said. "You've taken the only intelligent course and I feel sure you'll make a success of it. You'll find Mr. Parrott waiting for you in the outer office. You have your papers? You have your money? Very well, then, good-bye. As soon as you get on board I should advise you to study your instructions. They're extraordinarily complete, and I think you'll have no difficulty in following them. Good Luck."

Mr. Campion felt himself dismissed. In the outer office

he found Mr. Parrott making a very fair representation of
the stage idea of a plain-clothes policeman, in his tightly-
fitting blue coat and venerable bowler. The old lady was
still at her desk, and she nodded affably to Campion as he
appeared.

"You've got a nice cabin on board the *Marquisita*," she
said. "I've wired the stewardess to put plenty of blankets
on your bed. It's always cold when you start out."

Mr. Parrott, very grave and completely devoid of his
natural *bonhomie* in the rarefied atmosphere of the chief's
own room, took Campion by the arm.

"Come along," he said, and led him out into the corridor.

He seemed to revive a little as the door closed behind
them, and he lowered his voice confidentially. "There's a
lift down the end of the passage," he said. "Save us going
through the waiting-rooms. How's the tooth, ol' man?"

"Awful," mumbled Mr. Campion, whose handkerchief
now completely covered his mouth. "Seems to be getting
worse. I suppose I can't stop at a dentist's?"

The request was so mumbled that it was only with great
difficulty that Mr. Parrott caught the sense. At the word
"stop," however, he shook his head violently.

"Sorry, ol' man," he said, "but it can't be done.
Against the boss's orders. You're to go straight to the
aerodrome. Private plane, too."

A stifled squawk from Campion arrested them as they
came to the lift room. The young man's eyes were round
and horrified behind the horn-rimmed spectacles.

"If I catch cold in this tooth I shall pass out. You must
get me a scarf or something."

Mr. Parrott considered. At heart, it would appear, he
was a kindly man, but it seemed that Mr. Campion's
request was impossible.

"I'd pay a fiver for an ordinary woollen scarf," muttered the prisoner, turning up his coat collar and bringing
out yet another handkerchief to protect his swollen face.
He spoke despondently, but he caught the gleam of interest
in the other man's eyes. The next moment, however, Mr.
Parrott was his virtuous, self-righteous self again.

"Sorry, ol' man," he began as they shot past the second floor, when Campion clutched his arm.

"What would it cost me to call in at my flat, you watching me the whole time, of course, for a big coat and a bottle of toothache mixture? You can hold my hand for the entire outing, if you like."

Mr. Parrott drew a deep breath. Then he lowered his voice and spoke in a husky, confidential whisper.

"Five hundred quid," he said.

"Done," said Mr. Campion unexpectedly. "Seventeen A, Bottle Street."

As the two men stumbled into the little flat over the police station in the famous cul-de-sac off Piccadilly, the drawn curtains and sheet-covered furniture proclaimed its owner's long absence. Mr. Parrott followed his charge into the bathroom, where Campion rummaged through a cabinet until he found the phial he sought. Mr. Parrott asked to see it, and only the clearly-written label satisfied his curiosity.

"Now the coat."

Campion trotted into the bedroom, Parrott at his heels.

"Sorry if I'm a bit nosey, but orders is orders, you know."

His companion muttered something indistinctly about five hundred pounds, and Mr. Parrott had the grace to look discomfited.

"Every risk must be paid for," he said sullenly.

"Quite," agreed Mr. Campion without sympathy. "Now, my coat's in this cupboard."

"Is your tooth getting worse? I can hardly hear what you're saying." Mr. Parrott came closer.

Campion pointed to the door of a wall cupboard with his unoccupied hand.

"Blob, blob," he said.

His guard appeared to understand, for he nodded and stepped aside and the young man went in.

"Half a moment, I can't see very well," Campion's voice was still very indistinct.

Mr. Parrott glanced at his watch. "Here, hurry," he demanded. "Here, Campion, where are you?"

His momentary alarm was dispelled, however, by the reappearance of a tall slender figure, who now wore a scarf wrapped over the lower half of his face to hold the handkerchief in place, and who carried an immensely thick overcoat in his arms. His hat he retained upon his head.

Mr. Parrott helped him into the coat, and together they groped their way out of the dismantled flat. When they were safely back in the car Mr. Parrott's charge thrust an envelope into his hand. The sandy man glanced at its contents and something like wonderment spread over his face.

"I don't know who you are or what you're up to," he said. "But you're the first man I've ever met—and I've met some rich men—to pay up so handsomely for a little thing like that." He lowered his voice still more confidentially and came closer. "I say, your name isn't really Campion, is it?" he muttered.

"Blob, blob," said the figure at his side mysteriously, and Mr. Parrott, translating this remark as a refusal of confidence, leant back sulkily in his corner as the car sped on towards the aerodrome.

CHAPTER XII

Visitation

It was opening time at the "Gauntlett" on the evening of the day on which Mr. Campion's letter had arrived at the mill, and Eager-Wright and Farquharson hurried out of the bar as the Lagonda appeared in the yard, and Guffy climbed slowly out. This meeting had been arranged at the hasty conference that morning when it had been first decided that Mr. Randall should go to town to "get the truth" from Xenophon House. Amanda had been told nothing of the letter, and since there was Lugg also to be kept in the dark, the prince-bereft Court of Averna had decided to confer at the inn.

The three young men went into the deserted saloon bar together. So far Guffy had said nothing, but his woebegone expression told them that their best hopes were dashed.

"Well, I went there," he said at last, a faintly pugnacious expression creeping into his round, good-natured face. "And quite frankly I made a row. It's not a thing one likes to do, but in this case there was no help for it. Finally, I got to see a man called Parrott—an awful bounder—but he seemed sincere, although naturally I didn't feel like trusting him. He didn't seem to be a fool, and he took a great deal of trouble to find out who I was before he'd give me any information. But finally, when I'd convinced him that it really was my business, he opened out a bit."

He looked at his audience with troubled blue eyes.

"His story is that Campion was offered a hell of a job. He hinted that the amount involved was colossal, but it necessitated prompt action. According to him Campion's on his way to South America now.''

"I don't believe it," said Eager-Wright, who was becoming more and more wide-eyed as the regrettable story continued.

"Nor do I," said Guffy stoutly. "But the person Parrott went into a lot of details. Apparently he insured his life with the firm and then Parrott saw him onto the *Marquisita* himself. They flew from Croydon to Southampton—or so he says.''

"Campion was doped," said Farquharson with conviction.

"They obviously shanghaied him some way or other. If only that damned note hadn't been so horribly convincing I should feel like starting a hue and cry.''

Guffy was silent for some moments, and when he spoke it was with the utmost reluctance, his good-humoured kindly face red with shame.

"He can't have been shanghaied," he said. "Not in the ordinary way. This place, Xenophon House, is a cross between the Regent Palace and the Bank of England, with a spot of the Victoria and Albert thrown in. Of course, I believe in Campion. Whatever he's done, he's done it for the best. But I think we've got to face the fact that he's gone—for the time being, at any rate. I wish that letter of his had contained some sort of code. I've gone over it again and again. The beastly thing looks almost genuine. What we've got to do is to decide if we're going to drop the whole thing, or if we're going to carry on exactly as if he were here.''

"Oh, we must carry on." Farquharson spoke impulsively. "I don't see that we've got much authority, but we can't back out. I think Campion knows us well enough to realize we'd carry on. That's probably what he's relying on.''

Eager-Wright nodded. "I agree emphatically," he said. "Frankly, I couldn't drop this thing now if I tried. I feel we're on the verge of discovering something at any minute. Did you take that copy of the inscription on the oak to the man you spoke about?''

Guffy nodded. "I left it with Professor Kirk at the British Museum. I didn't explain much to him, but he didn't mind. He's an extraordinarily nice old boy and absolutely brilliant in his own line. If he can't make anything of it no one can. Then I came straight back. There didn't seem anything else to do after my interview with Parrott."

His despondency would have been comic in any other situation. Cowardice, and the letting down of friends, were the two cardinal sins in Mr. Randall's calendar.

"We went up to the church and had a look at the drums there," said Farquharson in an attempt to change the conversation from a topic which was painful to them all. "But I'm afraid there's not much to report. There are eleven of them in the gallery, all in an appalling state of repair. It's evident that no one thinks much of them. They're very dusty and one supports a pile of ancient hymn-books. We examined them carefully, but we couldn't find anything of particular interest save that they are certainly a good deal earlier than Malplaquet."

"As a matter of fact," Eager-Wright continued, "we put in a spot of 'strickening'. Farquharson played 'God Save the King' on each drum, but without any result, save that we stirred up a cloud of bats in the roof."

It was at this moment that Mr. Bull appeared for orders.

"You don't look so well to-day, sir," he remarked, peering at Guffy with bright, inquisitive eyes. "Some people'd tell you you looked well even if you didn't, but I wouldn't, because that wouldn't be right. You don't look so well as I've seen you. Try some Colne Springs. There's nothing like a good dark beer if you're not quite up to the mark. Now some people would say that just to make custom," he went on shamelessly, "but I wouldn't. If I didn't think that'd do you good I wouldn't serve you, and that's the truth now."

Before such a simple confession of virtue Guffy was stricken dumb. Mr. Bull went off to get the more expensive beverage without hindrance. When he returned with the three pewter tankards, discovering no opposition, he pursued his favourite subject.

"I'm honest," he said, gazing at his visitors with a self-satisfied smile. "That's what's made this house as popular as it is. I've turned away nearly a dozen visitors to-day, or the promise of 'em, which is as good. A person came along here this afternoon in a little car and asked me if I could put up twelve members of the party who were coming to dig for remains—something to do with history. I put him off. 'We don't want a lot of people here,' I said. And you can believe me, because I'm telling you the truth: he went to every other house in the village and not a soul would put his friends up. And why? Because we want the place to ourselves, and I'm not being offensive neither. We've kept ourselves to ourselves and always have done, and always will do until the great bell rings again."

At this remark Eager-Wright roused himself sufficiently from a gloomy reverie to regard the landlord thoughtfully.

"I don't suppose there's anyone left alive who actually heard the great bell ring before it was melted down," he observed.

"No," said Mr. Bull. "I do suppose not. Mrs. Bull's father lived to a hundred and eight, and he heard it," he went on cheerfully, but unhelpfully. "And that's the gospel truth and you can believe it because I've said it. He was a wonderful old man in his time. He remembered the Pontisbrights theirselves, and he could drink half a gallon without drawing breath. He wore the same pair of boots for twenty years and died in 'em. He could shave himself, too, and pull his own teeth," he went on, to the glory of his wife's house. "And his youngest daughter—that's Mrs. Bull—was born when he was eighty-five. That shows you, don't it?"

"What's this story about the voice of the old bell being heard in times of storm or disaster?" enquired Guffy.

The landlord looked dubious. "I've never heard it," he said. "And if I told you I had I'd be a liar. But old Fred Cole heard it—or always said he did. Anyway, he died and the devil took him, three or four days before you come down. He was a wicked one, he was. Both Fred and his wife and their little girl that used to live with them down in the little cottage by the church, they all three said they used to hear it when there was a tempest. But they were all three uncommonly evil-minded, and, finally, the devil come for Fred."

"What about the wife and the little girl?" enquired Eager-Wright.

"Oh, they've been dead these ten years," said Mr. Bull with relish. "Fred used to thrash 'em, and one after the other they died. Some on us reckon he killed 'em. Anyway, after he beat 'em they died."

"It almost looks as if he did," said Farquharson reasonably.

"Ah," said Mr. Bull, "it do, indeed, yes, yes, and that's the truth now. He were a powerful wicked old man."

There seemed no point in pursuing the conversation with the determinedly worth landlord, and they paid their score and went out to the car.

"What about Lugg?" enquired Farquharson as they drove over the heath. "And everyone else, for that matter. What do we say about Campion?"

"Detained in London, don't you think so?" said Guffy. "After all," he added hopefully, "it might even be true."

There were more lights in the house than usual when they drew up in the mill yard, and the old place looked very lovely against its peaceful background of feathery trees, half hidden in the mist rising up from the river.

As Guffy sprang out he glanced towards the door. He had half expected Mary Fitton to come out when she heard the car. He had no reason, but still he had expected it. The whole house was unnaturally quiet, he thought, and he wondered that at least Amanda had not come bouncing to the door.

But as no one appeared he turned the handle and stepped over the threshold, closely followed by the others. It was dark in the hall, but he thought nothing of it, and turned to the stand to hang up his coat.

It was at this precise moment that something dull and heavy was thrust over his head and pulled down round his shoulders. Similar scufflings in the gloom behind him told him that his assailant had companions, who were attending to Eager-Wright and Farquharson.

After the first shock of surprise Guffy's reaction was intense anger. The sack which enveloped him was damp and smelt abominably, and his captor had contrived to catch the bridge of his nose with the raw edge of the bag. Guffy began to swear in a savage undertone and, stiffening himself, proceeded to heave at his enemy with his shoulders, since his arms were pinioned. A grunt of pain escaped him; the swines were kicking. This was the final insult. Mr. Randall went berserk. He struggled wildly in his canvas prison, and actually succeeded in finding the lower end of the sack. He had wrenched an arm free when the butt of a revolver smashed down across his wrist, numbing his hand and arm from fingertip to elbow.

Once again the sack was dragged down almost to his knees and this time a narrow rope was pushed round his shoulders, and wound so tightly that the strands cut into his flesh.

He was helpless, blinded, and without the use of his arms. He crouched and butted in the direction in which he fancied his enemy to be, and he had the satisfaction of feeling a man's yielding ribs beneath his weight and of hearing the smothered grunt as their owner collapsed. Crippled without his arms he stumbled over yet another struggling figure, missed his footing, and crashed on top of his winded assailant. The two rolled over and over together.

He had no time to think clearly, and he did not realize at first that no word had been spoken by the attackers, and that he had no clue at all as to their identity. His own fury obsessed him. The sack was nauseating. Its dank and musty folds clung to his skin.

To outrage him still further, his adversary seemed to be gaining the upper hand. He squared his shoulders and took a deep breath of sickening sack-tainted air. The cords took the strain; they cut deeper and deeper into his flesh. He felt the veins in his neck swelling until his head sang, and the pain between his eyes was unbearable. Then, just when it seemed that he must relinquish the effort or burst, the cords snapped with a report like a pistol shot. He heard a muffled exclamation from his enemy as the man strove to rise out of the knee-grip in which he held him.

Guffy rode the man like a recalcitrant horse for a second, while he strove to free himself from the insufferable sack. He had his shoulders out, and was already rewarded by a deep breath of comparatively pure air when a sense of impending danger swept over him. He ducked forward a second too late. A blow so heavy and savage that even the thick hessian with which his head was covered proved little or no protection crashed down upon his skull. He fought wildly to retain his senses, but the terrifying numbness which the blow had produced spread in spite of him, and he felt himself falling, falling, and finally drifting away into unconsciousness.

He came to his senses some considerable time later to find himself sick and dizzy, and still a prisoner in the unbearable sack. His shoulders had been rebound, and his arms and hands were numb. He moved cautiously and discovered that he was not lying on the flagstones of the hall, but upon some slightly softer material, which he suspected to be the threadbare drawing-room carpet.

Gradually, he became aware that he was not alone, but that someone was breathing very close to him. He held his own breath, rolled a few inches forward, paused and listened. Then to his complete astonishment he heard a whisper barely more than a foot away from him.

"Who are you? Are you—are you dead?"

The terror in the familiar voice saved the question from banality. Guffy's heart leapt.

"Mary," he whispered back. "Where are you?"

"Here." The small voice sounded pathetically unsteady. "Tied to a chair. I can't move."

Guffy's anger began to reboil. The pain in his head was almost unendurable, however, and since he was now conscious he was particularly anxious not to collapse again.

"Where are they?" His lips grazed the sodden sacking as he spoke.

"Hush, I think they've gone, but I'm not sure. Be careful."

"Where are the others?" Guffy found that the hard mound beneath his head, which he had been cursing a moment before, was the instep of his informant, and the discovery comforted him unduly.

"In here, all except Amanda," she said. "We were all gagged, too, but I got mine off by wriggling. I—I'm afraid to scream."

"How about Wright and Farquharson? Are they tied up too?"

What with fury, pain, and tender solicitude, Guffy was almost demented.

"There are two more bundles—er like you," said the voice diffidently. "I can only see where the moonlight falls, so I can't tell who they are, even by the legs."

The young man settled himself as comfortably as he might. "I say, am I hurting you?" The idea occurred to him irritatingly.

"Not at all."

Guffy leant on.

"They came when we were in the dining-room," she continued in a hushed but penetrating whisper. "We were waiting for you three, as a matter of fact. There were six men, I think. They came in an enormous Darracq which they left in the yard at the back. We saw the car at the corner and we thought it was you until they all swooped down on us. I don't know where Amanda is. I heard her scream once. It sounded as though she were downstairs, but they bundled the rest of us, Aunt, Hal, and I, in here and tied us to chairs."

"Did you see them or get their idea?" Several futile efforts had convinced Guffy that his bonds were considerably stronger than those which had been used upon him before, and he gave up trying to escape them.

"Of course I saw them." Her tone was plaintive. "They were very ordinary people, like furniture movers, really."

Remembering the strength and ruthlessness of the blow which had knocked him out, Guffy wryly reflected that she was probably right.

"I don't know what they wanted," she went on. "But as far as I can see they just turned the house inside out. They went over this room like customs men. They pulled up the carpet on one side, and it wasn't until they realized it had been down so long that it had practically grown to the floor that they gave up the idea. They looked behind all the pictures, too. We heard them shifting furniture all over the house."

Guffy grunted. He could think of no adequate comment.

"I heard the car go off about half an hour ago," she ventured after a pause. "But I didn't yell in case there was still someone left behind. I haven't heard a sound since, though, so I suppose it's all right now."

Guffy struggled to rise but gave it up, breathless and groaning.

"How about you? Can you move?" he demanded.

"No. I've been trying, but my arms are tied behind me to the back of the chair, and I think the rope goes on to my feet. Anyway, my ankles are bound to the chair leg. I've tried wriggling, but it just hurts and the rope seems to get tighter."

"Keep still, then. I'll have another go."

It soon dawned upon the valiant Mr. Randall, however, that for once in his life he was beaten and he might struggle till doomsday and never get free.

"Wright!" he called softly. "Wright! Farquharson!"

"Hallo! Is that you, Guffy? I say, I can't stir."

Eager-Wright's voice, stifled and breathless, sounded somewhere near at hand.

Guffy swore. "How's Farquharson?"

An inarticulate sound from somewhere across the room indicated that Mr. Farquharson, besides being bound, was also gagged.

The minutes ticked on, and the company, having realized that silence was no longer politic, began to exclaim in their violent efforts to get free. It was when the struggle seemed to have gone on for hours that the miracle occurred.

"Well," said Aunt Hatt's cheerful American voice, vibrant and comfortingly strong. "Attacked in the home for the second time in one week, and they call this a quiet country. For crying out loud! I certainly feel better for that gag out of my mouth. Now just unfasten my hands. That's right. And the feet. That's better. Now let me see if I can give you a hand with the others."

The surprise made them incredulous at first, but it soon became evident that the indomitable lady was certainly free. She set to work on the task of loosening the others with remarkable energy, considering the cramped position in which she had been sitting for so long.

Mary and Hal were released within a few moments, and the girl and her brother immediately turned their attention to the three pathetic bundles on the floor.

Guffy emerged from his hated sack battered and filthy, but a hero in Mary's eyes, and was thereby appeased.

Eager-Wright appeared to be comparatively unharmed, but Farquharson was unconscious when they ripped the gag from his mouth. Aunt Hatt took charge of him with a brisk efficiency that was tremendously comforting, and Guffy left him in her care when with Eager-Wright and young Hal they set out to search the house for Amanda and those unlucky watchdogs, Lugg and Scatty Williams.

They found the girl almost immediately. She was in the dining-room, lashed to the heavy old-fashioned Chesterfield, a rag thrust into her mouth. Her wrists and ankles were raw where the cords had cut her as she struggled to get free, and there were tears of fury and frustration in the eyes which glared at them through a tangled mesh of flaming hair.

They released her and she staggered up, stiff and breathless and quivering with rage.

"Six of them!" she burst out. "Only six of them, and we let them get us down! Why, we were almost even numbers, and yet they beat us and tied us up in our own house. I bit someone's hand through, though, and I'd have got away if they hadn't had guns. I've been trying to get free for hours."

Tears choked her. Then she stood before them speechless, angry, and forlorn, while they looked at her helplessly. She pulled herself together.

"Come on," she said; "we must get Scatty and Lugg out. They're locked in the cellar. I've been listening to them swearing for the last two hours. The cellar grating is just outside this window."

Hal and Eager-Wright went down to release the crestfallen bodyguard, and Guffy and Amanda adjourned to the drawing-room, where the others were still assembled. But it was not until Farquharson had revived and Aunt Hatt had made a tour of the house, to discover that the place had been ransacked, but apparently not pillaged, that Guffy put the question which had been worrying him for half an hour.

"Miss Huntingforest," he demanded, "who set you free?"

The good lady stared at him. "Why, you, of course," she said. "Don't look at me like that, boy. You came up behind me and whisked the gag out of my mouth and the next thing I knew both my hands and feet had gotten free."

"But I let Guffy loose," said Mary. "And you untied me, Aunt Hatt, and—" she broke off, a terrified expression creeping into her eyes. "Who?" she demanded, looking round the dismantled room where the whole household was assembled. "Who set Aunt Hatt free?"

There was a long silence as they looked from one to another, startled enquiry in the face of each. No one replied, and all around them the great ancient house was silent and empty as a deserted tomb.

CHAPTER XIII

'Ware Amanda

The letter addressed to "The Rev. Albert Campion" arrived by the post on the following morning and it lay upon the side table in the hall, an object of curiosity to all beholders from the moment of its arrival to the time of its disappearance and subsequent recovery.

Since it had not been re-addressed, bore a Northamptonshire postmark, and was labelled "Urgent," the feeling in the family that it might contain useful information was acute.

The household had spent an uncomfortable night in ransacked rooms, and Guffy at least was considerably more grim and morose when he descended the stairs, a lump the size of an egg on the back of his skull.

At a hurried council of war on the evening before it had been unanimously decided not to call in the police. Nothing had been taken, as far as could be discovered, and the visitors were convinced that in the circumstances County Police investigation was the last thing to be desired. Aunt Hatt had been curiously amenable to this arrangement, and the residents of the mill had decided to undertake their own defence, and, when possible, to wreak their own vengeance.

Guffy caught sight of the letter on his way in to breakfast. He stopped in his stride and stood looking at it thoughtfully. He saw himself faced with a minor but irritating problem. If he followed the simple course which his instincts and upbringing dictated, he reflected, he would re-address the letter "c/o Xenophon House," and dismiss the incident from his mind. But, weighed down with the responsibility of his new vocation, he hesitated. His head was hurting abominably, and, hearing Amanda whistling happily as she clattered down the staircase behind him, he made a dive for the breakfast room, leaving the letter where it lay.

Amanda's reaction to the envelope on the table was very different. As soon as she saw it she paused, and, after a single guilty glance round to make certain she was unobserved, she whisked it off the polished wood and tucked it into that schoolgirl reticule, the knee of her knickers, and strode on in to breakfast.

Her whistling had not ceased throughout the incident, and Guffy would have been prepared to swear that she had followed him straight into the room.

The group gathered round the breakfast table in the warm morning sunlight was still considerably shaken by the events of the preceding night. Farquharson looked pale and unsteady, and Eager-Wright had serveral ugly bruises round his jaw. Young Hal possessed a black eye, of which he was inordinately proud, and only Aunt Hatt looked her compact, unruffled self.

A constraint had arisen between Guffy and Mary, and there was a slightly old-world shyness about the girl which enhanced her somewhat Edwardian beauty, and reduced the young man to a state of pleasurable idiocy pretty to watch.

Amanda alone had a light of triumph in her eye, and an even more pronounced jauntiness than before. Her wrists and ankles were disfigured by bandages, but her spirit appeared to have been strengthened rather than diminished. She planked a heap of wireless catalogues on the table next her plate, and began to turn over the leaves with tremendous interest.

"It seems to me the radio's like drink; it just gets a hold on you," Aunt Hatt remarked cheerfully to the table at large. "Amanda, will you drink your coffee before you spill it? This girl spends half her time reading advertisements of fearful machines which she never even hopes to buy."

"Not at all," said the miller with a certain amount of justifiable resentment. "I'm going to purchase four outsize valves—the plates run white hot at a thousand volts—a bunch of loud-speakers, and something rather sensational in the accumulator line. Very probably a new dress, too, if I feel like it."

Her brother and sister laughed politely at this exuberance, and passed each other the honey, but Amanda was not content to let the matter drop.

"Do you think," she enquired gravely of Eager-Wright, who sat opposite her, "that it would be better to buy a new accumulator for the car or a new car altogether?"

"Not to-day, Amanda. No bright conversation to-day. We're all a bit rattled."

Young Hal's voice had the genuine note of authority in it. It was evident that he took his position as head of the family with becoming seriousness.

The girl turned upon him coldly. "I'm perfectly serious," she said. "As it happens, I've come into a certain amount of money and I'm debating how to spend it. I think, perhaps, a new car after all. A last year's Morris would be fun. I've been talking to Scatty out of the window this morning, and he thinks we could pick one up in Ipswich for about ninety pounds. I thought I might go in and see about it this morning. The car would take me as far as Sweethearting and I can get a bus from there."

Hal, Mary, and Aunt Hatt exchanged glances.

"Poor Amanda, it's the excitement," said the elder lady compassionately.

"Wait a minute, Aunt." Hal put out his hand apologetically and then turned to his sister, his young face grave and politely enquiring. "Do you mean this, Amanda?"

His sister granted him a single truculent stare. "Of course I do. You don't imagine I'm sitting here making a fool of myself. I've got a first instalment of three hundred pounds, as a matter of fact, and as there are naturally a few things I want, I'm deciding how to spend it to its best possible advantage."

Recollecting suddenly that the Fittons possessed an income of one hundred pounds a year, apart from their various activities, Guffy understood the expression of blank amazement on his host's face.

Amanda remained calm, but a little sulky.

"Three hundred pounds? Where is it?"

"In my dressing-table drawer. In your collar-box, if you want to know. It was so lumpy I didn't know where else to put it, so I borrowed your box."

Hal frowned. He was leaning forward in his chair at the head of the table, his eyes wide and puzzled.

The two faced one another, Amanda superficially casual and ridiculously truculent, and the boy startled and incredulous. They were absurdly alike; the Pontisbright hair glowed and shone above their expressive faces.

"Do you mean to say you've got three hundred pounds in notes in the house?"

"Yes, I do." Amanda's tone was plaintive. "Why shouldn't I? Lots of people have three hundred pounds all at once. You often do, don't you, Guffy? Don't be so *bourgeois,* Hal."

Flushing under the injustice of the final admonition, the head of the Fitton family stuck to his guns.

"Where did you get it? And what's all this about a first instalment?"

"That," said Amanda calmly, "I am afraid I'm not at liberty to tell you. Now I must go and get ready to go to Ipswich. I'll take Scatty, I think, if you don't mind."

"But, Amanda, you're joking," Aunt Hatt appealed nervously.

"Of course I'm not, darling. I happen to have three hundred pounds, that's all. I may also have some more. I'd like to say, too," she went on, eyeing the assembly severely, "that, in my opinion, all this interest in my money is a trifle vulgar."

"Was the money in the house last night?"

"It was."

"And they never took it!" burst out Aunt Hatt, who could not get the burglary idea out of her head. "What a mercy!"

"Perhaps they were just six Santa Clauses in unorthodox costume," said Hal contemptuously.

Amanda's cheeks flamed. "That's mean, mouldy, and
unfortunately typical," she said, and rose to her feet.
"Now I'm going to Ipswich."

As the door closed behind her Hal coughed deprecatingly, the gesture of a man three times his age.

"Very extraordinary," he observed, and went on with
his breakfast with studied deliberation.

Eager-Wright caught Farquharson's eye and stifled a
desire to laugh.

Guffy was thoughtful. It occurred to him that, amusing
though Amanda's attitude might be, the facts were certainly odd, if true, and when he recalled her indignant
outburst at Hal's suggestion concerning the possible identity of their visitors of the night before, an uncomfortable
suspicion flashed through his mind. He put it from him
hastily, but it still hovered there, and he could not get it
out of his head that three hundred pounds might not be
such an inconsiderable mess of pottage if one needed it
badly enough.

It was evident that something of the same idea had
occurred to Hal, for he suddenly put down his table-napkin
and rose to his feet.

"If you'll excuse me for a moment," he said with that
grave courtesy which was his chief characteristic, "I think
I'd like a word with Amanda before she goes off." And
leaving the table he hurried after his sister.

Amanda's room was situated directly above the apartment in which they sat, and although Aunt Hatt and Mary
skilfully fielded the conversation it was impossible not to
overhear the staccato sounds which emanated from the
floor above. It began with angry voices and continued in a
series of rumblings which suggested that the rightful Earl
was beating his sister up and that she was defending
herself with true Pontisbright spirit. Eventually, the noise
ceased and Hall reappeared in the breakfast room looking
flushed and a little ruffled, but outwardly dignified and
composed as ever.

He came in at the door, glanced round to make sure that they had all finished, and then turned to his aunt deferentially.

"I wonder if you would mind, dear," he said in exactly the tone which his father and grandfather must have used before him in their more pompous moments. "There is something I would like to discuss with our guests, as I feel it concerns them."

Aunt Hatt, who was extremely fond of her nephew, withdrew immediately without so much as a smile, beckoning Mary to follow her.

Hal went over to Guffy, who was standing on the hearthrug reflecting that the Fitton family had a charm which made even their quarrelling delightful.

"Look here, Randall,"—the boy's tone was gravity itself—"I've got a confession to make on behalf of my sister Amanda. I'm sorry she's behaved like this, but you know what women are—no manners when it comes to it. I don't think they can help it. Just natural weakness, I imagine. I say," he went on, suddenly forgetting his head of the family pose, "she really has got that money. I've seen it. Three hundred pounds in five-pound notes. It's awfully fishy, isn't it? However, that isn't what I was going to talk to you about. I'd like you all to hear about this, although it's rather disgusting. When I went up to Amanda just now I came on her somewhat unexpectedly. She was reading this letter. I asked her whom it was from, but she wouldn't tell me. And then I saw the envelope lying on the bed. Look, here it is. It's addressed to Campion."

He stood before them, the envelope which Guffy had seen in the hall held out in front of him. It was considerably crumpled and explained in some measure the noise of five minutes before. Hal was blushing painfully.

"I can't tell you how sorry I am, and I don't want to make excuses for her. She's behaved atrociously, and I've told her so. I would like to say, though, that she doesn't always do this sort of thing. She's not that kind of girl at all. Perhaps," he added hopefully, "they knocked her on the head rather badly last night. It might be that, you

know. Still, I think you ought to read the letter. It's not
my affair, I know, but it does seem important. Aunt Hatt
and Mary and I can't very well help gathering what you're
up to down here, and—well, it seems important.''

He thrust a ragged piece of notepaper into Guffy's hand.

"I'm afraid Amanda's read it,'' he remarked. "But she
didn't seem particularly interested. I think she took it in a
fit of wanton mischievousness.''

He pronounced the last phrase as a single word, and
seemed considerably relieved to get it off his chest.

Guffy read the letter carefully. It was a remarkable
document, written in a flowing, somewhat affected hand
on a large sheet of buff-coloured notepaper, ornamented
by a crimson facsimile address stamp.

"My dear sir: In reply to your civil letter I may say that
I was profoundly interested in the question you raise. In
my letter to *The Times* of July 4th last year, which you are
pleased to quote, I referred to the reprehensible habit of
the curators of our lesser-known museums of relegating some
of their most interesting exhibits to the more musty and
inaccessible corners of the ugly, ill-ventilated mausoleums
over which they preside.

"As it happens, I am able to answer the question which
you raise, and let me take this opportunity of assuring you
that it is *no* trouble at all, but that I take a very *real*
pleasure in being able to perform what I regard as a public
service. I may say that in a long, and, I trust, useful,
pursuit of correspondence with the public Press, I have
seldom attempted to reply to a question which has interested me more. The Pontisbright drum, which you refer to
erroneously as the Malplaquet drum—its generally accepted
appellation being the *Pontisbright* drum of Malplaquet—
was placed in the parish church at Pontisbright when the
ancient mansion was demolished and the title fell into
abeyance.

"Some years later, in 1913 to be exact, it was loaned,
by whose authority I know not (although I should certainly
like to have a word with that gentleman!), to the Brome

House Museum at Norwich, where it remains to this day, a shocking example of laxity in the preservation of ancient relics. I feel sure you will respect my confidence in this matter and not bruit it to the Press until you, in your position (which is, I trust I am right in assuming, the incumbent of the parish), have been able to secure its return. As I know the curator of the Brome House Museum slightly, I have taken the liberty of dropping him a note by the same mail informing him that his little delinquency has been surprised, and that I fear he must surrender the prize he has held so long. (I am afraid the good people of Norwich have long since ceased to regard the drum as the eighth wonder of the world, as it is now, I hear, in a very inferior position.)

"My friend Mr. Formby (I feel sure he will remember my name, although we are only correspondent acquaintances) held his present post at the time of the original loan, so there should not be any irritating formalities.

"Thanking you again for the many civilities, and, I fear, flatteries, which you have been kind enough to write about my little hobby, and expressing the hope that I have been of some slight assistance in your estimable quest,

> "I beg to remain, my dear sir,
> "Your obedient servant,
> "RUDYARD GLENCANNON."

"Well, I'm damned!" said Guffy "What a genius Campion was—is, I mean. Well, that settles that, doesn't it?"

Hal coughed discreetly. "I don't want to interfere, of course," he said, "but who is Mr. Glencannon?"

"One of the prime busybodies of the world," said Farquharson, grinning. "You're bound to come across his name sooner or later. He's an old boy of independent means who spends his life writing to the newspapers. He must spend half his day reading them and the other half writing to them. He's been going for fifty years or so, and, of course, by this time he's a mine of information. Just the one person in the world to appeal to on a question of this sort. Campion must have written to him as soon as Amanda showed him the oak.''

Hal still hovered and it occurred to Guffy that the boy's position was invidious.

''Look here,'' he said, ''I don't know how much you've gathered, but I'd like to assure you that we're definitely on the right side and all that sort of thing. I know we can count on you at any time, can't we?''

It was just the right attitude to adopt, and Hal, who was so precocious in some things, and such a child in others, regarded him gratefully.

''Any time,'' he said enthusiastically. ''Rather! I say, are you going to dress up as parsons and get the drum?''

Guffy was silent for a moment. The call to action contained in the letter had not before occurred to him, and he was somewhat taken aback by this startling suggestion.

''Why, no,'' he said, and laughed. ''Of course, we can hardly do that.''

Eager-Wright joined him, but Farquharson grimaced.

''It's rather the sort of thing Campion would do, isn't it?'' he said. ''I mean, after all, we've got to get hold of the drum somehow or other, and in the circumstances the way seems open for us to go right in and ask for it.''

''There's something in that, you know,'' agreed Eager-Wright quickly. ''We can't very well dress up as parsons, of course; it's a rather serious, unpleasant offence, to start with, and I don't think any of us could bring it off, for another thing. But, after all, I don't see why we shouldn't turn up as lay-readers or something—zealous parishioners who have called to take the parish property back to its old home.''

Guffy looked profoundly uncomfortable. A naturally law-abiding soul, he was appalled by the illegality of the project.

''I say, you know, it's stealing,'' he objected.

Eager-Wright shrugged his shoulders. ''We could always call it kleptomania of an unusual kind. And, besides, we can put it back in the church when we've finished with it. It belongs there, anyway. Hang it! we should be performing a valuable public service, as old Ramsbottom, or Glencannon, or whatever his name is, points out. Look here, let's do that, Guffy. We'll all go up to Norwich this afternoon and interview the curator. If we mention Glencannon's name I don't see why we shouldn't get away with it. We can explain we've offered our services and our car to save the parish the cost of transport. People often do that sort of thing."

"Not a bad idea," agreed Farquharson. "I'm afraid we shall have to leave you in the town, Wright. With your face in its present condition, you hardly look *bona fide* as the Reverend Campion's right-hand man. How about it, Guffy?"

Mr. Randall hesitated. "It's rather an extraordinary thing to do," he said cautiously. "We shall have to do the thing properly. If we make a hash of the interview we shall never get hold of the drum. Perhaps if we wore dark suits and called about four o'clock in the afternoon just before closing time we might get away with it. We may be getting on the right track at last."

"What about defence here?" enquired Farquharson. "Lugg will be your only assistant, Hal. Look here, shall we leave Wright behind?"

"Oh, Lord, no." The boy was polite but firm in his refusal. "We shall be ready for anyone this time. Besides, I imagine they did everything they wanted to do last night, or else satisfied themselves there was nothing here."

The inference of the first part of his remark dawned upon Guffy before the others and he glanced up to see the boy staring gloomily out of the window, suspicion and discomfort in his eyes.

As though in answer to their thoughts, there was a whirr and a rustle from without, and the "car," every inch of its crimson surface a-quiver, slid out of the coach-house and shot across the drive. Amanda, bolt upright and impudent, sat at the wheel, with Scatty, huddled and a little scared, beside her.

Moved by a sudden impulse, Hal threw open the casement and shouted to her:

"Amanda! Come back! I want to talk to you."

His sister waved her hand with blissful disregard, and was gone.

"Where are you going!" he bellowed.

Very faint, but clear and triumphant, her voice returned to them on the wind.

"To spend three hundred pounds, you poor fish!"

CHAPTER XIV

The Churchworkers

"Ever stolen anything before, Farquharson?" said Guffy as they pulled up in the market place at Norwich to drop Eager-Wright and enquire of a policeman for the Brome House Museum.

"Hundreds of things," said Farquharson. "What's a little drum, anyway? If I see anything else I like I shall bring it back as well. If we get away with this we might start on the South Ken. There's a large-size model of a flea there I've always had my eye on."

Left to themselves, however, their mood sobered. Neither was particularly keen on the task, and the prospect of misrepresenting themselves to some eagle-eyed guardian of the city's treasures appeared uninviting in the extreme.

Since Mr. Campion's mantle had descended upon him, however, Guffy was determined to see the thing through. The only museum he ever remembered visiting was the Victoria and Albert, and he pictured himself being thrown out ignominiously by resplendent officials and delivered to the local police to be brought up on the following day, on a charge of attempted theft, before his old acquaintance Sir Geoffrey Partington, the magistrate for the district.

Farquharson sat quiet and placid, prepared, apparently, to take everything in his stride.

Guffy swung the car into Maple Street, and sought for Number 21. To his surprise this building turned out to be an ordinary house, presenting an even greater problem than an impersonal stone palace. It was not even a particularly large house, but a pathetic, rather dingy late Georgian edifice with a small brass plate on the front door which announced timidly to the curious that the "Brome Grotto and Museum" lay within.

Here was no magnificent *concierge,* no stream of people, no confusion under cover of which they might secure their treasure and depart. Even the door was latched.

Guffy rang the old-fashioned iron bell-pull and waited, his heart thumping ridiculously. So great was his alarm that he almost turned and fled when heavy footsteps on the tiles within warned them that someone was coming to obey their summons. The next moment the door was opened and the two nervous desperadoes were confronted by a somewhat disastrous spectacle.

A man who had once been tall and broad, but who was now both bent and shrunken, stood before them. He was clad in a shiny blue serge suit, which had evidently been made for him in the days of his former pride, and a dull red face, greasy eyes and dusty sandy hair completed his unedifying appearance. He smiled at them hopefully.

"You've come to see the Grotto?" he enquired. "I shan't be half a minute. I'm just getting a letter off to the post, so perhaps you'll go round by yourselves. If you'll just step in I'll give you a ticket. That'll be threepence each—thank you."

While he spoke he backed, waving his hands in front of him with a curiously enticing movement, and they found themselves in a very ordinary narrow hall adorned with a few cases of stuffed birds and some packets of faded picture postcards spread out on a decrepit table. From among these the unpleasant person produced a roll of tickets, two of which he traded for a sixpence.

"Well, there you are," he said, pointing to a room on their left. "Go through the museum, down the steps and across the garden to the grotto. I'll just finish my letter and then I'll come and give you the history."

He had wandered off and disappeared through a small archway at the end of the hall before either of them could speak. The closing of a door seemed to jerk Guffy back to his senses.

"Perfectly absurd," he muttered. "I say, it wouldn't be difficult to lift the thing completely and simply walk out with it. Hang it, we're the only people in the place. I expect it's in here."

They turned into the room vaguely described as the museum to find themselves confronted by a heterogeneous collection of curios. Here were stamps, fossils, more stuffed birds, flints and Roman pottery, a large boat in a bottle and a mummified two-headed calf. But of the Malplaquet drum there was no sign at all.

They went on still further and discovered yet another room devoted to the same distressing confusion. One or two pleasant pieces of china and a vast amount of worthless material, an ancient boneshaker and a miscellaneous collection of swords and early sporting guns were heaped upon one another with the profusion of a second-hand shop.

A neatly printed notice directed them to the grotto, and they were about to follow it hopefully when the person who admitted them returned.

"It's very dull," he remarked from the doorway. "Very dull, isn't it? The exhibits are not good. Very ordinary. I don't suppose you thought much of the grotto, either."

He had a sing-song voice with a suggestion of tears in it, and as he stood looking at them a wave of hopeless melancholy seemed to flow over the entire room. He did not give them time to speak but continued unhurriedly, his voice plumbing even greater depths of wretchedness.

"I've been here thirty years. When old Dr. Poultry died and left this house and collection to the town, I was appointed Curator. And I've been Curator ever since. It's been growing duller and duller every year. I don't know why I stay. It's a rotten life. People used to come once; they don't come now. Hardly anyone ever comes. I don't blame them. It's a rotten collection. You're tourists, I suppose, at a loose end? You must have an old-fashioned guide book, too, because the newest ones don't even mention this place. I can't complain: it's a terrible show. Have you seen all you want to? No one stays here long."

He was backing out of the door with the same beckoning motion of his long damp hands, and they were in serious danger of being hypnotized out of the place by his very gloom. Farquharson nudged Guffy, who took the plunge like a hero.

"Oh, so you're the Curator, are you?" he said, his voice becoming unexpectedly severe in his efforts to sound confident. "Well, we've come from the—er—Vicar of Pontisbright. I am one of his parishioners, you see, and I've—h'm—lent my car for the purpose."

The man was looking at him blankly and he floundered on.

"I'm afraid I'm not making myself very clear," he said fiercely. "You may have heard from Duncannon—hang it, man, it's about the drum." Nervousness and a sense of guilt were making Guffy irritable and inarticulate.

The faded sandy person in the doorway began to betray a flickering gleam of intelligence.

"Oh, the drum," he said. "You've come from Pontisbright. It ought to have gone back, I know that. It's been here for years. Nothing remarkable about it. No history attached to it. Just an ordinary drum. Very dull. Always in the way. Still, if you want it there's no reason why you shouldn't have it. People are very funny over church property. I suppose they're justified."

Guffy heaved a sigh of relief. It was going to be easy after all, in spite of the hash he had made of his opening.

"Oh, well, that's very satisfactory," he said. "There was some doubt in our minds as to whether you would be willing to part with it. After all, it's hung in the church for a long time and we—h'm—people of Pontisbright felt that it ought to go back in its proper place, don't you know."

"Very natural, I suppose," said the Curator wretchedly, his sing-song becoming well-nigh unbearable. "Very natural. It's a rotten drum. You don't mind my saying so. Nothing of interest about it. It isn't even dated, or autographed by Marlborough. It's just an ordinary drum. Have it back in the church by all means. Sorry we've kept it so long. I'd have sent it back before, but we're so poor. There's no money for carriage."

This pronouncement, unflattering though it was, was definitely encouraging, and Guffy and Farquharson already felt the glow of triumph.

"Oh, well, then, that's perfectly all right then," said Farquharson. "Since we can have the drum, we've no complaint to make. Although I may add," he went on with a brilliant effort at improvisation, "our last parish council meeting was a somewhat fiery gathering. Now I imagine there's a certain amount of formalities to attend to and then we can call the matter settled."

"There's no formality," droned the deplorable person, now actually hovering on the brink of tears. "It's all been done. Done this morning. And I'm glad to get rid of the drum."

"It's all been done, has it?" Guffy's jaw fell open. "Oh, I see," he went on with an effort. "When you got Mr. Glencannon's note I suppose you made the necessary arrangements?"

"There weren't any arrangements. It was only the receipt, and I've got that. Naturally I didn't part with the drum until I got the receipt."

The monotonous voice did not alter in tone in the least on these momentous words, so that it took some seconds before their sense actually percolated to his two visitors.

Guffy sat down heavily on a chair which was providentially behind him. Farquharson, however, kept his head.

"Oh, it's gone already, has it?" he said, striving to make his voice sound casual. "I see there's been some slight mistake. My friend here, Mr. James, was under the impression that the Vicar wished him to call for the drum as he was bringing his car into Norwich to-day."

The Curator looked at him stupidly. Then he laughed, showing an unexpected array of craggy yellow teeth.

"Just like a vicar, isn't it?" he said, the gleam of cheerfulness dying out instantly. "Just like a vicar. A lot of old women, I call them. They're always bothering people to do things and then doing them themselves."

Farquharson repressed a start of surprise.

"Did the Vicar call himself?" he asked faintly.

"No," said the Curator. "Not exactly. As he's so deaf he stayed in the car. His wife came in. Hardly the sort of woman for a vicar's lady, I thought. I hope I don't give offence. But it wasn't that way when I was young. The vicar was expected to marry a woman of his own age, and she was supposed to know how to behave." He paused and looked at them dubiously. "I'm not being very gallant, am I?" he said. "I hope the lady isn't a personal friend. One gets indiscreet at this job. Hardly ever seeing a soul makes a difference. It wears down a man's spirit. It's all so dull!"

"Dull!" said Guffy explosively, and controlled himself instantly, granting the startled Curator a distrait smile.

"Dull," said the sandy man. "Dreadfully dull. Nothing ever happens here. We've never even had a burglary. Nothing here worth stealing."

Farquharson, catching sight of Guffy's eye, received the impression that the Curator's thirst for excitement was going to be gratified by a murder, and he hastened to intervene.

"So you didn't like our Vicar's wife?" he said with forced joviality. "Well, well, a lot of people don't. Er—which one was it?"

"Eh?" said the Curator.

"The old one or the young one?" floundered Farquharson. "I mean, the mother or the wife?"

"Oh, the wife, I think," said the sandy person gloomily as his one chance of a sensation was dashed before his eyes. "Dyed red hair; very unsuitable with her old-fashioned clothes. I haven't seen a leg-of-mutton sleeve since my wife left me. Oh, I am being indiscreet! I must apologize. But it's so dull. I haven't had a chat with anyone for so long."

"Dyed hair and leg-of-mutton sleeves?" said Guffy, who had apparently given up any idea of playing his part.

"It must have been the old lady," said Farquharson hastily. "Or his sister, perhaps."

"No, it was Mrs. Campion," said the Curator. "Mrs. Albert Campion. She signed the receipt and gave me twopence for the stamp. No money passed, but it seems to make it legal. Oh, well, I'm sorry you've had your journey for nothing, but it was nice to have someone to talk to. You'll find the drum in the church, I expect, when you get back, if Mrs. Campion got it safely home. She said she had a new car, and the old Vicar by her side didn't look too grand. But then these country vicars never do. They don't see enough of life, and so they get narrow-minded and dull."

His voice rose to a passionate wail of misery on the final word and he snuffed at a none too clean handkerchief.

"The Vicar," said Farquharson in a desperate effort to identify their precursor, "is quite an athlete in his way."

"Well, he didn't look it," said the Curator. "Bald as an egg, and deaf as the proverbial coot, according to his wife."

It was in that instant that inspiration came to both Guffy and Farquharson. For a moment they stood looking at their informant with glazed eyes. Then Guffy rose to his feet. He seized the astonished official by one damp, limp hand, shook it firmly like a man accomplishing some unpleasant duty, and walked out of the house.

Farquharson glanced after him and then bent confidentially towards the bewildered museum keeper.

"Mr. Walker is a little put out," he said. "You see, the Vicar especially requested him to call in here. There was a lot of feeling about it at the parish council meeting."

"I can understand it," said the Curator wretchedly. "But I thought you said his name was James?"

"Whose?" said Farquharson.

"Your friend who's just gone out, banging the door and raising the dust."

"So it is," agreed Farquharson rather stiffly. "James Walker."

"Oh, I see." The Curator seemed saddened by the news. "Well, good-bye. Come again and I'll show you the grotto. But you won't like it. It's a rotten show. As I tell the executors, it's dull.''

Farquharson fled. Guffy was waiting for him, the engine running. He let in the clutch the moment the other man was in the car. When they got to the end of the street he turned.

"Amanda!" he said thickly.

"Amanda," echoed Farquharson. "And, God bless my soul, Scatty Williams."

CHAPTER XV

The Stricken Drum

The sunny afternoon air was warm and pleasant as Hal leant over the half-door of the mill and gazed with thoughtful unseeing eyes into the clear water of the race, shooting out over the green stones towards the narrow bridge which marked the end of the Fitton territory.

Behind him the giant wheel was turning slowly and its gentle creak could be heard behind the whine of Amanda's dynamo.

On the cobbled yard in front of him stood a heap of packing cases, deposited there not half an hour before by a lorry from Ipswich. Hal had so far demeaned himself as to wander over and inspect the labels. They bore the name of a big electrical firm, and he had returned lowering to his position to await Amanda.

He was contemplating the complete subjection of Amanda, and while he was planning exactly what he would say and what she would reply—a natural but singularly useless proceeding at the best of times—he became aware of Dr. Galley's rotund figure striding down the lane. Having assured himself that the doctor had not already seen him, Hal, who did not feel like general conversation, withdrew a pace or two into the shadow.

Dr. Galley bounded forward, his peculiar springing gait creating the illusion that he bounced. Hal watched him idly.

When he reached the front door, instead of pulling the bell he peered about him furtively, and then, drawing something from an inner pocket, he stretched up to his fullest height and thrust the tiny object into a crack in tne plaster above the lintel.

Hal took a step forward in his surprise at these extraordinary antics, and now the little doctor, glancing over his shoulder, caught sight of him. He thrust his hands hastily behind his back, puffed out his chest and sauntered over towards the mill with elaborate carelessness.

"Hallo, my boy," he bellowed as soon as he was within speaking distance. "Glad to find you. I was coming down to see you all," he went on as he came up to shake hands over the half-door. "I really ought to see you all together. You must forgive me if I sound mysterious, but I feel that I've made a discovery, and I know you will all excuse me if I make a little occasion out of the telling."

There was no hint of jocularity in his tone. On the contrary, he spoke with a profound seriousness which Hal found embarrassing.

"I want you all to come up to my house to-morrow night," the doctor continued, permitting a hint of his excitement to creep into his voice. "When I say 'all,' I mean you, your sisters, and that man Randall, if he's still here. He seemed a nice person, didn't you think, Hal?"

The boy looked at the old man sharply. Dr. Galley's manner was always strange, but to-day there was something definitely odd about it. His round eyes seemed wider than usual, his plump face less rosy.

"You like the man Randall?" the doctor continued with such earnestness that it put the question quite outside the range of casual interest. "I mean, you think he's an honest, sober, decent, clean-living man?"

"Oh, yes, I think so, sir," said Hal, rather taken aback by this trend in the conversation.

"Splendid," said the doctor fervently. "Splendid. Just the man. Well, I'm afraid I can't tell you much about it now. I must go in to see your sisters and your aunt. I suppose she ought to come to-morrow. It's going to be a great day for you, my boy, a great day. I want you all to be up at my house at half-past six. It's an unconventional hour, but it's the best time for me. You wouldn't fail me, would you? You'd regret it if you did."

"I'm sure we'd like to come, sir," said Hal dubiously. "Of course. Thank you very much. The only thing is that we're tremendously busy down here just now and—"

"Oh, you'd regret it all your life if you didn't come, Hal." The little man bent forward as he spoke. "Look here, I'll tell you this much. Last night I was rummaging in my library when I picked up an old volume of *Catullus*. The cover slipped off and I found that it had been made with pockets in the binding." He lowered his voice mysteriously. "In one of the pockets I found a document written by my great-uncle. He was the incumbent here in Lady Josephine's time, you remember. And I found another thing: a page torn out of the church register of the period. D'you realize what that means?"

Hal stared at him. "Do you mean that you've found proof of the marriage between Mary Fitton and Hal Pontisbright?"

The old man put up his hand. "Not another word until to-morrow night. It's my discovery and I want it to be my party. You'll come now, won't you?"

"Rather! Of course. I say, this is wonderful of you, Dr. Galley."

The old man regarded him steadily. "I can show you greater wonders than that, my boy," he said solemnly. "Don't come into the house with me. I think I'll tell your aunt and your sisters alone, if you don't mind. I won't give any more away than I've told you. I want to keep it for a real surprise. I shall see you at half-past six, then, my boy. Half-past six to-morrow night. Oh—and, Hal, you'll forgive me for saying this, but it's very important. Could you—er—put on completely clean clothes?"

The boy stared at him, and the old man hurried on.

"I know it sounds peculiar to you, but put it down to an old man's fad. Completely clean clothes, all of you."

He hurried off before the boy had time to say anything further, and Hal looked after him in astonishment. He watched the little man until he disappeared into the house,

and then relapsed into his old position leaning over the
half-door. His natural impulse was to follow the doctor to
see if he could glean any more information on this exciting
theme, but he was an obstinate soul and he had made up his
mind to wait for Amanda.

He ceased to think about his sister, however, for Dr.
Galley's hints had raised all sorts of possibilities. If the
missing page from the church register had really been
found, and Mary Fitton's marriage could be proved, then
his own claim to the Pontisbright fortune and titles could
hardly be disputed.

This disturbing thought was followed by the recollection
of his father's disastrous attempt to fight the claim and the
penury to which it had reduced his children. The proof was
not much use without money, Hal reflected gloomily, and
the subject of money brought him back naturally enough to
Amanda.

However, he completely forgot to walk over to the door
and discover what Dr. Galley had hidden so carefully
above the lintel. His exasperation with Amanda had just
been aroused again when she appeared, seated at the wheel
of a two-year-old Morris Cowley which shot dangerously
down the lane, escaped the mill-race by inches, and pulled
up with a shriek of brakes as its inexpert driver, flushed
but triumphant, brought it to a standstill.

She waved airily to her brother and stepped out with
conscious pride.

"Hullo," she said. "If the Quinney children came down
for their battery I hope you didn't give it to them. It isn't
nearly done. I didn't put it on until this morning. I know
you're impressed, but don't stand there gaping at me. Get
the garage open and I'll see if I can steer this bus in."

Hal felt that this was hardly the opening for the tremendous chastening which Amanda was due to receive. He was
also extremely interested in the first petrol engine to be
owned by the Fitton family, and it annoyed him to find
that his desire to examine it was becoming overwhelm-
ingly strong. He let himself out of the mill and walked
towards the car with as much dignity as he could muster.

"I say, you can't see it here," said Amanda hastily before he was within six feet of her. "Get the garage open and I'll show it to you in there. Scatty is bringing the brougham from Sweethearting. I dropped him there. Do you think we shall be able to get them both in?"

"Now look here, Amanda." Hal strove to make his tone authoritative rather than querulous. "You've got to explain. You're disgracing the whole family; putting us all in an awkward position. And I, for one, am not standing it. Leave that smelly little sardine tin alone and come into the house, and let's have a full explanation. Fortunately our guests are out of the way, and if you insist on making a fuss it won't matter."

"It isn't a smelly little sardine tin," said his sister, touched on the raw. "The exhaust smells a little, but that's nothing. Get that door open or I'll run over you. I did fifty coming home."

Hal strode forward and placed his hand on the side of the car as though he would hold it down by main force if necessary. As he had feared, Amanda was going to be difficult.

"Before this car goes into our coach-house," he said firmly, "I want to know where you got the money to buy it."

He stopped abruptly, his eyes resting on a bundle lying on the back seat.

Amanda saw his changing expression and sprang forward, but she was too late. Hal whipped off the covering and there lay exposed in the clear sunlight the Pontisbright Malplaquet drum.

It was a side drum, a little longer than the pattern now in use, but its dark blue sides were still gay with a faded crest, and worn white cords long since devoid of pipe-clay hung gallantly from the under-hoop.

The two faced each other across the car, the drum between them. Amanda was scarlet and inclined to be truculent, while Hal was pale with rage and shame. Slowly he stepped down off the running board and went round to his sister. Amanda did not follow his intentions, so that

when he came up behind her and jerked her wrists together
behind her back she was taken completely off her guard.

As soon as he began to march her into the mill, however, she protested violently. But he was angry and in no
mood for half measures.

"I'm so furious with you, Amanda," he said, speaking
like a child through clenched teeth, "that I simply can't
trust myself not to beat you up. I'm going to lock you in
the granary to cool your heels for a bit, until I decide
what's best to be done with you."

Amanda knew when she was beaten. Early tussles with
Hal had proved to her beyond doubt that he was by far the
stronger. She kept her dignity, however, as she permitted
him to guide her into the concrete-lined chamber on the
ground floor of the mill, whose only exits were a heavy
oak door which bolted on the outside and a small grated
window high up in the wall.

The sense of satisfaction as he slammed the door to and
thrust the bolt home was the sweetest balm his outraged
sensibilities had received in the whole afternoon. He hurried back to the car and, having made sure that he was not
overlooked, he rewrapped the drum in its covering, and,
armed with the bundle, crept into the house by the side
door and up the back stairs to his bedroom.

This room, situated under the roof on the second floor,
ran the whole depth of the house on the eastern side, and
from its narrow casement window he had a clear view of
the yard and the approaching lane. He set the drum down
upon the bed and stood for some time looking at it, a sense
of excitement tightening his heart.

It was a beautiful romantic toy, so bravely coloured, so
gallantly braced. The belt hook was still shiny, and with
pardonable vanity he was constrained to hitch it clumsily
to his belt and peer at himself in the mirror. He tapped it
gently with his knuckles, and the hollow sound was comforting, but it did not produce any startling or untoward
results.

He put his head out of the door and listened. Mary and
Aunt Hatt, he guessed, were still in the drawing-room with

Dr. Galley, and he went softly back into the room and rummaged among the odds and ends in a drawer of his dressing-table until he found an old ivory ruler. Armed with this, he advanced upon the drum and beat it vigorously.

The head was loose and the sound buzzed hollowly round the room.

He gave it up. In view of Amanda's behaviour, he reflected, the only thing he could do was to hand over the trophy untouched as soon as the others returned. He wandered over to the window and looked down, to be rewarded by the sight of Scatty Williams returning with the ancient brougham. He shouted down to him:

"Don't go into the mill, Scatty. As soon as you've put that away you might trundle Miss Amanda's new car in after it. Then go round to the kitchen and stay there."

The old man touched his hat without looking up and set about the work obediently.

Hal continued to lean out of the window. He saw Dr. Galley depart, and some ten minutes later Aunt Hatt set out, a shallow basket containing white flowers on her arm. He guessed she was going up to the church. On Friday evenings Miss Huntingforest made it her business to attend to the altar vases, and she went off now looking very businesslike in her tweeds, a stout ash-plant held firmly in her gloved hand.

From where he stood Hal had a wide view of the surrounding country. He could see Lugg fishing placidly in the millpool. Only Mary was unaccounted for, and he guessed that she was in the kitchen preparing Scatty's tea.

Once a light sound from the mill startled him and he turned to look at the gaunt white building. The skylight in the room where the oak was kept was shut, he noticed, and it puzzled him, for he could have sworn that it had been open a moment before. Still since there was no one there to close the window, he dismissed the matter from his mind.

He was still keeping vigil when the others returned. He caught sight of their disconsolate faces as they clambered out of the Lagonda. He glanced behind him. The drum was still lying on the bed, and, bursting with excitement, he hurried down the back stairs and into the hall where they were standing round the table.

Guffy held a letter in his hand. It had come by the second post, and had been lying there ever since twelve o'clock. He glanced up from the document as Hal appeared.

"Where's Amanda?" he demanded sternly.

"Yes," put in Farquharson. "I'm afraid we want an interview with her rather badly."

"I know," said Hal hastily. "I say, I'm awfully sorry this has happened. She's gone completely off her head, of course. But don't imagine I'm standing for it. I've locked her up. She's in the granary, and you can deal with her yourselves afterwards. But first of all you've got to come upstairs with me. Don't you see? I—I've got it!"

"The drum?" enquired Guffy eagerly as they crowded round him.

Hal nodded. "I've got it. It's upstairs on my bed. I say, I've given it a tap or two, but nothing's happened."

Guffy's grip bit into the boy's shoulder. "That's great. I've got a letter here from Professor Kirk, our expert." He put the sheet of paper on the table. "Look, here you are. Here's the only paragraph that matters. 'In my opinion the word *stricken* when used in reference to the Malplaquet drum probably means broken or riven. I should suggest that when you acquire the trophy you should bring it to London for expert examination.'"

"Good heavens, let's get our hands on the thing!" said Eager-Wright. "Where is it, Hal?"

The boy led them up the main staircase triumphantly and into the bedroom, which he had left barely five minutes before.

"I couldn't lock the door," he explained. "Because there isn't a key. And, anyway, I knew where everyone in the house was. Look, there it is."

He pointed to the blue-and-white cylinder which still lay upon the bed. They hurried forward, and Guffy was the first to emit an exclamation which sent a chill of alarm down Hal's spine.

"Look here," he said, "when did this happen?"

The boy stood staring down in helpless amazement at the sight which confronted him. Although the Malplaquet drum remained where he had left it, in his absence the bracing cords had been slashed through, and the underhead had been removed. The discarded hoop lay loose upon the coverlet.

The boy stared at his friends, scarlet-faced and stammering.

"It wasn't like this when I came down five minutes ago," he ejaculated. "And there was no one in this part of the house. Aunt Hatt has gone out, Scatty and Mary are in the kitchen, Lugg's fishing. Amanda's locked up in the granary, bolted on the outside—" He broke off helplessly.

From the yard below came the sharp, ominous sound of splitting wood. They crowded to the window and looked out. Amanda stood on the cobbles, hammer and chisel in hand. With the calm of one setting out on a pleasant but arduous task, she was breaking open the largest of the three packing cases.

CHAPTER XVI

Before the Storm

Guffy Randall lay on his back, and stared at the fluted beam which sprawled across the bedroom ceiling. It was just dawn. Through the casement on his right he could see the tops of the elms in the meadow gilded with morning light, but the beauties of Pontisbright held no longer any attraction for him. He was contemplating his failure to complete the task Campion had left undone. Even now he could not trust himself to think about the Hereditary Paladin. His somewhat sentimental heart had been wrung by his old friend's desertion. His own position at the moment kept him occupied, however, and as he lay gloomily regarding the ceiling it reoccurred to him that things were bad.

He heaved over on to his side. There was Amanda, for one thing. Whom was she working for? And the odd little doctor with his fishy invitation and crazy astrological talk. There was the terrorized village, the vanishing of Widow's Peak, and the mysterious raid of the night before, which had ended more mysteriously still.

He had been inclined to welcome the raid. After all, when it came to a straight fight he was up against something to combat which he could at least lend a hand. But even that adventure had proved unsatisfactory. The only comforting thing it had shown was the fact that wherever the Averna proofs might be, they were not then in alien hands.

He sat up in bed and clasped his knees. After the disappearance of the drumhead on the previous evening he had been so sure on this point, especially when an exhaustive search of the house and mill had revealed nothing.

Amanda, of course, had hardly been helpful. Her airy account of walking out of the granary on discovering that the door had been unbolted had not been convincing,. and her absorption in her new radio apparatus had proved frankly exasperating. Even the good-natured Eager-Wright was finding it hard to champion her.

With the end of the search had come the certainty that the under-head had vanished, and whatever the drum might have contained was in enemy hands. Complete failure had seemed obvious until Aunt Hatt had returned from the church with her extraordinary tale of the camp on the heath.

In the chill morning light, Guffy turned the story over in his mind. A party of hikers, quite twenty of them the good lady was convinced, had descended upon the village, and put up in tents on the heath. Mrs. Bull, who had been distributing hassocks in the church at the same time as Aunt Hatt had been attending to the flowers, had volunteered the information that they were the same archaeological students that her husband had refused to accommodate the day before. Aunt Hatt, her suspicions aroused, had walked boldly home across the heath and taken in as much of the scene as her sharp eyes could see of the strangers.

She had come back with the information that they were criminals, every man of them: most suspicious.

Guffy and Eager-Wright had walked down to the village later in the evening, ostensibly to visit the "Gauntlett," but they had seen nothing of the archaeologists save the little white tents grouped together like the sails of a schooner on the dark sea of the heath.

Guffy stirred restlessly. The faint air of inaction and the impression that they were waiting for some storm to break he found unnerving.

Finally, he rose to lean out of the window and inspect the morning. It was barely flve o'clock. A ground mist levelled the contours of the valley, although he could just see the course of the narrow river winding down through the low meadows on the southern side of the heath, picked out by the high brambles and pollard willows which lined its banks, and grew so thickly that in most places the stream was obscured.

The rest of the household still appeared to be asleep, and he returned to his bed cursing himself for his helplessness.

Had he stayed at the window a moment or so longer, the events of the day might have been considerably precipitated, for almost at the instant that he threw himself disconsolately onto his bed the coach-house doors in the yard below were swung cautiously open, and the nose of Amanda's new Morris emerged.

Scatty Williams sat at the wheel while Lugg, exerting his full strength for one of the rare times in his life, pushed the car silently into the yard. Scatty dismounted and together they disappeared into the mill, to return some minutes later, bearing most of Amanda's new radio equipment and a coil of rope. These were loaded carefully into the back of the car, and the vehicle was then steered silently down the lane.

Some minutes later, when the two conspirators judged they were out of earshot, they started the engine and drove off, turning down the lower road to avoid the heath.

For some hours after this secret departure the house and mill were perfectly silent. Even the water in the race was barely flowing, and behind the shuts the sluggish river mounted slowly.

As with many country mills where the local river boards are lax, there was not sufficient water power to move the wheel at all times, so that Amanda was accustomed to raise the shuts before a bout of work in order that the necessary force could accumulate for her purpose. It seemed that she had a special programme on hand to-day.

At seven o'clock Mary came down and the kitchen quarters sprang to life, and it was to the pleasant clatter of delf and the sizzle of bacon that Guffy arose and went down, missing for the second time that day a phenomenon which might have given him food for thought.

He had just passed the landing window when a dishevelled figure barely recognizable as Amanda crept out from among some shrubs in the garden and sprinted the last few steps to the side door. She slipped into the house and gained her own room without being seen. Her costume, which consisted of a bathing dress and a pair of ragged flannel trousers lifted from Hal's cupboard, was covered with green lichen, and her hair was wild and full of twigs. But there was a gleam of triumph in her eyes and her cheeks were red with excitement.

She washed and changed with the speed of a revue star, and trotted downstairs, demure and downy, to find Hal and Guffy conferring in the hall. Oblivious of the thought that they might not want her assistance, she joined them, and peered over her brother's shoulder at the note he held.

The boy glanced at Guffy enquiringly and, receiving his shrug of acquiescence, handed her the paper.

"Found on Lugg's pillow this morning," he said. "His bed hasn't been slept in either, or else he made it before he went."

Amanda read the message aloud. "To whom it may concern. I am bunging off. Yours respectfully, Magersfontein Lugg."

"Poor dear," said Amanda.

"Poor dear, my foot!" said Hal contemptuously. "Clearing out just when things are getting exciting. Look here, Amanda, your behaviour up till now has been very bad, but we're going to give you one more chance. We've been talking to the postman this morning, and he tells us that these so-called hikers on the heath have got five fast cars and about a dozen motor-bikes in that white barn on the Sweethearting Road. He's seen 'em."

As Amanda did not seem particularly impressed, he went on:

"There's more to it than that. When Perry went round with the letters he was naturally curious, so he rode over the heath quite near the tents, and he says he saw a man sitting outside one of them cleaning a revolver. Now what do you say? Archaeologists don't carry guns in England."

"Who said they were archaeologists? Come in to break-fast. By the way, Aunt Hatt says old Galley wants every-one to put on clean linen to go to his party. I hope you remembered this morning."

It was not until noon, and the heat which the early mist had promised had become a sweltering reality, boding thunder to come, that the second surprise of that amazing day burst upon the people of the mill.

Guffy was pacing up and down the dining-room in an agony of indecision, struggling with the premonition that something was about to happen, and the sober reflection that hardly anything else could when the car containing a self-conscious policeman and a bluff but didactic inspector arrived.

Mary, who had spent the morning devoted to household affairs with the sweet womanly abstraction which Mr. Randall admired, was the first to interview them. She came bursting into the dining-room a few minutes later, her face pale and her eyes starting.

"It's the police from Ipswich. They want Farquharson and Eager-Wright."

The two young men, who had been lounging in the window-seat, sprang up in astonishment and, followed by Guffy, clucking and anxious as a hen with a brood, hurried into the hall. Hal was already there pressing, with unerring instinct, beer on the perspiring but adamant inspector.

Amanda, too, had lounged over from the mill, and now stood draped against the doorpost, surveying the scene with calm, childlike eyes.

"Mr. Jonathan Eager-Wright?" enquired the inspector, consulting his notebook, as the young men appeared.

Eager-Wright nodded. "Anything I can do?"

"The official regarded him mournfully. "Yes, sir," he said. "Just stand on one side, will you? That's right. Now, Mr. Richard Montgomery Farquharson? Oh, that's you, sir, is it? Well, Jonathan Eager-Wright and Richard Mont-gomery Farquharson, I arrest you both and severally on a joint charge of attempting to obtain under false pretences valuable exhibits from the Brome House Museum, Norwich, on Friday, the 3rd last. I have to warn you that anything you may say will be taken down as evidence against you. Now, gentlemen, I must ask you to come with me. Here are the warrants if you'd care to see them."

Guffy was the first to break the frozen silence which followed this announcement.

"Really!" he exploded. "I say, Inspector, this is ridiculous. In the first place Eager-Wright never went near the place, and . . ."

He broke off in some confusion as he caught Farquharson's startled glance.

"Anyhow, it's absurd," he finished lamely.

The inspector thrust his notebook back into his coat-tails and sighed.

"If you've anything to say, sir, germane to the issue as they say, then you come back to the station and say it there. I'm sorry, but I must take these gentlemen along."

"I'll certainly come." Guffy was crimson with indignation and guilty alarm. "I'll phone my friend the County Commissioner, too. This is damnable, officer, frankly damnable." He advanced upon his hat on the stand as if it had been an enemy, and Amanda leapt forward.

"Don't leave us," she whispered, with just enough dramatic effect to flatter Mr. Randall's mood. "Don't forget we haven't even got Lugg now."

Guffy stopped in his tracks, and Farquharson, who had heard the appeal, spoke hastily.

"She's quite right, Randall. You can't leave the house. Don't worry, my dear old boy. We'll be back during the day. These fellows only want a satisfactory explanation. Don't you, Inspector?" he added, turning the full force of his lazy, charming smile on the policeman.

"I'm sure I hope you'll be able to give one, sir," said that worthy without much enthusiasm, while his attendant sprite in the helmet smirked irritatingly.

Eager-Wright joined in the discussion. "We're all right, Guffy," he said. "I'll phone my old boy if necessary. Don't get alarmed. You hold the fort until we return—

probably about tea-time. I hope nothing exciting happens until we do get back."

"You come along, my lad," said the inspector, suddenly growing tired of the conversation. "You'll get all the excitement you want."

A stricken group stood in the doorway and watched the departure of the police car. Eager-Wright and Farquharson were wedged in the back, the plump inspector between them.

Guffy passed a trembling hand over his brow. A long line of law-abiding squires had produced in him a subconscious horror of the police and their ways which no hardened criminal could equal.

"I ought to go and phone about those fellows," he said. "Where's the nearest place?"

"Sweethearting," said Amanda promptly. "And I don't think you ought to leave Mary and Aunt Hatt alone. After all, Hal and I aren't much good in a scrap. It was all right yesterday when we had Lugg and no one was about, but now all those people have arrived on the heath . . ."

She broke off. Mary frowned at her.

"Nonsense. We're perfectly all right," she said. "Amanda, you're simply behaving ridiculously."

Guffy became thoughtful, and his round, good-natured face was troubled.

"She's right," he said at last. "Of course, I must stay here. Those fellows can look after themselves. I imagine it's only a case of a phone call or two, establishing identity or arranging bail. It's infernally awkward, however. I mean to say, in a sense Farquharson and I are guilty. I wonder how they got hold of our names?"

No one volunteered any reply to this problem, but Mary sniffed the air suspiciously.

"My cakes," she said. "They're in the oven."

"I—er—I'll come and help you," Guffy offered, following her precipitate flight into the kitchen. "It may clear the air a bit," he added inanely.

Hal and Amanda exchanged glances and it seemed to

Hal that his sister was definitely more amenable. The sudden depletion in their numbers made for friendliness.

"Come over to the mill," she suggested. "I've something to show you."

He followed her dubiously. "I didn't smell burning," he said. "Did you?"

"No," said Amanda. "It was camphor. The policemen's clothes, I think. Didn't you notice something about those men?"

"What?" he enquired cautiously.

"That they weren't real policemen, of course," said his sister.

"Not real . . . ?" Hal stared at her, his jaw falling open. "But why didn't you say? We might have stopped them. Good Lord, Amanda, why on earth didn't you mention it?"

"Because," she said darkly. "I had my reasons. Come along and I'll tell you."

CHAPTER XVII

The Crown

"What do you think of it?" enquired Amanda.

Her brother, who was squatting among the reeds that fringed the millpool, peered down at the boat hidden so cunningly among the bushes before replying.

"It's not at all bad," he admitted. "Who fixed it up?"

"Scatty and I. It's all part of the scheme. I'm afraid you've got to trust me for an hour or two longer, though."

"I haven't trusted you for a minute yet," he observed drily, his eyes still fixed upon the boat.

In many ways it was an extraordinary craft. In foundation it consisted of the old ferry punt in which Amanda and Scatty got about in flood time, but its appearance had been considerably changed by a superstructure of light leafy branches and gorse, so that its real character was completely hidden, and while there was sufficient room for four or five people to crouch inside, to the casual observer it resembled nothing so much as a floating bush or a tangle of brushwood which had come adrift from some pile on the bank.

Amanda pointed downstream to the leafy tunnel ahead.

"In the dusk," she said softly, "no one from the road would notice that going down, would they? Once I lower the shuts there'll be enough water to send us downstream with a rush."

The boy straightened himself, and eyed her dubiously. "I hope for your sake that you're not playing the fool, Amanda," he said.

"I'm not, honestly I'm not," she assured him earnestly.

"I brought you round here to show you this because I may have to ask you to take it down to Sweethearting on your own. You could, couldn't you?"

"Naturally," he said. "A good deal better than you could, I should think."

"That's what I thought," said Amanda with unexpected humility.

Hal was about to enquire further, but he was interrupted. At that moment there sounded clearly and sharply from the other side of the mill the unmistakable crack of a revolver.

The two young people exchanged sharp, startled glances, and then the boy started off across the meadow to the footbridge, Amanda at his heels. As they reached the yard they heard another shot somewhere in the house, and Aunt Hatt screamed.

They hurried into the hall at the same moment as the good lady herself appeared at the head of the stairs. She was only partially clad, and a dressing jacket was clutched round her shoulders.

Mary and Guffy emerged from the kitchen a moment later, and Aunt Hatt screamed again.

"Oh, it's you two, is it?" she said with relief as she peered down into the darkness of the hall. "Where's the burglar? Be careful, he's got a revolver."

"What burglar, darling?" Mary stepped forward. "What's happened?"

"The burglar was in my bedroom. He stole my garnet necklace," said Aunt Hatt with some asperity. "It wasn't of any value, but I had a sentimental regard for it. It belonged to my mother. I'd just set out my things on the bed for the party and I stepped into my clothes closet for my black skirt, when I heard a sound in the room behind me. I came out and there he was, a perfectly strange man in my room, rummaging among the things on my dresser. He snatched the garnet necklace out of my trinket case—it only came back yesterday after having a new clasp—the necklace, I mean, not the box."

"What happened to the man?"

"He climbed out of the window on to that ledge above the coach-house roof." Aunt Hatt was more outraged than frightened and her kindly grey eyes flashed angrily. "I shouted at him," she said. "And he had the impudence to point a gun at me. I stepped back from the window, a little alarmed, I suppose, and the next thing I heard was firing. Oh, listen! What was that?"

Her last words ended on a little squeak of alarm as a third shot shattered the drowsy silence of the mill. Before anyone could speak, there was another report, and another, and another, until it sounded as though there was a pitched battle in the yard.

Guffy was making for the scene of action, with Mary clinging to his arm to prevent him, when the patch of brilliant sunshine framed by the doorway was obscured by the startling apparition of a strange gunman backing into its shelter. He was firing at some assailant hitherto unseen, and appeared to be a stranger to them all, a little thickset man with a roll of red fat between his coat collar and his cap.

Guffy disengaged himself from Mary's restraining hold, and took a flying leap onto the intruder's back, pinioning his arms to his sides with the grip of a bear. The man swore viciously, and struggled to free himself, but Hal stepped forward and snatched the gun from his hand.

"Here, let me go, can't yer?" said their captive, revealing an unexpectedly squeaky voice. "Don't hold me in the doorway. There's a female lunatic out there with a gun."

"Hold him!" shouted Amanda. "Hold him!"

"That's the man." Aunt Hatt advanced menacingly upon the now helpless captive. "That's the man who took my garnet necklace. Make him give it back."

"Look out!" bellowed the stranger, suddenly doubling up as footsteps sounded on the stones without. "Here she comes. She's a homicidal maniac, I tell yer."

The whole struggling group fell back a pace or two as once again the patch of sunlight vanished, to give place to an extraordinary individual who, revolver in hand, now appeared upon the threshold. It was a gaunt figure clad in a long dark skirt and skimpy blouse, and upon its head an old felt hat was unbecomingly tied with what appeared to be a bootlace. It stood for a moment in the doorway while they gasped at it, and then an unmistakable, slightly pedantic voice said clearly: "She walks in beauty like the night. I say, hang on to that fellow. Hysterical little soul, isn't he? He's blown a most unbecoming hole through my new blue bonnet."

"Campion!" said Guffy in a strangled voice. "Well, I'm damned!"

"Not necessarily," said the new-comer affably. "By the way, before we get chatty, let's tie this fellow up. Amanda, the clothes line."

Amanda was the only one of the party who was not temporarily dazed by this unexpected development, and she trotted out into the kitchen obediently.

Ten minutes later the man who had stolen Aunt Hatt's garnet necklace in what at first sight appeared an unnecessarily dramatic fashion, was reposing safely under the dining-room table, neatly trussed.

The party then adjourned to the cool of the hall once more. Guffy was shaken with a mixture of amazement and delight, and an overwhelming sense of relief. No restoration monarchist could have been more delighted at the return of his prince and leader than this foolish, but stouthearted Grand Vizier of Averna to see the Hereditary Paladin once again.

Mr. Campion sat down on the stairs where he was in the shadow and out of sight of the doorway, while they gathered round him, curious and as yet a little incredulous.

"Mr. Campion, you're wearing my old clothes."

Aunt Hatt peered at the skirt as she spoke.

"My landlady gave them to me," said Campion, casually indicating Amanda. "When I presented myself at her mill some days ago I explained my desire to get about unnoticed in the dusk, and she very obligingly obtained these garments to effect my disguise."

Guffy gaped at him. "Then you never boarded the

Marquisita?'' he said. "I knew there was something fishy about that letter."

The pale young man, looking somehow less foolish without his spectacles, had the grace to appear penitent.

"I admit my letter was a little misleading," he said. "As a matter of fact that whole incident was rather amusing. The engaging Mr. Parrott and I came to a little agreement."

As he spoke he kept his eyes fixed upon Guffy's face as though he were anxious to explain and to apologize.

"I had the toothache, you see," he went on airily, "and we called in at my flat for a scarf and a coat. Unknown to poor old Parrott (two t's, he tells me—that's to make it clear that he's nothing to do with the other branch of the family) my friend McCaffy was waiting for me in the cupboard wearing my second-best blue suit. I had the best one on, you see. I don't know if you're following all this, but there really isn't time to go into it very fully. Poor old McCaffy's a delightful soul, on for absolutely anything and one of the very best. He's always hard up, poor fellow, and occasionally I'm able to put a job in his way. This was one of them. You see, unfortunately for him he resembles me extraordinarily, except in the lower part of the face. To make the likeness more harmful he's made a study of my more revolting mannerisms, and if he can only wrap up his mouth and his chin he can pass very easily for me. Well—" he spread out his hands—"during the business interview I had with Pop Savanake, or whatever his friends call him, I rang up McCaffy, who was sitting in the outer office of my insurance brokers by appointment in case my interview turned out as I thought it might. As soon as he got my clever message, which was ostensibly to my broker, he handed on as much of it as was good for him to the fellow who does my business, and then doubled round to wait for me in the clothes cupboard. The rest was childish but so pretty. I went into the cupboard with a marble in my cheek and a hanky over it and McCaffy came out with a muffler round his face. He went off with Mr. Parrott for a nice sea voyage, with nothing but his passage money home at the end of it, for on examining the sealed orders handed to me by the captain of industry, he discovered them to contain just that. I hung about until it got dark, motor-cycled down to Sweethearting and walked the rest of the way over the fields in the dawn without seeing a soul. Then I burgled the mill and left the rest to Amanda, for whose creditable performance she will be mentioned in my will. By the way, remind me, Amanda, when the fun is over: I must wire McCaffy his passage money to Rio.''

Guffy shook his head. ''If you've been in the mill the entire time,'' he said, ''why on earth you chose to hide there, frightening the lives out of us and worrying us to death, I can't possibly imagine.''

Mr. Campion's pale, foolish face became regretful. ''I'm sorry about that,'' he said. ''But what else could I possibly do? I've had to keep you in the dark because it was absolutely necessary for you all to behave exactly as if I had deserted you. You see, in this instance it really is a case of 'spies everywhere.' The place is swarming with them.

Guffy was still dubious. His leisurely mind was recalling the incidents of the past few days.

''Then you explain Amanda's behaviour,'' he said. ''The three hundred pounds—the releasing of Miss Huntingforest after the raid—the new car. I suppose you engineered all that?''

Mr. Campion regarded his friend and the seriousness in his face was so unlike him that Guffy was silenced altogether.

''The exciting relation of my astounding adventures while in hiding I shall reserve for the club banquet,'' Campion continued. ''As it is, my appearance at this particular juncture is an accident. But for the unforeseen intrusion of our friend in the next room you would have remained in ignorance of my duplicity until this evening. So, my dear old birds, do carry on as usual. Everything depends on that.''

''You say 'everything,' '' said Guffy gloomily. ''Everything's over. Our failure is complete and utter.''

"Failure?" exclaimed the Hereditary Paladin with spirit.
"My poor dear imbecile friend, if we can screw our
courage to the sticking point, as we say on the halls, we
shall make good—succeed—win through—make the bell
ring and get our money back. It's only the next few hours
which are difficult, and they're so difficult and tetchy that
I feel that Miss Huntingforest and Mary ought to be out of
it, somehow. But as the whole success of the circus depends upon their complicity, I'm asking them to take the
risk."

"I imagine one more risk or so won't make much
difference to me," said Aunt Hatt grimly.

Guffy looked uncomfortable. "Miss Huntingforest, I
shall never forgive myself for the inconvenience and trouble we've brought upon you," he said.

"They started before you came," said the lady with
resignation.

"Count us in on it," said Mary firmly, and the older
woman nodded.

Mr. Campion leant forward, a comic figure in his remarkable garments.

"The situation, so far," he observed, "is definitely
sound. If it weren't for the simple-livers on the heath and
the evidence delivered so neatly by the gentleman in the
dining-room that our opponents are not so daft as I had
hoped, the affair would be almost plain sailing. As it is,
I'm afraid there's a risk, a much greater one than I dreamed
would ever be possible. These fellows are desperate. They're
working for a man who's never yet been disappointed in
anything he set his mind on."

"When you say the situation is sound," said Guffy,
"what do you mean? I don't see that we're any further on
than we were at the beginning."

"Not with the Charter well on its way to Whitehall?
That's a tremendous step. Oh, I forgot . . . Dear, dear, I
hope you're not going to be annoyed. You see, what
happened was this. When I heard about Glencannon's
letter from Amanda I asked her to drop into Norwich for
the drum. It never dawned on me that you three heroes

would undertake the same task or I'd have left it to you. However, when at last it came into the house I couldn't keep my hands off it. I watched Hal take it out of the car and then, seeing him looking out of his bedroom window, I guessed that he'd got it up there. I sneaked round the back of the mill, got in through the side door, and secreted myself on the upper landing, so that as soon as Hal went down to meet you fellows I was able to nip in and get the thing."

"But how did you know the Charter was inside?"

"I didn't, and it wasn't," said the Hereditary Paladin. "It was where I hoped it would be from the moment I read the verse on the oak. The Charter was written on parchment, you remember. Well, as a matter of fact, it formed the underhead of the drum itself. Rather a natty hiding place, don't you think? All the clerical work was on the inside, of course. It was genuine all right. Henry the Fourth's seal and everything. Lugg took it over the fields to the Sweethearting road early this morning, I hope, and from there Eager-Wright will take it to town."

Guffy, who had been listening to these revelations with the delight of a child, now became depressed.

"Of course," he said, "you don't know. Rather an awkward thing's happened to Wright and Farquharson."

"Yes," began Mary, but words failed her as she caught the gleam in Amanda's eyes.

Guffy looked scandalized. "Good heavens, Campion, was that you, too? I say, you know, it'll take a bit of explaining, won't it?"

"It was the only way," said the Hereditary Paladin shamelessly. "Consider: this village is swarming with potential trouble-mongers. They've made two attempts to discover if we've got hold of anything and if so to appropriate it. They're more or less convinced—or were until a few hours ago—that we have nothing. And yet they can't understand why we're still hanging about. They believe I'm safely on the way to South America, but at the same time they believe that you're on to something or you'd hardly remain here. Well, reflect. If Eager-Wright sets out post-haste for town in the ordinary way they'd naturally hold him up, search him and take whatever was going. The problem that faced your old friend Albert is obvious to you. Those two birds had to be got away out of the community without arousing any suspicion whatever, and the arrest notion seemed to be the only one that fitted into the case. Lugg fixed it up this morning by phone from Sweethearting. We have a lot of odd friends in town who have no difficulty in getting hold of a little thing like a uniform or two. I hope they did their stuff well?"

"Damned well," said Guffy, who was still not quite approving. "I suppose if they took us in they deceived those blighters on the heath."

"Oh, I think so. I told Lugg to see they did the thing properly. I imagine they called in at the pub, asked the way to the house, dropped a few elephantine hints about the young gents who were wanted for a motoring offence, and finally came down here and carried off their prize in triumph. Once they get outside Sweethearting they'll pick up Lugg and the Charter, and Eager-Wright will take the car and go on. Farquharson will wait at that pub on the river for further developments. Rather smart organization, don't you think? When, if ever, I come into my kingdom I'm thinking of making it into one of these new-fangled republics with myself as dictator."

"You talk about the importance of the next few hours," said Guffy. "Are we to take it that something really sensational is about to happen some time this evening?"

"Well, yes, it'll be sensational enough if it comes off. Oh, yes, quite definitely."

"We must put Dr. Galley off, then," said Mary quickly.

"Oh no, please don't do that." Campion turned to her gravely. "That little jaunt is tremendously important. And that brings me to the subject of Dr. Galley. He presents a rather interesting problem. While I know for a fact that he's not definitely in league with our over-attentive friends, I observe that he's up to something very queer, although what it is I can't for the life of me imagine. When I first heard of his invitation I felt that it was the most awkward

thing that could possibly have happened, but now I'm not
so sure. Those good souls who are taking such tremendous
interest in your movements just now will be taken completely off their guard if you all dutifully go out to tea, as
it were, at this stage of the proceedings. All I dare tell you
at the moment—and I've got to implore you to put your
trust in little Albert—is that during your visit to old Galley
you will receive the signal. You can't miss it. It will force
itself upon you. Then follow Amanda back here as hard as
you can and leave the rest to her.

"I'm sorry to be so mysterious," he went on unhappily,
"but you must see how touchy the whole thing is. If all
goes well to-night we shall have the third and last proof,
the most important one, the Metternich receipt. The other
two are important, but without this third trophy I'm afraid
any suit would fail at the International Court at The Hague.
Now you see just where we stand."

He was looking at them appealingly, and they responded.

"Rely on us," said Aunt Hatt with unexpected vigour.
"I'm glad we're going to Dr. Galley's," she continued,
displaying once again her vein of practicalness, which
never seemed to desert her, no matter how fantastic the
situation became. "His story interested me. He might
really have those proofs of Mary Fitton's marriage."

"I thought that," said Campion, who appeared to know
everything. "I heard the story from Amanda last night,
and it seemed to me that it might be very likely. There's
something odd going on there, though, something I don't
understand at all."

Amanda looked startled and hastily diverted the conversation.

"You say we've got *two* proofs," she said. "We know
about the Charter, but where's the Crown?"

"The Crown!" said Mr. Campion, aghast. "I forgot
it." He rose to his feet, and dived into the dining-room
where their captive lay.

It was some minutes before he returned, and then he
came back triumphant, something shining in the palm of

his outstretched hand. They pressed round him, and Aunt Hatt emitted a squeak of astonishment.

"My garnet necklace!"

Mr. Campion peered at her quizzically through his spectacles.

"They're not garnets," he said. "They're very old square-cut rubies."

"Rubies? Why, it might be valuable."

Mr. Campion grinned. "It is. This exhibit, ladies and gentlemen, is the Crown of Avera."

He held the necklet up so that they could all see it. It consisted of a roughly made chain of early red gold, worked to resemble a daisy-chain, and at uneven intervals three rust-red stones were set between the links. Three large white agates completed the circle, and a latter-day jeweller had inserted a very modern fastener, so that the round now appeared nothing more than a fashionable choker necklace of a somewhat unusual design.

"There you are," said Campion. "Three drops of blood from a royal wound, three dull stars like the pigeon's egg, held and knit together by a flowery chain."

"But it belonged to my mother," said Aunt Hatt in astonishment. "It was given to her by my father and it was always kept, I remember, in a walnut bureau which stood in the parlour, since it wasn't fashionable to wear such ornate jewellery in those days. I remember that bureau quite well. It was inlaid, you see, with a little diamond-shaped panel in the writing flap. When you pressed the diamond at the bottom it came up and opened in two halves to show a tiny secret drawer behind."

She stopped abruptly before the expressions on their faces.

"The diamond!" ejaculated Guffy. " 'The diamond must be rent in twain Before he wear his crown again.' That bureau must have been part of the household furniture that went to America with Guy Huntingforest."

"But how did you know? And how did they guess? Why wasn't it stolen before, when they searched the house?"

Not unnaturally Aunt Hatt was still finding the story difficult to believe.

"If we take those questions backwards, the clever gentleman will endeavour to explain," said Campion. "In the first place, it wasn't stolen when they searched the house because it wasn't here then, and even if it had been no one knew quite what they were looking for.

"Then for the second question. They guessed, I imagine, because in the last two days the man in authority has seen fit to appoint men of brains on this business. That's what makes it so awkward for this evening's performance. The gentleman in the next room is quite an eminent professional thief in his own line. He seems to have been told exactly what to look for. The thugs who descended on you last Thursday were hunting for something more obvious, I imagine, something they could take away in a hatbox."

"How did *you* guess?" demanded Mary.

Mr. Campion glanced down at the chain in his hand.

"Last night," he said, "a rather pathetic figure, clutching her weeds about her, paused outside the lighted window where the family sat at their evening meal—just like you see on the pictures. If I had time I could bring tears to your eyes on this theme. However, when I was peeking in my eyes fell naturally upon Miss Huntingforest, and there she sat smiling and serene with the Crown of Averna round her neck. Stifling my hysterical shrieks of delight and astonishment, I went back into the darkness and decided that, as I didn't want to give myself away, the Crown was probably as safe there as anywhere."

"But I don't see how you could have guessed from just seeing it," said Amanda.

"Oh, we master minds, we jump at things like that," said Mr. Campion solemnly. "Of course, it seemed incredible at first, but I couldn't get the description out of my head. However, it was not until I noticed something else that I was absolutely certain."

"Something else? What was that?"

"Well," said the young man slowly, "the quotation from the manuscript goes on, you know. 'And when a

Pontisbright do wear it, none shall see it but by the stars.'
Last night Miss Huntingforest was sitting between Hal and
Mary, and what I noticed was this.''

He beckoned Hal towards him, and when the boy stepped
forward obediently Campion placed the circlet upon his
head. The effect was extraordinary, and somehow miraculously
convincing. The flaming Pontisbright hair swallowed
up the red gold, and the dull sheen of the strangely
coloured rubies, so that all of the Crown that was visible
were the three agates, the ''three dull stars like the pigeon's
egg,'' creamy clear above the boy's wide forehead.

CHAPTER XVIII

Doctor Galley's Unusual Practice

"If you, Amanda, will only think of me as Hannibal," said Mr. Campion, tucking his threadbare skirt round his ankles as he sat huddled up on the stairs, "or Julius Caesar, or even that other great organizer, Policewoman Webb, the Limehouse Fairy-Godmother, you will see that my system for this evening is neat, snappy, quite the thing and well worth following."

They were alone in the hall. The others had already set out for Dr. Galley's house, and only Amanda had lingered behind for final instructions. Now she stood leaning against the wall, her face pale with excitement and her eyes wide and questioning.

"It's all ready," she said. "We've got the boat down to the join in the river. It's completely hidden. The trees meet in a tunnel there. Hal's going to get the others aboard, and I shall let down the shuts. The river is very high, so it'll come down with a rush and we ought to make good speed. I've had it all out with Hal, and he knows exactly what to do. I'd like to go over it again just to see I haven't made a mistake. When we get to Sweethearting we take the car that will be waiting at 'The George' and we go round the back way to Great Kepesake, where we wait for Scatty and Lugg, who will come by the fens."

Mr. Campion nodded. "I'm very proud of that bit," he said. "If your friends on the heath miss you they'll take it for granted that you've made for London. It won't occur to them to look further inland. However, if it should be necessary to go further afield leave it to Guffy. He knows West Suffolk very well. Anyway, most of it belongs to his father.''

Amanda shrugged her shoulders. "We shall be all right," she said valiantly. "Don't bother about us. What I want to know is what's going to happen to you? You'll never do it all alone without me. Why not leave the escape to Hal, and let me stay behind to give you a hand?''

Mr. Campion's pale eyes met hers gravely. "Sorry, old lady," he said. "Can't be done. Put it down to a natural desire on my part to hog all the glory.''

"I do," said Amanda coldly. "And I think you've bitten off more than you can chew. I'm the technician, remember, and I don't think you've got any idea the sort of noise this . . .''

"Signal," said Mr. Campion quickly.

"Signal," agreed Amanda, "is going to make. They'll hear it in Ipswich. You'll have the whole hive down on you like a sandstorm.''

"So I shall," he agreed cheerfully. "But I've provided for that. The boy's got brains. I've always thought that it was only spite that kept me from getting into the sixth form.''

"What have you provided?" demanded Amanda ruthlessly.

Campion sighed. "I was going to take you into partnership as soon as you were over school age," he said, "but I'm hanged if I shall now. You're much too nosey. You ought to look on me with reverence. You ought to see me as the hand of fate, a deity moving in a mysterious way.''

"What have you provided?" persisted Amanda.

Campion shrugged his shoulders. "At precisely ten minutes to seven o'clock," he said, "the two officials who arrested Mr. Farquharson this morning will obligingly bring him back, and the outside world will assume that they have discovered that he wasn't the man they wanted after all. They will bring him back here, exciting a certain amount of comment but, I trust, no alarm. As soon as they get here they will remove their uniforms, the inspector will

take our Morris, the policeman will remain at the wheel of
the hired car he's driving, and Farquharson will take the
Lagonda. The moment the signal is given they will shoot
out of the lane. Farquharson and the inspector will take the
heath road round the camp, driving at great speed. They
will dash past the 'Gauntlett' and on to the road which
skirts Galley's side of the wood. Meanwhile, the bobby—
you'd like him, by the way, drives at Brooklands quite a
lot—will take the lower road on the other side of the
wood. They will circle the enclosed area as often and as
noisily as is possible in the time, and the moment the
signal ceases, will drive off ostentatiously down the three
different roads which lead out of this charming village.
Behind them, I hope and trust, will dash our enemies,
leaving little Albert time to take the hat round and clear off
with the collection. It should also cover your departure, or
flight out of Egypt, or whatever you like to call it."

"It's good," said Amanda after a pause. She nodded.
"Very hot."

"That's what I thought," he agreed modestly. "Now
you see the kind of man I am."

"I'm conceited, too," said Amanda. "But I wish you
luck. I'll go now. You can think of me as Moses, leading
my relations out of the wilderess. By the way, have you
noticed Guffy and Mary? I think it must be because she's
led such a secluded life and has been starved for compan-
ionship of her own age, don't you?"

"Without any modicum of disrespect for my old friend,
Mr. Randall," said Mr. Campion judicially, "perhaps so.
Er—life's very beautiful, isn't it?"

"Speaking as a soul not yet mated, nerts," said Amanda.

Campion rose to his feet. "I'm going to get out of these
clothes and sneak into the wood and bide my time. You
run along. Don't forget. Hold them there until the signal at
all costs."

She did not turn away, but stood there hesitating, and at
the expression on her face he came over and stood looking
down at her.

"Look here," he said gravely, "what's the matter with

this visit to Galley? You've been so tremendously against it all along, and now I believe you're funking it."

She shook her head defiantly, and a gleam of the old defiance showed in her brown eyes.

"I'm not really afraid of anything," she said, but he knew the words were sheer bravado and he continued to look down at her, for the first time a trace of anxiety appearing in his eyes.

"What do you know about Galley?" he demanded.

She did not move away, but turned her head and gazed thoughtfully through the open doorway into the yard beyond.

"He's very harmless, really," she said suddenly, her voice unusually soft. "I don't suppose he ever kills anybody who wouldn't die anyway, and I do believe he does a lot of good. Of course, it's all childish and not at all serious, but there's always that uncomfortable feeling that there might be something in it."

Mr. Campion's eyes were very stern. "Does he take some sort of dope?" he demanded. "I didn't recognize it when I saw him. What is his poison?"

"Oh no, it's not that," said Amanda, still not meeting his eyes. "I've never said anything because I thought he might get kicked out of the profession for it, and I do think he does a lot of good in a way. But all the really queer things you've noticed around here—the fear sign and that sort of thing—are mainly due to him and his habits for the last twenty years or so. He's mad, you see."

He laughed. "Most people are a little."

She turned her head sharply and looked him full in the eyes, and he was startled by her expression.

"I mean insane," she said. "Or at least that's the only comfortable way to look at it."

Something about her calm sincerity was very convincing and he reseated himself upon the stairs.

"Out with it."

Amanda stirred uncomfortably. "I haven't told anyone this," she said. "In fact, I once swore a most frightful oath I never would. But I think you'd better know." She paused to consider her confession, but finally the words came with a rush. "This is how I worked it out," she said. "Dr. Galley was only just qualified when he came down here forty years ago. I don't know much about it, but as a rule doctors learn a great deal after they're qualified, don't they? When Dr. Galley came down here at first he didn't have anyone to talk to except country people, and I think he had a lot of time on his hands. Naturally, he took up reading.

"Well"—her voice sank—"that library he inherited from his great-uncle is an enormous affair, and it contains some very queer books and manuscripts."

She paused and glanced dubiously at Campion, but he was following her intently and she continued:

"This is only my theory," she said. "And, of course, I know hardly anything about it. But even fifty years ago medicine and—and superstition were rather mixed, weren't they?"

Campion was frowning and his eyes seemed to have become darker as he stared thoughtfully into her face.

"You're suggesting, I take it, that Dr. Galley is actually practising archaic medicine, herbalism and that sort of thing, I suppose?" he said.

"Oh yes," agreed Amanda with a flash of her old cheerfulness. "He's always done that. But what I'm getting at is this. Ever since I've known him he's gone a step or two further than that. You see, what it boils down to is that ancient medicine was often—" she paused again.

"A variety of witchcraft," said Mr. Campion dryly.

The girl regarded him with complete gravity. "Yes," she said at last. "That's it. It sounds silly, doesn't it?"

Mr. Campion was silent for some moments. In a long experience of the more out-of-the-way corners of life he had met with some curious phenomena, some odd forms of mania, and some amazing cases of retrogression. Suffolk, one of the oldest counties, was virtually unexplored, and little local papers whose very names were unknown to the great London dailies sometimes printed strange tales of ignorance and superstition which had found their way to tiny rustic police courts. It did not seem incredible to him, therefore, that, in a county where whole districts go for years without seeing their local police constable, very strange things should occur which never reached the maw of any printing press.

The more he considered Amanda's revelation the less unlikely, if not the less extraordinary, it seemed to be. The fact that the little doctor had bought no practice, but had put up his plate uninvited, would have automatically ostracised him from any professional folk in the district and his patients would have been gathered naturally from the ignorant, trusting country people, very few of whom could read at the time of his arrival.

Campion considered Amanda's theory set forward so ingenuously and found that with her he could imagine any impressionable youngster left to solitude and a library delving amongst the ancient volumes, and consuming greedily anything which touched his own subject, however remotely. He could guess at the temptation to try an early remedy thus discovered on some unsuspecting patient, and the surprise at some coincidental cure. He could see the man growing older, becoming more and more bigoted, obsessed by his dangerous hobby.

He glanced at Amanda. "The first night we came to the village Lugg saw—or thought he saw—a corpse laid out on the heath," he said. "Was that anything to do with Galley?"

Amanda took a deep breath. "It isn't often done here," she said. "Anyway, it did no harm. The village only consented because Galley wanted it. Fred Cole died quite naturally, and really he was rather a bad lot. You wouldn't understand or I'd explain."

"In certain uncivilized countries," remarked Mr. Campion, his eyes still fixed on her face, "the natives believe that if one of their number dies, whose private life has not been quite as beautiful as it might have been, then it is a good idea to let the corpse lie out in the moonlight for three nights running so that the evil spirit may escape completely and not be shut in a grave where it may grow fierce and dangerous. The bravest natives watch the body to see, so they say, the hour at which the spirit escapes, so they may be able to tell to which angel they must appeal for protection from it."

Amanda sighed, a little escaping breath of pure relief.

"You know all about it. I'm so glad. It saves a lot of explaining. Yes; that's it exactly. I'm not sure whether old Galley had ever actually had it done before, but he's talked about it for years. I fancy Fred Cole was the first person to die with a reputation bad enough to allow Galley to make the experiment without offending anyone. Well, that's all there is to that, so we can forget it, can't we?"

Campion had not taken his eyes from her face.

"You were there, I suppose?" he said.

Amanda grew slowly crimson. "It was wrong," she burst out at last. "Wrong, and rather horrible. But you see, Galley's brought the whole village up—and me, too, in a way—to believe, or at any rate to know, a lot about witchcraft, and when he actually summoned me I didn't like to disobey."

Mr. Campion remained very grave. "Did Dr. Galley tell you that according to superstition to perform this rite satisfactorily one of the watchers should be a magician and the other 'a fair young maid, chaste and untaught, so that the spirit may enter into her, and when she runs mad may be kept close and of no danger to her fellows'?"

Amanda stared at him. "No," she said at last. "No, he didn't. Perhaps he didn't know about that bit," she went on, wrestling with this new sidelight on Dr. Galley's character. "Or perhaps he realizes there's nothing serious in it after all."

"Optimism and loyalty will be your downfall, young woman," said Mr. Campion grimly. "To my less charitable mind this story shows one thing very clearly: Dr. Galley has a mania and his malady has at last reached a point when his concern for his friends is less important to him than his rather nasty hobby. This is very disturbing, Amanda."

She was silent for some moments. She seemed to be considering the situation gravely, for her brown eyes were dark and troubled, and there was an alarmed expression in their depths.

"I've had my doubts about this party all along," she said at last. "You see, I found a bit of vervain stuck up on the lintel over the front door after Dr. Galley went yesterday, and he asked particularly if Hal and I and Guffy and Mary would wear clean clothes for the party. The others put it down to sheer eccentricity, but I did wonder . . ."

Campion bounded to his feet. "I'm going up there with you," he said. "You ought to have come out with this before. As soon as I've discarded this hampering garment we'll clear off through the wood."

"But what about the signal?" demanded Amanda.

"Signal be hanged!" said Campion unexpectedly. "D'you realize that we've sent your poor aunt, the unfortunate Guffy and those two children into the hands of a lunatic with a mania for demonology, and the black art, a form of madness which, after all, had all England by the ears three hundred years ago? And now we find two evidences of the more common preparations for sacrifice planted neatly under our noses."

CHAPTER XIX

Pourboire

Mr. Campion strode along the narrow footpath through the woods which had once formed part of the grounds of the Pontisbright house. Amanda plodded at his heels. In spite of their haste they went cautiously. An ominous silence hung over the village, and the storm which had been threatening all day was now billowing up out of the south in great inky clouds of trouble. It was insufferably hot, the air stifling.

Once, when they had almost traversed the clump of pines which grew on the western extremity of the open space where the house had stood, Campion paused, and whistled softly.

The sound was echoed from somewhere high in the branches of a cedar which stood just to the right of the cavity which had once contained the foundations of the Hall.

Mr. Campion seemed satisfied, for he pushed on, Amanda still pattering behind him.

By the time they reached the low hedge that separated Dr. Galley's garden from the Hall grounds the storm was perceptibly nearer, casting an unnatural light over the vivid flowers which grew round the rectory. The flowers of the sun, Mars and Jupiter, which were all in the front garden, seemed to favour peculiarly bright colouring, and it was not difficult to remember that spellmongers of ancient times professed an ascendancy over the weather and plant life.

Mr. Campion glanced back at Amanda, and the glimpse

of her white face suddenly brought home to him the full
drama of their mission.

"They'll be in the long room at the back," she whispered.
He nodded. "Is there a window we can look through?"

"I think so. Come on."

She slipped in front of him, and set off down a path
between two great banks of giant sunflowers. The battered
white house stood out startlingly amid the swirling shadows. The aromatic scent of the garden was so strong that it
was almost overpowering. The wind had risen in the last
few minutes, and it was as though the doctor's garden had
been caught by a fury. The flowers and leaves danced
wildly in the breeze.

When they reached the side of the house the girl mo-
tioned her companion to keep back, and they crept along
the mouldering wall until they approached a window set in
an alcove and partially hidden by heavy curtains on the
inside.

Pulling herself up cautiously Amanda peered in and
Campion looked over her shoulder. They were looking
down upon the scene within, for the ground sloped away
in front of them.

Amanda nudged Campion. She dared not speak, for the
window was partially open. He nodded, but did not take
his eyes off the little group within.

Dr. Galley's drawing-room had been dismantled. The
furniture was piled against the walls and a dark curtain hung
across the bay window in the far wall.

Aunt Hatt, looking comfortably conventional in her walking suit and serviceable hat, sat nursing her gloves in a
chair by the fireside. Guffy and Mary sat on a couch
opposite her, while Hal stood directly beneath the window
through which they watched. An awkward silence appeared to be in progress and it was some time before
Amanda located Dr. Galley. When she saw him at last he
was bending over a side table on which were a decanter
and glasses. Presently his voice sounded fretfully out of
the shadows.

"I wish Amanda would come. We really can't get on

without Amanda. It's most important. The time's going, too.''

"I'm sure she won't be long," said Aunt Hatt comfortingly. "I really don't think we need wait for her, Doctor. Won't you tell us some more about your exciting discovery?"

The old man looked at her vaguely. "Oh yes," he said at last. *"That* discovery. Yes, yes, of course. But there's no time for that now. The hour is at its height."

It was evident to everyone that he was labouring under some tremendous emotion, and Campion, who caught a glimpse of his eyes as he looked up, felt that sudden thrill of mingled pity and nausea which a healthy mind must always feel before such a revelation.

"The hour is at its height," the doctor repeated. "We must begin without her. Mary, my dear, will you pour a glass of wine for each of you? Don't worry about me; I shan't drink myself. I have to keep my mind very, very clear."

Aunt Hatt and Mary exchanged glances as the old man brought the table into the very centre of the room. His hands were trembling, and the glasses tinkled and rattled alarmingly. The two outside the window caught the dull gleam of the wine in the white decanter.

It was evident that Mary felt the sinister atmosphere in the room, for she did not stir, and for some seconds after the doctor stood back the table remained unattended.

Mr. Campion frowned and Amanda noticed that his usually expressionless face showed definite signs of alarm. He felt in his pocket.

"It's a pity," he whispered. "Such a nice bottle. Still, they really mustn't drink that stuff."

And before the girl realized what he was doing, he had raised his revolver and fired through the narrow crack between the lower sash and the sill. She had just time to see the slender cut-glass bottle split to atoms, and its crimson contents spurt out over the floor, when Campion seized her hand and dragged her headlong over the grass to a vantage spot among the sunflowers.

They crouched there, waiting, but no one came to the

window, and, although there was the sound of voices from the room there was no banging of doors or hurrying footsteps.

"They're all right for a bit," said Campion, sighing. "He was relying on that stuff. It was something to make them sleep, I hope, nothing more serious."

Amanda blinked, and was silent for some moments. "Look here," she said at last, "it's getting late. You ought to go down to Lugg and Scatty. I'll keep the others in there until the signal. You must let me. I can manage it. I see now: he's as batty as a coot."

Mr. Campion regarded her thoughtfully, and she went on:

"Don't be obstinate. If anything goes wrong with the plan we shall all be in the soup."

Mr. Campion took his revolver from his coat pocket and handed it to her.

"If you take this," he said, "at least you can't come to any serious harm. Although, be careful."

Amanda did not waste any time in argument. She took the gun from his outstretched hand.

"You get back to the wood," she said. "When I hear the signal I'll get them out."

She rose cautiously to her feet, slipped the gun in her jacket pocket, and turned towards the house. Then, looking back suddenly, she stopped and kissed him unromantically on the nose.

"That's by way of *pourboire*, in case we don't meet again," she said lightly, and hurried out onto the garden path, whence she walked boldly into the house, the unnatural light turning her blazing hair into a flame.

CHAPTER XX

To Meet Ashtaroth

When the decanter standing upon the small table in the centre of the room was suddenly shivered the atmosphere in the doctor's drawing-room, which had been tense enough before, was instantly brought to fever pitch. Aunt Hatt screamed, Guffy sprang to his feet and Hal, over whose head the shot had passed, made for the window.

But Dr. Galley's reactions were so much more startling than the phenomenon itself that they forgot their own alarm in their surprise at his behaviour. He threw up his hand and with eyes blazing and face transfigured exclaimed loudly: "He strikes! He shows his will!"

He gave no explanation for these cryptic utterances, but, finding that he was the centre of interest, turned and addressed the company in a voice completely unlike his usual diffident murmur. The change in him was extraordinary. He held himself very stiffly and there was a suggestion of new strength about him as though he had become possessed of a new and powerful personality.

"Since he has decided to act without my aid, we will leave it to him," he said. "You will all keep very still, please."

Aunt Hatt would have spoken, but he silenced her with a gesture, and she sat looking at him, frank bewilderment written clearly on her kindly face.

Guffy coughed. The whole thing struck him as being incomprehensible. Campion's sudden return had exhausted his powers of surprise, and, besides, the atmosphere of the room, which seemed to be full of acrid smoke not unlike incense, but less pleasant, was beginning to cause him discomfort. He felt dizzy and inexplicably sleepy.

It was at this moment that a third diversion was caused by the arrival of Amanda, who walked coolly into the room, her right hand resting negligently in her jacket pocket. She smiled at the doctor, who turned towards her eagerly.

"You're late," he said testily. "The hour is past its height. It is the hour of Casael—you know that. Stand over there."

He pointed to a chair set on the right of the bay window. As Amanda walked towards it she disturbed the folds of the curtain which covered it, and the choking aromatic smoke in the air became more dense.

"Quarter to seven," wailed Dr. Galley. "Quarter to seven and we have not yet begun."

He moved the table from the centre of the room and preceeded to roll up the carpet. Since his behaviour had become really eccentric only with the smashing of the decanter, and Aunt Hatt, Guffy, and Mary were all three slow-thinking, conventional people, they sat there looking at him stupidly, too astonished to move.

He kicked the folded rug across the doorway and they sat looking at the boards which he had revealed. These were oak and blackened with age, and upon their dull surface a curious design had been chalked. This consisted of a nine-foot square with a line drawn parallel to each of two opposite sides, forming rectangular margins. These were occupied by crosses and triangles, whilst in the central area between them a circle had been drawn to touch the parallel lines. A smaller circle lay within, concentric with the first circle, and this contained a square again. In the space between the first and the second circles the name *Casael* was written three times, and on all four sides of the inner square the name *Ashtaroth* was printed in large letters.

The full significance of this display did not dawn on anyone, save Amanda, for some time, but Aunt Hatt rose to her feet.

"The air in here is stifling, Doctor," she said. "I think I'll go out into the garden."

He wheeled upon her. "Sit down," he said sharply.

Aunt Hatt sat down meekly; why she never quite understood, save that curiosity played a large part in her mixed emotions just then.

Dr. Galley leant over the back of the sofa and produced a long black dressing-gown, which he put on. And then, stepping carefully to avoid the chalk lines, he placed himself in the centre of the inner square.

"Now," he said, "I will explain."

Outside the storm had broken and the sigh of the wind, coupled with the sound of rain pouring down upon the leaves, made the scene in the room somehow more fantastic, more convincing, than if the sun had been shining.

A violent crack of thunder above their heads drowned the old man's voice for an instant, and even the phlegmatic Guffy was conscious of a thrill. Sometimes things are so utterly inexplicable, so unexpected, that they stun the senses into at least momentary acceptance. After the thunder-clap had died away there was complete silence in the little room as the five sat with smarting eyes and suddenly disturbed breathing, watching the figure in the black gown.

"There are many sciences," began Dr. Galley, "which have been forgotten. There was a time when men willingly gave up their lives in a search for power such as is undreamed of by modern pettifogging students. Forty years ago I made up my mind that I would emulate those men and perhaps beat them at their own game.

"For years," he went on passionately, "I strove with the aid of the remarkable books left to me in this house to make myself a master of those occult sciences which have been neglected so foolishly in the present day.

"I have studied diligently," he continued, turning a glittering eye upon them, "and, in countless little ways, I have proved that I was right. I could tell you of remarkable cures worked upon the good people hereabouts with the aid of the powers of the air. Some of the country people know me for what I am and respect me for it, even as their forefathers not so long ago respected the great Dr. Dee, Court Magician to Queen Elizabeth.

"But," he went on with growing fervour and so much nervous power behind his words that now they could hardly have moved had they wished, "although in small things I was successful enough to know that I was right, in the large things I had always been disappointed. I thought at first that my books were at fault, or that I myself by my early training had rendered my being too gross, too materialistic to achieve my ends. But seven nights ago I was successful. He came at last. Ashtaroth himself appeared.

"Wait!" he continued, throwing out his hands. "Wait! You shall hear it all. You shall see to what a triumph my studies have brought me. Seven nights ago in the hour of Methratton I was alone in this room, standing within my circle conjuring him to appear. I had fasted for three days. This room was strewn with coriander, sorcelage, and henbane, and I had done all the other necessaries which it is not right for you to hear. After I had repeated my conjuration he appeared.

"He did not come in his usual guise, but in his own person as a man. When I conjured him he came up to me and I knew that my spells were strong enough to hold him. So that he would not harm me I became his servant. He stayed in my house and hid himself, and I obeyed him. I failed him in one thing. I thought he had left me, but after"—he turned to them and his face lighted up until he became positively terrifying, and Amanda gripped the gun in her pocket until the steel bit into her flesh—"but after," he continued, "he was delivered into my hands I became his master. I found him on the heath so stricken that the spirit could not leave the body. I brought him back here and he has been my captive. But I have been afraid. The body is dying, and although I have fed the spirit on those things which my books tell me are his chief food, the smoke of ambergris, frankincense, red storax, mastick, and saffron, he has not yet recovered."

He paused to allow this announcement to sink in and

then went on, speaking with the same horrifying earnestness as before.

"If the body in which he rests should die, then he must find other habitation. Now perhaps you see why I have brought you here. It is written in my books that Ashtaroth, Prince of the Criminators, that great group of fire spirits, can be placated with the blood of two maidens, and two young men taken on the appointed day in the hour of Casael.

"I had arranged," he went on, a flash of cunning creeping into his face, "that you should take a little morphia with your wine, so that his task of subduing you might be easier. But, you see, he knew his power and disdained a modern drug.

"Now the time is at hand. Ashtaroth, come forth!"

He threw up his hand and stood facing the curtained bay window. He was trembling, his eyes were blazing, and there was a thin line of foam between his lips.

The storm added to the impressive effect. A distant rumble of thunder emphasized the words and a flash of lightning flickered through the room, this time accompanied by a much louder crash.

"Here!" ejaculated Guffy, suddenly stumbling to his feet. "You must stop this tomfoolery, Galley. This is madness, you know."

"Oh, look! Look!" Aunt Hatt's voice was hardly recognizable as it cut through Guffy's husky outburst. "There's something behind the curtain. It's moving!"

It needed only this to produce a state of genuine fear in Dr. Galley's audience. All eyes were turned upon the heavy curtain. The choking fumes were now growing stronger in the room, and even while they stared, the curtains stirred a little and from behind them there issued a strange inarticulate sound, something between a gasp and a groan, but which in the circumstances sounded very much less than human.

"He comes!" screamed Dr. Galley, quivering in an ecstasy of excitement. "Ashtaroth, come forth! By the masters of the demons who people the upper air, by Python, by Belial, by Asmodeus and by Merizim, come you out! By the Psoudothei I conjure you. I charge you by the Prestidigitators, by the Furies and by the Ariel powers who mix themselves with thunders and lightnings, corrupting the air, bringing pestilence, and other evils, I summon you! O Ashtaroth, come hastily and tarry not. Make your appearance visible to my sight. I bind you in this hour of Casael to whom you be captive that you remain visible here before the circle as long as my pleasure is, and not before my license to depart.''

As the doctor's chanting died away the curtains billowed forward and were then dragged open, to reveal in the aperture, surrounded by the choking fumes of burning herbs, a terrifying spectacle. The figure of a man so emaciated that he appeared almost a skeleton, partially draped in a crimson cloth and otherwise entirely nude save for cabalistic designs which appeared to be painted on his skin, stood swaying in the aperture. His face was contorted and his red-rimmed eyes were glazed. It was only by his hair that they recognized him. It grew down to an unmistakable widow's peak, almost reaching the bridge of his nose.

The doctor was chanting like a maniac in the centre of his circle, and now his voice rose to a frenzy as he besought the new-comer to take his ancient right and drink his fill of blood prepared for him.

The others, who had been momentarily stunned by this apparition, now sprang to their feet, and the pitiful thing in the curtains suddenly caught sight of Guffy and a strangled cry escaped him as he tottered forward.

"For God's sake," he mumbled through cracked lips, "get me out of here! He's mad—he's torturing me!"

The effort of speech seemed to be too much for him, for the next moment he had pitched forward onto the floor, where he lay sprawled out across the ancient circle at the feet of the doctor.

Guffy swept the man out of the way and dropped down beside the terrible thing on the floor. When he looked up again his face was white with alarm.

"I think he's dead," he said shortly. "We must clear out of here. Dr. Galley, you'll have to see the police about this, I'm afraid."

His quiet voice, which had yet something of a tremor in it, was almost drowned by a recurrence of the thunder. The storm had returned and the angry roar of the rain upon the windows made a fitting accompaniment to the extraordinary scene in the room.

Dr. Galley seemed oblivious of everything and everyone save his captive devil, Ashtaroth, from whom he had so pathetically expected so much. He stood now, an expression of startled bewilderment on his face, all the more terrible because of his strained pupils and twitching lips.

"If the body is dead," he shouted suddenly, "I have stepped out of my circle. I am no longer protected. The spirit has entered me. I am possessed by Ashtaroth. I feel his power in my blood. I feel his power in my hand. I am possessed—"

Guffy leapt upon the maniac just in time. From the folds of his robe the doctor had drawn a long slender-bladed knife. The little man seemed to have developed superhuman strength, and Hal and Amanda went to Guffy's assistance before at length they got him to the ground.

Then, just at the moment when the magician who had been Dr. Galley had become transformed into a frothing, screaming homicidal maniac, and the storm outside was at the height of its fury, a clock somewhere in the house struck seven, and instantly a sound which none of them ever forgot swelled and reverberated through the valley until the whole world seemed to reel before its clamour.

It was as though a bell of gigantic proportions was tolling a peal to summon mankind. It was impossible to tell where the noise came from. It seemed to be all about them, an angry sea of sound.

And then, quite suddenly, it stopped, and in the peace which followed they became aware of an answering note, a shrill clear humming. It lasted for perhaps a minute and then the clamour of the great bell rang out again, drowning everything else.

Amanda, who in her position of superior knowledge had not been quite so shaken by these terrifying developments as the others, kept her head and remembered her part.

"Guffy," she whispered, "lock Galley in the first room across the hall, and the rest of you beat it back through the wood. We've got to. I can't explain now; there's hardly any time."

The urgency in her tone lent her authority, and since her advice embodied the natural desire of everyone present, they obeyed her. Hal put his arm round Aunt Hatt's shoulders and seized Mary by the hand.

"Come on," he said. "We'll go straight to the boat, Amanda. You follow with Guffy. You'll see to the shuts, won't you?"

She nodded and on a sudden impulse thrust Campion's gun into his pocket.

"You take this," she said. "I can leave everything to you, can't I?"

He looked at her meaningly and nodded.

When Dr. Galley had been disposed of safely in his own dining-room, Amanda and Guffy paused for a moment in the darkened hall.

"This way," she whispered. "We've got to get back to the mill before the bell stops ringing."

The storm had abated a little, but the sky was still dark and a fine rain was falling as they came out into the tangled garden, thankfully leaving the house behind them. The body of Ashtaroth lay where it had fallen, its face hidden against the rudely decorated boards.

The rain had not cooled the atmosphere and a wave of hot scented air, heavy with moisture, met them as they plunged into the path between the sunflowers. All the time the tremendous clangour of the great bell, which now seemed louder even than before and was interrupted by fierce splitting sounds like rending stone, deafened Guffy's senses and added to his bewilderment.

Suddenly it ceased again and once more that high sweet echoing murmur soothed the battered valley.

Amanda turned to Guffy, her eyes dancing. "It works!" she said triumphantly. "It works!"

"I don't understand," he said. "What the hell is it?"

"Oh, of course—you don't know. It's the great bell of St. Breed, the convent in the Pyrenees. Campion fixed up with them to broadcast it on a private wavelength. That's what the wireless stuff was for. Scatty has the loud-speakers in the cedar as high as he could get them, so that they correspond more or less with the real bell in the old tower. Those awful crashes are atmospherics. This storm isn't very helpful. But it's the sympathetic vibrations that count. Don't you remember what it said on the oak? Don't you see, there's an answer!"

She dragged at his arm and forced him to plunge on through the undergrowth. As they crossed the narrow lane to the home wood a car, apparently driven by a madman, roared past and turned to skirt the old Pontisbright estate.

Amanda's eyes glinted. "The system" was beginning to work.

CHAPTER XXI

Truth in the Well

At the moment when Dr. Galley was conjuring Ashtaroth to appear, Mr. Campion was crouching in the hollowed-out centre of a bramble bush beneath the cedar tree talking to Lugg. The big man, looking even more unhappy than usual in his ear-phones, was expressing his views with his customary forthrightness.

"We're askin' for trouble," he said, looking down at some six square feet of accumulator while storm and lightning played round him and his paraphernalia. "Askin' for trouble," he repeated. "If you want my views on this scheme of yours, it's perishin' awful."

"I don't," said his master frankly. "Is Scatty ready?"

Mr. Lugg held up his hand. " 'Ullo," he said. " 'Ere it comes. With these atmospherics it sounds like a vaudeville turn."

He jerked a string which hung down beside the bole of a cedar tree and received an answering tug from Scatty, who was superintending the loud-speakers above.

"Well, 'e's not bin struck by lightnin' yet," he said. "Shall we let 'er rip?"

Campion nodded and his aide bent over the amplifier.

" 'Ere goes," he said. "Eight times as loud as real. I'm very fond of bells."

Instantly from above their heads came the sound which had such a profound effect upon the little group in Dr. Galley's drawing-room and which was to be one of the wonders of Suffolk for many years to come. Even Campion was not prepared for the stupendous uproar which the

broacast bell of St. Breed, sister bell to the Pontisbright
giant, could make when amplified. He could picture the
effect which this mighty clangour must make upon the
superstitious village folk, and, more important still, upon
the camp on the heath. There the forces had been massing
all day and now they would be stirred into action.

He permitted himself an anxious glance through the
leaves towards Dr. Galley's white house. If that little party
came to any harm, he reflected, he could never forgive
himself.

But behind all these considerations which raced through
his mind was the one great hope which possessed him.
When the deafening clangour above his head ceased for a
moment's respite he would know the answer to a question
which had been uppermost in his mind ever since he had
read the couplet on the oak.

Everyone has noticed that in a room where there are
hollow vessels certain sounds will produce answering mur-
murs. The sharp bark of a dog may set a row of cups
ringing on a dresser. Certain notes on a piano will provoke
answering vibrations from metal trays. Campion had hoped
that some such phenomenon might give meaning to the
remarkable instructions carved so laboriously under the
sundial.

As he waited the great bell ceased and his heart leapt as
from somewhere in the depths of the wood before him
came the answering murmur he longed to hear; clear, high,
sweet, and unmistakable, a humming beckoned him.

He turned to Lugg. "Don't forget they're broadcasting
five times. After the fourth time get Scatty down, and as
soon as the fifth is over smash a couple of valves and clear
out."

"What if 'Is Nibs' boy friends spot us before?" demanded Mr. Lugg not unnaturally.

"Then you must fight for it. But they won't. They'll be
following the second note. They're not fools. Good-bye.
See you to-morrow."

"I 'ope," said Mr. Lugg, but this pious wish never

reached his master, for, his lank figure bent against the storm, Mr. Campion had plunged into the trees.

Although he had spent the best part of the past three nights in making himself familiar with the overgrown paths and ruined boundaries of the once magnificent garden, he found the task he had set himself to be quite as difficult as he had anticipated.

Another shattering peal from the bell of St. Breed made him stop in his tracks and wait anxiously for the clatter to subside. The storm was still raging and the atmospherics tore through the pealing of the bell like miniature thunderclaps. He could hear the sound of a motor-car engine in the lane and recognized the Lagonda. Farquharson was doing his part, then.

From the heath there were other noises, only faintly discernible through the clangour.

Then again the noise above him stopped, followed by the sweet musical call ahead. He forced his way on towards it. There was very little time. The great bell would ring only thrice more. Between now and the dying away of the final vibration he must find the source of the answer.

As he pressed on he realized to his relief that it was nearer than he had suspected. It led him across the site of the old lawn and down a narrow path to what must once have been the stables, but over which the grass now grew in uneven mounds. It was risky business coming out into the open, but he ploughed on recklessly.

He had just reached a clump of overgrown laurels when again the loud-speakers in the cedar bellowed forth the challenge of the sister bell. Again the answer came, beckoning him ever forward through the rain-soaked leaves. Alarm seized him: only twice more now.

He pressed on. He was coming to the open field which skirted the lane below the church, the same lane which lay between Dr. Galley's home and the heath. As in many meadows that have once been parkland, a fine group of elms stood in the centre, forming a ring round a little depression in the grass. As soon as Campion saw them his heart sank. He wormed his way down the hedge and stood

there, waiting, while for the fourth time the bell chimed
and received its answer.

Yes, there was no doubt about it: the echo came from
the elms.

There was no hedge between the meadow and the lane
and the stately park railing had long since disappeared.
Already two cars had passed. There was no time to be lost.

He sped across the short grass, trusting to the rain and
the uncertain light to hide him. When he reached the trees,
the humming had died away and he stood there, flattened
against the trunk of an elm, while for the last time the
great booming voice of the twin sister of the Bell of
Pontisbright startled the countryside and reawakened old
echoes long since forgotten.

Campion stood waiting and was rewarded. From somewhere among the trees, almost, it seemed at his very feet,
the high clear voice of the answer rose to meet him.

He saw the explanation suddenly, an old half-broken
wellhead, the mossy stones quite clear among the short
grass. He glanced about him and even as he did so a sleek
black car, followed by three motor-cycles, swung round
the bend and on to the meadow.

In his present position he was hidden, but discovery, it
seemed, must be inevitable. If he were found then the
hiding-place was found also. The short branches of the elm
invited him. He caught at one and swung himself up
swiftly into comparative safety among the leaves.

He went high and at length found himself in a position
from which he could see down into the shadows and still
descry the faint outlines of the well-head some twenty feet
below.

He was craning round in an attempt to catch a glimpse
of the occupants of the car when another sound reached
him which he recognized immediately as the roar of the
mill wheel down in the valley. Amanda had reached the
shuts, then.

He turned involuntarily towards the sounds and found
that although he could not see the mill the lower portion of
the river was visible to him from the height at which he

sat, and he caught the chill gleam of water between the overhanging trees.

He watched it anxiously and it seemed to him that he saw a shadow passing swiftly down the stream; something that might have been a bundle of brushwood or some trusses of straw swept down from some flooded yard.

His attention was recalled immediately, however, by the sound of voices just below him. The light was getting worse at every moment in the shadows beneath the elm, but as a dark-coated figure leant for a moment against the trunk of the very tree up which he sat a thrill of surprise passed through him.

Those giant shoulders were unmistakable. Savanake had come himself.

There was still a murmur from the well-head. It was more than he could hope that they should not notice it, and when a voice which revealed startlingly the presence of Mr. Parrott said clearly, "It's somewhere here—hark," Campion's thrill of despair was mitigated by the knowledge that it was only to be expected.

The light was fading rapidly. Now he could no longer see the well-head himself, and the river was only visible in little silver patches among the grey meadows.

"Yes," said the voice of Savanake suddenly. "It is here. Of course, something like this was perfectly obvious from the time we first heard about the amplifier in the wood, but I didn't quite follow it until I heard the bell." He laughed. "It's amusing that they should have taken all the trouble and left it to us to do the finding. We must hurry."

"Two cars left the mill, sir," said one of the motor-cyclists, and Campion could see his dark form coming forward. "One turned to Sweethearting. The other took the lower road."

"That's all right," said Parrott quickly. "Our people are following. They're making a get-away with the crown. Probably realize that this is too much for them. We shall collect all they have before morning."

"Why waste time?" said Savanake testily. "This all-important thing is at our feet, probably. It's infernally dark, isn't it?''

There was considerable movement at the foot of the tree and from Mr. Campion's point of view the figures had almost melted into the darkness. But for the red tips of their cigarettes, and their voices, he would not have been able to locate them.

''It's too dark to see anything,'' grumbled Parrott. ''If we use torches we shall be seen. Does that matter?''

''I don't care what you do. Find the thing. Here, Everett.''

Campion heard the car door open and a figure stumble through the gloom.

''Yes, sir.''

He guessed it was the chauffeur who spoke.

''Bring the car up here and turn the headlights full on this dell. Understand?''

''Yes, sir.''

Almost immediately the soft purr of a car engine sounded through the field as the Rolls crept forward and two great beams of light stretched out over the short grass.

''I say, Mr. Savanake.'' Mr. Parrott's voice sounded nervous and protesting. ''We'll have them down on us.''

''Who the hell cares if we do? We're armed, aren't we? They've gone off in those three cars with the rest of our fellows after them. We shan't get any villagers here for days. They're probably saying their prayers in pious terror as it is. Get on with it, Everett.''

Slowly the great car slid into position and the enormous headlights picked out each blade of grass in the dell with startling vividness.

The well-head seemed to jump at them, and Campion's last hopes were dashed as Parrott started forward.

''Well, that's a bit of luck, isn't it?'' he said, his voice shrill with excitement.

The little group closed round the well save for the chauffeur, who still lingered by the side of his car, although even he had dismounted. The men who had come on motorbicycles produced a crowbar and a pickaxe. They set to work at once on the stone slab, which had grown into its position and was firmly cemented there with weeds, moss, and soft earth.

Campion watched them anxiously. His position was desperate. He had even no revolver. He crouched there peering down at them, and although Savanake's broad back obscured the scene most of the time, he heard the grunt of satisfaction as the slab gave beneath the pick, and saw the crowd scattered for a moment as it was heaved out of its position.

They were all engrossed now; too excited by their discovery to heed anything else. Mr. Campion began to descend. He came down cautiously, feeling his way on the side of the tree most in darkness.

At length he found himself on a branch not ten feet from the ground, and beneath him, leaning forward and craning his neck to catch a glimpse of the well-head, was the chauffeur. The shaft from the parking lamp lit up his wide shoulders.

Mr. Campion felt for his only weapon, a heavy stone twisted in his handkerchief. He had armed himself with this elementary life-preserver when he had first made his way from Dr. Galley's garden to find Lugg.

"There it is! There it is!" said Parrott's voice excitedly. "Another bell slung on a crossbeam."

"Don't worry about that." Even Savanake's voice sounded nervy. "It's the thing itself we want. Probably an iron box or a cylinder. Look for a hole in the brickwork. Don't fall in. We have nothing to get you up with. Hullo, what's that?"

There was a movement among the group, a ripple of smothered exclamations. The chauffeur took another step forward and at that instant Mr. Campion dropped.

The interior of the well was dark. Its rounded sides were grey with lichen. From its depths a dank unpleasant odour arose, breathing the decay of centuries. But the excited men round the edge were oblivious of anything save the object of their quest.

Savanake himself was kneeling on the stones, wrenching at something embedded in moss just above the ear of the bell. Once his hand slipped and his arm shot back, so that his elbow struck the iron and a faint high note sounded for an instant in the night.

"Here, you get it," he said savagely, rising to his feet and rubbing his arm vigorously.

A man took his place eagerly. There was the sound of iron on the stones and someone swore.

"Look out, it's heavy, sir."

They dragged a square iron box on to the slab.

"It's locked, of course?"

"Shall I smash it open with the pick, sir?"

"No, no. Isn't there a key somewhere?"

Once again the crevice in the well was explored, but without result. Savanake seemed to make up his mind.

"I'll take it as it stands," he said. "You three replace this stuff. You can use your torches. We're evidently not going to be disturbed. Then get back to town. Report to Mr. Parrott to-morrow. Come on, Parrott. You and I will take this with us."

He picked up the box by the iron rim in its lid and strode towards the car. In spite of its weight he carried it easily, as though it had been a toy in his hand.

"Back, Everett," he said, as he climbed into the body of the Rolls, his assistant scrambling after him.

The figure in the chauffeur's coat touched his peaked cap respectfully and the great car shot back over the grass and then, with rather more of a jerk than might have been expected from a man used to his machine, leapt forward on to the lane.

Down the narrow fling road, past the darkened "Gauntlett," Campion brought the great car like a whirlwind. The man in the seat behind him was ruthless, a giant, and armed; also he had a companion. But in his hands was the one thing above all others which at that moment Albert Campion most desired, and with a whirring flurry of wheels he brought the great car round the bend and down the narrow cul-de-sac at the far end of which stood the mill.

CHAPTER XXII

The Millpool

The car sped down the narrow lane, its giant headlights picking out the familiar scene and lending it a strange unreality as if the mill and the silent house had been part of some enormous stage set. Only the roar of the water and the steady chugging of the wheel were alive.

Unarmed save for his improvised sling, Campion drove on savagely and brought the car to a standstill within a foot of the race.

"Lost your way, Everett?" Savanake's voice sounded hearteningly casual.

Campion made an inaudible reply and, springing out of the car, threw up the bonnet. He bent over the spotless engine for some moments, trusting to the shadow of the hood to hide his face.

Presently, as he had hoped, the car door opened and footsteps advanced. Mr. Campion gripped his handkerchief in which the heavy stone still rested.

The new-comer proved to be Mr. Parrott. He came up out of the darkness, officious and trembling.

"I say, Everett, this is disgraceful at such a time. You'll get into trouble. Mr. Savanake's very upset."

Campion raised his head and looked at the new-comer. The expression on the pompous little face as Mr. Parrott recognized the man he thought he had put so safely on board the *Marquisita* was remarkable.

Campion did not permit his surprise to subside. On top of the realization that the incredible does sometimes occur,

208

Mr. Parrott received a blow on the skull which sent him down like a sack.

But even as he fell a voice in which there was an unmistakable ring of satisfaction said sharply: "Put your hands up, Campion. I've got you just where I want you."

Mr. Campion, looking lanker and more pale than usual in the chauffeur's cap and the coat which was much too wide for him, had no alternative but to obey. He had no illusions concerning the man with whom he had to deal. He raised his hands above his head, therefore, and waited.

Savanake came towards him. The side-lights fell upon the gleaming barrel of the revolver he levelled. In his left hand he still carried the iron box, as though he had been loath to set it down even for an instant.

Campion felt the gun muzzle in his ribs. His captor glanced down at the race.

"That's no good," he said suddenly, and went on, his voice still soft, his tone still conversational. "You're going to walk in front of me, Campion, with this gun just where it is now, until you get to the millpool. For obvious reasons I don't want you to be found with a bullet from my gun in your body. But any sidestepping, any tricks, any stumble, and I pull the trigger. Understand? This time I'm doing the job myself, so that there can be no mistake."

Mr. Campion did not reply, but his silence was pointed. They might have been standing at the end of the world, so remote did they seem from any interruption. Parrott lay where he had fallen.

The big side door of the mill stood open, as it always did, and through it, across a concrete way, a faint gleam showed in the darkness where the second door, which was the main exit to the sluices and the gangway round the river, stood wide also.

Mr. Campion walked slowly into the mill. On the threshold the increase in the pressure of the muzzle against his ribs arrested him.

"Why are you leading me in here, Campion?" demanded the same ominously soft voice. "You know me well enough not to play the fool."

"This is the only way to the millpool," said Mr. Campion plaintively. "The gangway at the back of the mill below the grille is so rotten that the millers have put a barrier of hurdles across the path, and unless you intend us to swim the river this is the only means of reaching the pool. I don't mind you shooting me so much, but I won't be bullied."

"Go on," said the man behind him. "Lead me to the millpool. I've heard a great deal of your cleverness lately, but how you could have come out on a job like this without a gun is beyond me."

"I don't like the idea of being hanged," confided Mr. Campion in the darkness. "You just don't worry about that, I take it?"

They passed through the mill and now came out on the mouldering wooden way which skirted the dynamo wheel and led on to the top of the millpool floodgates. On their right the river flowed silently through the grille and under the broken gangway, which was so badly in need of repair that for safety's sake Amanda had placed a couple of hurdles across the path, one in the angle of the wall near the door through which they had come and one farther on at the opposite bank of the river.

They passed the shed over the dynamo wheel and came out on to a narrow bridge with the river on their right and the steep sides of the millpool on their left. There seemed to be more light here and the water which surrounded them looked sinister and uninviting.

The floodgates, a little farther on down the path on which they stood, were closed to permit the full force of the river to flow through the mill into the main stream.

"This will do very nicely, I think," said Savanake quietly. "Turn around."

The lank figure in front of him turned obediently. The expression on his face was still affable and vacant. Savanake could see him clearly in the faint light.

As they faced one another the incredible loneliness of the spot became more apparent. Both men were deadly serious, but while Savanake betrayed a certain tension,

Mr. Campion remained foolish-looking and ineffectual as ever.

"One moment," he murmured. "Would you like me to take off my coat? It belongs to your chauffeur, you know. The police get hold of a thing like that. They're great lads for the obvious."

"Keep your hands above your head," said the other man warningly, but the notion evidently appealed to him, for he set the precious iron box down on the path and with his left hand caught the coat collar firmly. "Stretch your arms out behind you."

He stripped the garment off his captive and laid it on the ground, but did not pick up the iron box again.

"I'm quite sorry to have to kill you," he remarked. "And it may seem foolish of me, although there seems to be plenty of time, but I should like to explain that I am not taking this way of getting rid of you as a form of revenge for the insignificant little trick you played upon the arch-idiot Parrott. I have only one reason for wishing you out of the way, and that is sufficient. You are the only man who knows exactly what it is that I have obtained to-night. None of my assistants have any idea what is in the iron box, or of the story concerning it. You see, in the circumstances the course I am taking is the only intelligent thing to do."

Mr. Campion shrugged his shoulders. "I don't know why it should occur to you that my last moments would be comforted by an assurance of your intelligence," he said. "What method are you thinking of employing? I hate to seem lowbrow, but in the circumstances that subject interests me more. Or perhaps it's a secret?"

Savanake laughed. He towered over Campion and the young man became suddenly aware of his enormous strength.

"There's no secret," he said. "Your body will be found floating in the pool. You will be bruised, naturally, but it will be assumed that you met your death by accident. There will be no awkward bullet, no ridiculous clues for half-educated policemen to follow. How do you imagine I'm going to kill you, you little rat, you? With my hands."

There was a tinge of satisfaction in the tone, an almost brutish savagery which lurked behind the soft voice.

Mr. Campion remained thoughtful.

"I see," he said slowly. "But there's something you've overlooked. I can't worry about your affairs now, though. I've got my own eternity to think of. Still, perhaps I may as well mention it. This iron box"—he glanced down at it on the gangway—"what exactly *is* in it?" And moving his foot sharply he toppled the precious trophy over the edge and in to the millpool.

The splash it made as it hit the water was audible above the throbbing of the wheel.

Savanake, taken off his guard for an instant, swore violently and turned instinctively to the dark water. In that moment Campion leapt.

He caught the man round the shoulders and swung himself up, kicking the gun out of his hand. It fell to the path but did not slide on into the water. Any ordinary adversary would have staggered back or fallen beneath this sudden attack, but Savanake was a person of no ordinary strength. He braced himself to meet the onslaught, exerting the tremendous force concealed in his huge body. One mighty hand closed round Campion's ankle like a vice, and with a wrench of the gigantic shoulders the young man's grip was prised open. Campion slipped down and caught his enemy round the knees, thrusting his head forward savagely into his stomach.

Savanake grunted and pitched forward, but his grip on the young man's ankle did not loosen as together they plunged down into the cold dark waters of the pool ten feet below.

When Campion came to the surface some seconds later his first feeling was of relief. He was free. The paralysing grip on his ankle had gone. He struck out cautiously, swimming half under water. His clothes weighed him down and it was numbingly cold after the storm.

He found himself just below the alcove in the brick wall of the pool which housed the floodgates. When the main shuts were closed and the mill was not working the water was released through the pool by means of these gates, and at such times the alcove, or "apron," was a race, with the water pouring down from above. But now all was quiet and the little trickle of water escaping through the gates barely wetted the stones.

Campion stretched out a hand to grip one of the iron staples in the brickwork. His fingers closed over it gratefully and he was about to haul himself up when the unexpected occurred. Another hand came out of the blackness of the little cavern, a hand unmistakable in size and strength. It caught him by the throat and Savanake's voice said distinctly: "Now!"

Realizing his danger a second too late, Campion caught the wrist and threw his weight upon it to drag his enemy forward into the water again. He could see the eyes, bright and dangerous, in the face so near his own, and he guessed the man was lying on his stomach, one hand grasping the iron staple let into the brick floor of the race while with the other he gripped his victim.

Campion's efforts were unavailing. He realized they were hopeless immediately.

Savanake laughed. He spoke, and the words reached Campion through the mists that were gathering about him. Their sense dawned upon him slowly.

"Found drowned."

The grip upon his throat tightened and he was forced down until the water met over his head. He struggled, but the grip was relentless. The man was drowning him deliberately, holding him under until the life should have been forced out of his body.

It came to Campion with something like a shock of surprise. This was the end, then. This was the finish. It seemed a pity.

He made a last desperate effort to free himself, but the hand which held him and the icy water which imprisoned him had become as one. The veins in his head had ceased to feel that they must burst. He felt calm, almost sleepy.

Then quite suddenly he was aware of a change. He felt
himself shooting up to what seemed an incredible height.
He felt the air forcing itself into his lungs, choking him. A
dark form shot past him in the water, the surface of which
had become frothy. A current was sweeping him out into
the centre of the pool. In the single moment, during which
he regained consciousness before the black shadows once
more closed down upon him, Mr. Campion realized the
explanation of this phenomenon.

Some third person had opened the floodgates and the
sudden sheet of water belching through the alcove had
swept Savanake and his victim out into the pool again.

He struggled to rouse himself, but the old peaceful
feeling returned and he floated limply through the pool to
the tunnel of trees over the stream.

Brett Savanake clambered up out of the water on the far
side of the floodgates where the bottom of the pool sloped
up sharply to the bank. He had no clear idea what had
caused the sudden rush of water which had swept him back
into the pool. Vaguely he supposed he must have touched
something, pulled some lever or otherwise disturbed some
crude mechanism.

It was typical of the man that he did not give another
thought to Campion. The Campion episode was over and
best forgotten. He went back to the spot where his gun lay
and from which the young man had kicked the iron box.

As he paused to look down a faint sound disturbed him
from the shadow of the dynamo-wheel shed and he stood
listening. But as nothing else occurred to arouse his suspicion he continued on the task he had set himself.

Flattened against the wall in the shadow of the shed,
Amanda stood trembling, hardly daring to breathe. She
had watched the proceedings at first from the window on
the first floor of the mill and then from her present hiding
place. She knew Campion too well to interfere, and had
lent a hand by opening the floodgates only when the situation had seemed desperate enough to warrant her assistance. At the moment, for the first time in her life, she was
almost paralysed with fear.

Where was Campion? She listened, her heart beating so loudly and heavily that it hurt her side. She could just see Savanake from her present position, and as she watched him he removed his coat and boots and plunged into the pool again.

She listened anxiously for sound of Campion, but there was no noise above the wheel save the splashing of the man who had just entered the water.

The revolver still lay on the path by the chauffeur's coat. She had not noticed it at first, but now she caught sight of it and had just made up her mind to creep out and get it when she heard Savanake coming out again, and once more she sank back into the comparative safety of the shadows.

From where she stood she could see him coming up to the path where his coat lay.

The storm had completely cleared and the sky was bright with stars, so that she could see he carried something, an iron box suspended by a ring in its lid.

The explanation of the whole thing dawned upon her as she caught sight of it, and her courage, which had temporarily deserted her, now returned as she realized that here was something definite to be done.

Savanake sat putting on his boots not ten paces from where she stood. She felt that he must hear her breathe. But he seemed principally concerned with dressing himself as soon as possible. The iron box lay unprotected at his side.

Amanda stopped and picked up a loose pebble at her feet. Then, waiting her opportunity, she hurled it out across the pool with all her strength. It struck a tree on the opposite bank, and the sharp sound, followed by a gentle plop as it ricocheted into the water, brought the man to his feet, straining his eyes to see the least sign of movement on the further bank.

Amanda darted forward like a shadow, snatched the box and fled down the gangway to the mill. She heard his startled exclamation and the next instant a bullet tore the shoulder of her dress.

She gained the mill, however, and swung the door to behind her. The heavy iron bolt was stiff; it took her a moment to force it home, and as she bent over the task there was a roar, a shriek of splintering wood and a sharp pain stabbed her in the chest. The box dropped from her hand on to the stone with a clatter, and as she bent down to snatch it up a strange giddiness overtook her and she dropped to her knees.

Another shot cut through the door. Amanda struggled to get out of the line of fire. Her mouth felt full of blood and a numbness was spreading over her body. She reached her feet only to fall again, pitching headlong into the arms of a figure who had burst through the further doorway of the mill and who now held her in wet arms.

"Amanda!" Campion's voice was strained. "For God's sake get out of this, you little fool!" And then in a new tone: "Hullo, I say, Amanda, are you hurt?" And finally, as she did not speak but lay limp and heavy against him, an exclamation escaped him and he set her down gently against the wall.

Outside the door Savanake had ceased shooting and appeared to be putting his shoulder to the boards. Campion advanced cautiously, keeping out of the line of fire as well as he could, but before he could reach the bolt the hammering ceased and he caught the sound of the scraping of wood above the rumble of the wheel.

Campion was not as a rule foolhardy. His adversary was armed and not fifteen minutes before had been all but successful in an attempt to murder him. Moreover, the iron box was temporarily safe. Yet because of something which he would not have explained even if he could, and which was definitely to do with Amanda, he went out after Savanake with the intent to kill.

He worked back the bolt as silently as possible and opened the door an inch or two. At first it seemed that the man had vanished, but suddenly he caught sight of him and his heart leapt.

In Savanake's anxiety to get round to the front of the mill before the girl with the box could have reached the car, he had disregarded the warning of the hurdle and had scaled it, to fall almost immediately through one of the gaping holes in the planking over the river. At the moment he was up to his armpits and was clutching feverishly at the mouldering boards, which broke under his hands, while the river sucked at his body eagerly.

Campion stared at him and the sudden realization of the man's terrible danger came home to him. The planking through which Savanake had fallen was above the grille, that grid of iron which keeps debris floating down the river out of the wheel of every mill. The man's helpless body was immersed on the inner side of the grille and the great wheel rumbled and spluttered within a few feet of him.

In spite of the fact that a moment before Mr. Campion had come out with the intention of killing his enemy if he could, such a death was too terrible for him to contemplate.

"Hold on," he said. "I'm coming."

The white face on whose forehead the veins stood out in weals was raised to his own for a moment. Recognition gleamed in the eyes, coupled with bewilderment and a flush of superstitious fear. Then, as Campion reached the hurdle, the right hand crept forward and snatched the revolver which lay where he had dropped it on the edge of the hole. A sudden smile spread over the contorted face, but although the lips moved no sound issued.

With a superhuman effort the man raised his arm and fired. The bullet passed harmlessly over Campion's head, but the movement had been too much for the man in the water. As he raised his arm the river carried away his hold and he slipped under the boards.

The steady throb of the wheel, so monotonous, so relentless, seemed to Campion's horrified ears to pause an instant, and a tremor so small and yet so terrible passed through the great white building. Nothing more.

Then all was silent save for the steady throb of the thirty-foot metal paddle.

CHAPTER XXIII

Late Extra

Kneeling in the dark mill beside the silent bundle which was Amanda, Mr. Campion listened anxiously. At first the entire village seemed silent save for the steady throbbing of the wheel and the chatter of water in the race. He stood up, therefore, and braced himself to lift the girl. His head was dizzy and his clothes dragged upon him. Besides being irritated by his own weakness, he was frantic in his alarm concerning her.

He had just raised her up and was preparing to carry her and the iron box into the house when a beam of light swept across the face of the mill and the one thing he most dreaded occurred.

A car, the sound of whose engine he did not recognize, came rattling over the loose stones of the lane and pulled up beside the Rolls.

He leant back against the wall, Amanda in his arms. The darkness hid them for the moment, but they were completely unprotected should a dark form loom up in the open doorway and flash a torch round the chamber. He held his breath and strained his ears to catch every sound. His alarm increased.

The new-comers, whoever they were, seemed to take it for granted that the mill was unoccupied. One of them was talking loudly, although as yet he could catch no words. He heard them rattling the front door of the house and then stamp round to the back.

Campion staggered forward. Some hiding place must be found immediately for them both. Even though Savanake were dead, his lieutenants were still at large.

He had just reached the centre of the floor when thundering footsteps sounded on the stones outside, a moment afterwards someone rattled on the door panel with the head of a cane, and a voice, old, kindly, and faintly pompous, demanded briskly: "Anyone about here?"

Mr. Campion froze. He felt the hairs rising on his skull. Death was one thing, but to find oneself suddenly bereft of one's senses was another.

"Anyone about?" the voice repeated querulously, and at the same time the sharp beam of a powerful torch stabbed the darkness.

It came to rest on Campion's face and he stood there blinking, the girl in his arms.

There was a startled but satisfied grunt from the doorway before the voice said astonishingly: "Well, Campion my boy, what the devil do you think you're up to now? Little lady hurt? Glad I came along."

Mr. Campion's knees only just upheld him. "Colonel Featherstone!" he said. "Good heavens, sir, how did you get here?"

"Confidential orders from the top, my boy." The old voice had a self-satisfied ring in it. "Stationed at Colchester, don't you know. Only heard of this an hour ago and here I am. Young Stukely-Wivenhoe is out there beating round the house with a couple of men. Hark at 'em. Sounds like a herd of buffalo. I've got a subaltern with sergeant and three sections in two lorries coming along. They had some little trouble with a car-load of blackguards on the road, but they'll be here any moment now. I saw they didn't need any help so I pushed on. There's a fellow out here lying by a Rolls-Royce. Seems stunned. Campion, that girl's been shot or something. Blood on her bodice."

Mr. Campion did not speak but stood swaying. The peaceful sensation he had experienced under water was returning and only Amanda's weight in his arms forced him to cling to consciousness.

There was a commotion in the doorway and Colonel Featherstone's huge dark form loomed forward.

"Here, my boy," he said, "I didn't realize, dammit.

You're done up. Give me the little woman. There, that's right. Wivenhoe!''

The final word was bellowed in the famous voice at once the pride and despair of every sergeant-major in the brigade.

Instantly a clatter of boots sounded on the stones outside and Mr. Campion relapsed into a species of coma until he found himself sitting in the hall of the mill house, while old Featherstone, assisted by the lean and handsome Wivenhoe and two wooden-faced but excited private soldiers, laid Amanda upon the couch in the drawing-room.

Colonal Featherstone came back blowing with kindliness, importance, and unusual exertion.

"Doctor in the village, Campion?"

The young man glanced up sharply. "No, not at the moment," he said, pulling himself together. "Someone had better get into Sweethearting and fetch the man there." He went into the drawing-room while the Colonel despatched his chauffeur with orders which were pithy and concise to return with a competent doctor in the shortest possible space of time.

Wivenhoe and the other men went out to inspect the condition of the unlucky Mr. Parrott.

Amanda was still unconscious, but Campion was sufficiently familiar with revolver wounds to hope that the danger was considerably less than he had feared at first.

He left her at last and went back to the hall. The Colonel and company commander, Captain Stukely-Wivenhoe, were waiting for him. Both men were naturally curious. The atmosphere of mystery and excitement which enwrapped the whole place like a blanket was unmistakable. Campion glanced at their knaki uniforms and was thankful and comforted. Old Featherstone's bright pink face and voluminous white moustache were other emblems of peace and security, and for once in his life Mr. Campion was grateful for such assurance.

Proceedings were interrupted at the outset by the return of the orderly from the dining-room whither Mr. Parrott had

been carried. The man was plainly startled and Featherstone nodded to him to speak.

"Excuse me, sir, but there's a man under the table in
the other room."

"Hiding?" Old Featherstone clumped forward with
interest.

"Hardly, sir. He's bound and gagged."

"Oh yes, of course," said Mr. Campion. "Of course. I
forgot."

The Colonel's little blue eyes rested enquiringly on the
young man for a moment before he coughed noisily, and
returned to his subordinate.

"That's all right, Bates. Run upstairs and see if you can
find a dressing-gown and a pair of trousers for Mr. Campion. Can't stand about like that, Campion," he continued
as the man went off. "Might catch a chill—never know."

The young man smiled faintly. There was something
fantastic about old Featherstone's imperturbability.

"Look here, sir," he said, "I'd better explain a bit,
hadn't I?"

"All in good time my boy, all in good time. First of all,
is there anything you want done? We're here primarily to
give a hand, and secondly to convey—ah—something or
other to Whitehall. Orders were a bit hurried, don't you
know. Young Oxley will be along with the men at any
minute now."

Campion considered. "Someone ought to go along to
Great Kepesake to collect Miss Huntingforest, the elder
Miss Fitton, her brother, and Randall," he ventured.

"Guffy Randall?" enquired the captain with interest. "I
was lunching with his father yesterday. Really! Well, shall
I go along, sir?"

"Yes." Old Featherstone stuck his head out of the door.
"I hear the lorry. You take that Rolls, Wivenhoe, and
bring 'em all back here. Any objections, Campion? Your
car?"

"No, sir, but I think that's an excellent idea, if I may say
so. That car will get through anywhere unquestioned. I
should take someone with you, Wivenhoe, all the same."

"Right. I'll pick up a man from the lorry."

Old Featherstone watched him go and then returned to Campion, who was struggling into the dry clothes the orderly had unearthed.

Mr. Campion turned the events of the past few hours over in his mind. The iron box stood on the table and he laid his hand over it absently.

"There's a man's body in the river below the mill," he said slowly. "It's probably in a bit of a mess. He went through the wheel. Then there's that fellow tied up in the dining-room; he's a case for the police."

"Oh, well, we'll leave him there." Old Featherstone seemed relieved. "We're just here to protect your party and to convey the two—ah—objects which you've discovered to headquarters. In confidence, I don't understand this business, Campion, but as far as I can gather, someone—I heard young Eager-Wright's name mentioned—went to town carrying something or other which set the whole department by the ears, and they phoned to me."

Mr. Campion's nod of understanding was interrupted by the arrival of the lorry and the unexpected appearance of Farquharson, followed by the subaltern Oxley. The young officer made his report briefly to Featherstone.

"We found Mr. Farquharson's car overturned, sir, on the Sweethearting road. He was being attacked by the occupants of a second car, who were armed, and who fired on us. One of our men has a shoulder wound. Mr. Farquharson appealed to us for assistance and as his story showed that he was—well—in this business, sir, I ventured to bring him along."

"Quite right. Unorthodox, but quite right. Where are the blackguards who fired on you?"

Old Featherstone's pink face was almost luminous.

"In the back of the second lorry, sir."

"Splendid. I suppose we shall have to turn them over to the civil authorities. Pity. Good work, all the same. Now, Oxley, send the sergeant and a party to search the river for a body. Corpse of a man. Been through a mill wheel, poor fellow. Bring him in."

"Yes, sir." The young man saluted and went off, while Farquharson, pale and battered, but bursting with excitement, came forward.

Old Featherstone shook hands with him. "Didn't think I should find you in this sort of mess, my boy, when we met last year. That was a dull affair at the Bletchleys', wasn't it? God bless my soul, it was. Well, had a bit of scrap?"

"Just that, sir. Oxley put the story in a nutshell."

"They caught you, I suppose?" Campion enquired.

"Yes, in the end. But I gave them a run for their money first. What happened? Did you get it?"

"Amanda did."

"Amanda? Where is she?"

"In the drawing-room. He got her pretty badly, I think."

"Good Lord!" Farquharson sat down suddenly on the edge of the table.

The doctor from Sweethearting arrived at practically the same moment as the scouting party under Oxley reported that the heath was deserted, and the barn which the invaders had used as a garage was now empty.

Farquharson and Campion waited in the hall for the doctor to come out of the drawing-room. They were both silent, but while Farquharson looked frankly anxious there was no expression at all upon Mr. Campion's face.

At length the doctor, a squarely built, eminently practical young man, came out to them, and at the first glimpse of his face Farquharson seemed relieved.

"Is she all right?"

The doctor glanced at him suspiciously. Revolver wounds were rare in his experience, and ever the precursor of a day in the courts giving evidence.

"I don't know about all right," he said brusquely. "She's not in danger, if that's what you mean. Can we get her to bed upstairs anywhere? There'll have to be explanations about this, you understand."

Mr. Campion, whose appearance was not improved by the enormous pair of flannel trousers and gay dressing-gown, both the property of Guffy Randall, in which he was arrayed, nodded gravely to the doctor.

"That's all right," he said. "Don't worry. Farquharson, will you see to all this? I must go to Featherstone."

When Farquharson descended the staircase some time later, Amanda was lying safely in her bed, conscious and comparatively comfortable. The doctor remained with her until Mary and Aunt Hatt should arrive, not that he was in any way alarmed at her condition, but his curiosity was thoroughly aroused, and he was conscious that it might be his duty to make some sort of report to the police.

On reaching the hall, Farquharson found a soldier on duty outside the drawing-room door.

"Here you are, sir," he said. "The Colonel's compliments and will you join the conference?"

Farquharson hurried through the doorway to find a typically Featherstonian scene within. The furniture had been pushed back save for a small rectangular table which was placed in the centre of the room, and behind which the old man sat with Wivenhoe on his left, and, rather surprisingly, an anxious, but still game Aunt Hatt on his right. Mary sat behind her aunt, while Campion, Guffy, and Hal were placed on a long, narrow music stool parallel with and in front of the Colonel's table.

Campion had just finished speaking as Farquharson came in, and Aunt Hatt, who was too worried about Amanda to be silenced by any military etiquette, sprang up.

"How is she? Can I go up to her?"

Colonel Featherstone turned a shade darker, but his manners did not desert him. Lumbering to his feet he clumped over to the door and held it open.

"Give the brave little woman my compliments, ma'am," he said. And as Aunt Hatt fluttered out he strode back to his chair without dreaming for an instant that he had spoken, save in the most simple, natural manner in the world.

"Ah, Farquharson, my boy," he said. "Sit down, will you? Campion's just told us a most remarkable tale. If you'll forgive me, my dear"—he nodded to Mary—"damned remarkable. Well, Campion, let's have that iron box and open it, shall we? Don't want to make any mistakes at this juncture.''

The iron box was placed on the table, where the Crown of Averna already lay, and Captain Wivenhoe and Campion set to work on it with a steel pike in the captain's clasp knife. The long secretion in the damp well-head had told upon the metal, and finally the lock burst with a crack like a pistol shot. In spite of the Colonel's discipline, they crowded round the table.

The box contained a small parcel wrapped in oilskin, which, on being unfolded, disclosed a stout linen bag, a little yellow and clammy with age. Within this again was a sheet of old coarse law paper, and a folded slip of parchment, the seal which had bound it, broken.

Colonel Featherstone produced a pair of glasses, and his stubby fingers played over the papers clumsily.

"This looks important, Campion," he said. "But I'm hanged if I see what it means. Have a look at it.''

Campion took the sheet of paper and read the faded, brown script aloud:

"The bell hath kept this secret well
If Pontisbright you be.
But evil dog thee, death until,
If stranger taketh me."

"Huh!" said old Featherstone and added, turning to Hal: "Here, my lad, look at this, will you?''

He passed the parchment to the boy, who opened it carefully. An array of seals met their eyes and a fine Latin screed, too legal and archaic to follow, but the word "Avernium" re-occurred again and again, and at the foot of the page was the signature too well known to be doubted, "Metternich," and the date, 1815.

"That's it!" Guffy met Campion's eyes, and a sense of exhilaration swept over the whole room.

Featherstone replaced the documents carefully in the linen bag, and put the crown in with them.

"Well, Campion, my boy," he said, "I'll take charge

of these, shall I? Daresay you'll be glad to hand over the responsibility, after everything. Don't worry. They shan't leave my tunic until I place them in the secretary's own hands. You're going to get recognition for this, you youngsters, and in my opinion you deserve it."

They watched him while he buttoned the linen bag carefully in the inside pocket of his tunic.

"There," he said with unconcealed satisfaction. "Now I must consider myself a royal courier, don't you know. We'll do the thing properly. Mustn't take any risks. I'll take Bates and a section under a corporal in one lorry by way of escort. Wivenhoe, I'll leave these good people in your care until you can hand over everything to the civil authorities. Well, good-bye, Campion. Congratulations, sincere congratulations."

They followed him to the door and saw him safely installed in the back of his car. Bates and the chauffeur sat in front, and the lorry lumbered along behind. There was something slightly absurd, slightly magnificent, and mightily romantic about this gallant departure, and even had Brett Savanake not lain mangled in the sweet waters of the Bright, Mr. Campion felt he would have been unperturbed about the safety of the precious proofs.

Captain Wivenhoe proved as capable, if less colourful, as his superior officer.

"Look here, Randall," he said as they trooped back to the drawing room, "we both know the County Commissioner pretty well. Dear old Tenderton is an understanding, intelligent old boy. I feel like putting the whole thing, or most of it, before him. After all, I gather there's a bit of a mess to clear up, and that will fall to his department. They found the body, by the way. The mill wheel stove his head in against the race."

Guffy turned enquiringly to Campion. "Shall we appeal to the Commissioner?" he enquired.

Mr. Campion nodded. "Fine," he said. "Fine, if you can fix that up between you. The doctor chappie will want appeasing, too, and there are several things to be considered."

"Good heavens, yes." Guffy blinked as he spoke. "Dr. Galley. I'd forgotten him."

They listened appalled, while he sketched a brief account of their terrible experience of the afternoon, his inarticulation and under-statement lending a much more awesome gravity to the tale than any more elaborate telling could have done.

Mr. Campion was silent after the recital, but when Wivenhoe went out to dispatch a man with a note to the County Commissioner he spoke:

"That kid Amanda," he said; "what a nerve she has! She stayed behind after all that."

Guffy glanced across the room to where Mary stood with her back to him talking to Hal.

"They're marvellous women, all of them," he said, and his round solemn face brightened. "I'm a very happy man. Campion," he announced gravely. "Very happy, indeed. Mary's as keen on the country, the estates and that sort of thing, as I am. Fortunate, isn't it? There's only one thing that's worrying me. We got engaged this afternoon," he said, "and at that time I assure you I had no idea at all that this revelation of old Galley's was going to break. You see, as it is, in view of everything, the P.M. can hardly refuse to interest himself personally in the family's claim, and with this sheet from the register to go on it seems to me to be a foregone conclusion. That means that I shall marry Mary just when her brother gets the earldom and the estate. Rather awkward, isn't it?"

Campion passed his hand through his fair hair. "My dear old garrulous," he said, "let me assure you first that the idea of anyone of your house marrying for wealth or position is one of those absurdities which could not take root even in the embryonic mind of the lowliest of gossip-columnists. Then let me enquire gently and kindly, as of a man demented by love or drink, what the hell are you blathering about? What page from what register?"

Guffy blinked at him. "Of course," he said. "Of course, you don't know. Oh, well, here it is. When we first went to see that unfortunate fellow Galley the man produced an envelope containing, so he said, a page or so from his uncle's diary, and a sheet from the parish register. He was going to show it to us when the clock struck the half-hour, and the sound seemed to bring on his—er—paroxysms. Well, naturally, I forgot about it in the excitement which followed, but apparently Aunt Hatt—that woman has guts, Campion—simply picked it up before she went out. When we came off the boat and went into the 'George' at Great Kepesake she produced it. Hal's got it. It's unmistakably genuine.''

The boy came over and unlocked the rosewood bureau in the corner.

"I've just put it in here for safety," he said.

Campion took the envelope, and they gathered round the table and pored over its contents.

There were two leaves from the diary, two small discoloured pages written in a ragged, crabbed hand. The first entry was dated June 30th, 1854.

"Rose early. Cow still sick. Mrs. Padditch dropped my best salad bowl and cracked it, so was forced to dismiss her. This evening young Hal from the Hall came to visit me, looking very gallant in his soldier clothes. Gave me twenty guineas (20 gns) to marry him to Miss Mary Fitton of Sweethearting without his mother's knowledge. Felt myself in a quandary, but since he is the heir and I am still a young man, and may live here many more years, I salved my conscience and agreed. Married him at seven o'clock this evening to the girl, Mrs. Parritch and her father's man, Branch, standing witness. The little Miss looked peaky. I wonder if she will live to see him back."

Campion set the page down. This intimate glimpse of another life so long vanished was sobering even at the end of so much modern turmoil.

The second entry was even more enlightening.

"January 5th, 1855. Have consented at last to Her Ladyship's way. My conscience pricks me but I see no

way out of my dilemma. Hear the poor little Miss is near
to death, anyway, at the loss of her man, so it may well be
the same in the end for her. Her Ladyship is very bitter. A
hard woman. I find myself helpless in her hands. Have
taken out leaf from Register and find that I thereby also
render Elizabeth Martin and Thos. Cowper unmarried in the
sight of man, if not in God's sight. Prayed diligently that I
should be forgiven my sins. N.B. Have hidden page from
Register in cover of *Catullus*, leather bound copy.''

"There you see," said Mary. "He was afraid afterwards that his diary might be read, so he took these pages
out and hid them with the sheet from the register."

Campion spread out the last sheet. It was a page from
the Church Register. The signatures were faded, but still
clear: "Hal Huntingforest. Mary Fitton. June 30th, 1854."
And underneath the record of the marriage which had so
disturbed the accommodating vicar: "Eliz. Martin. Thomas
Cowper. Sept. 18th, 1854."

"What do you think?" Hal's young voice was eager.
"Can we get it proved? We haven't any money, you
know."

Campion glanced up from the documents and grinned.

"That's all right," he said. "I think we shall find that
in view of everything we can get it through without the
least difficulty in the world. As for money, the Hereditary
Paladin of Averna should come in for a packet. As Pretender, I, Albert, abdicate in favour of thee, Hal, and all
that."

Hal shook hands with him gravely, and Mary slipped
her arm through Guffy's.

Eager-Wright put his head round the door.

"I say, Campion," he said, "half a minute. The sergeant and a patrol have just brought in those two prize
idiots, Scatty and Lugg. They've walked from Kepesake.
Come and swear to 'em, will you?"

Mr. Campion hurried out to the rescue of his henchman.
Lugg, lugubrious and sorry for himself, was sitting on the

doorstep of the mill with Scatty at his side, while their captors stood round, amused and tolerant.

"The *army*," said Mr. Lugg, casting a baleful glance at his employer, his voice packed with scorn. "The blinking *army*. Can't do a little quiet job without the *army* turning out. It's Yes, mister sergeant. No, mister sergeant, the whole time. I get sick of it. Yes, sir," he added hastily before the expression in Mr. Campion's face. "Yes, sir. Come to report, sir. All quiet, sir."

After satisfying the sergeant Mr. Campion turned away. He was unbearably weary. His head was burning, his mouth was dry. The adventure was over, then; the victory complete. He walked slowly upstairs.

As he passed Amanda's room Aunt Hatt came out. She was smiling.

"She's better, I do believe," she confided. "Quite herself again, but a little weak. Go in and see her. She's anxious to hear that everything's all right."

Campion went into the gay little room. Amanda, white and a trifle pinched, but very much alive, grinned at him from the bed.

"Hallo, Orph.," she said. "Come to report to the Lieut? What's the worst?"

"There isn't any," he said, sitting down on the end of the bed. "This sensational business has come to a successful close, as we say in the board room. The treasure has gone to town in the charge of a minute but magnificent portion of the British army, the missing earl is well on the way to his place in Dod, we're both alive, thanks to you, and I'm half asleep."

"Good," said Amanda and sighed. A spasm of pain passed over her face, and her eyes fluttered open, surprise in their brown depths. "It hurts when I do that," she said. "But I'll be all right in a day or two. I'm very healthy, my teeth are good, I never snore, my relations say I have a sweet temper."

Campion sat looking at her, and she lifted a hand with some difficulty, and laid it on his arm.

"Don't be frightened," she said. "I'm not proposing

marriage to you. But I thought you might consider me as a partner in the business later on. You see, when Hal comes into the estate Scatty and I are going to have a thin time. I don't want to go to a finishing school, you know."

"Good Lord, no," said Campion, aghast at the prospect.

"That's all," said Amanda. "Get that well into your head. No higher education for me. I say, do you ever think about Biddy Pagett? You know—Biddy Lobbett."

Mr. Campion, dishevelled, and unbeautifully clad, met her frank enquiring gaze with one of his rare flashes of undisguised honesty.

"Yes," he said.

Amanda sighed. "I thought so. Look here," she went on. "I shan't be ready for about six years yet. But then— well, I'd like to put you on the top of my list."

Campion held out his hand with sudden eagerness. "Is that a bet?"

Amanda's small cold fingers grasped his own. "Done," she said.

Mr. Campion sat where he was for a long time staring out across the room. His face was expressive, a luxury he scarcely ever permitted himself. At last he rose slowly to his feet and stood looking down very tenderly at this odd little person who had come crashing through one of the most harrowing adventures he had ever known and with unerring instinct had torn open old scars, revived old fires which he had believed extinct.

"What's going to change you in six years, you rum little grig?" he said slowly.

She did not stir. Her eyes were closed. Her lips were parted, and her breath came regularly and evenly.

Amanda was asleep.